WOUNDED HEART

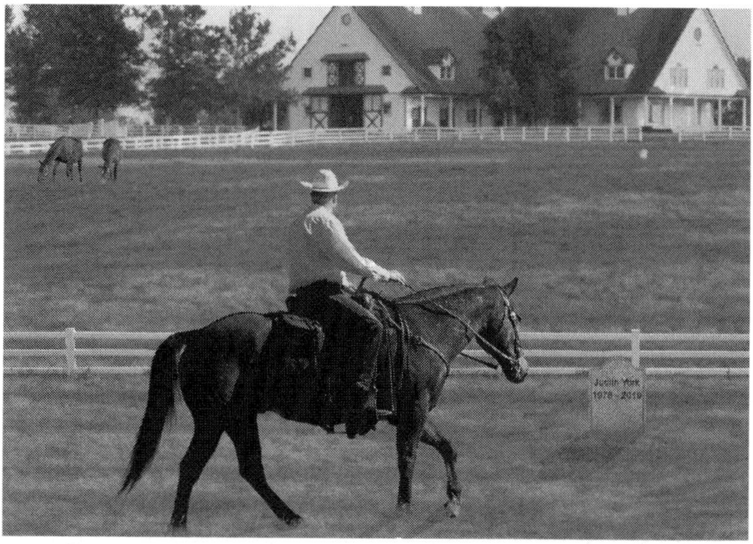

WOUNDED HEART

Broken Spirit

Michael R Emmert

Copyright

Copyright © 2024 Michael R Emmert

All rights reserved. No portion of this book may be reproduced, stored in a retrieval system, or transmitted in any form or by any means—electronic, mechanical, photocopy, recording, scanning, or other—except for brief quotations in critical reviews or articles, without the prior written permission of the author.

For permissions, contact:

Michael.Emmert@Gmail.Com

The author has taken all scripture quotes from the Holy Bible, the English Standard Version, unless otherwise noted.

DEDICATION

<u>My wife</u>

Lottie

<u>My Daughter</u>

Cheryl

<u>My Granddaughters</u>

Anna

Grace

Rebekah

Caitlyn

Bethany

Rachel

The human spirit can endure in sickness,
but a crushed spirit who can bear?
Proverbs 18: 14

A joyful heart is good medicine,
but a crushed spirit dries up the bones.
Proverbs 17:22

Memory gives us pictures of the past which can ...
be a huge problem in moving forward
Frank Ball

Disclaimer

    <u>Wounded Heart, Broken Spirit</u> is a work of fiction. Names, characters, businesses, places, events, or incidents are the product of the author's imagination or are used fictitiously. Any resemblance to actual persons (living or dead) is entirely coincidental.

    This story begins in 2020 and the setting is in Nebraska, in the south-central part of the Corn Husker state. The events carry through into 2021 and end in Cass County, Iowa, the Hawkeye state.

    The views and opinions expressed in this novel are those of the characters and may or may not reflect the views of the author.

Book Plot

Philip York had a perfect life until his wife, Judith, died two years ago, and her death shattered his life. Memories of her imprint every corner of the ranch, and it's almost impossible to get through the day. His love of ranching and rodeo competition has come to a halt. His daughter Beth plans to heal his broken heart by setting him up with a mystery woman. Her scheme goes insanely awry at a New Year's Eve party. Now, Phil must make a choice.

When two men, at an off-season rodeo, attempt to take his deceased wife's champion Quarter Horse, Phil's stellar integrity is questioned and his reputation is sullied. His memories of Judith keep rushing back and won't leave him alone. Will he gain victory over his endless memories of Judith? Will he find peace?

Chapter 1

Friday, December 25th, 2020, evening

Beth's sigh punctuated the darkness like the whoosh from a soda bottle.

I glanced at my daughter. *What scheme was she plotting now?* "What's the matter, Princess?" Did the plan have anything to do with corralling me into taking her home after our family Christmas because her husband had left earlier to put their two toddlers to bed?

"Beth, what's the matter? You seem uneasy."

She leaned her head against the side window, and puffs of moisture blossomed on the glass. "I missed Mom today because she wasn't here to celebrate the Lord's birth. It was important to her."

My fingers tightened on the steering wheel. Judith, my wife of twenty-four years, should have been at today's get-together. I still wasn't used to living alone.

I should have known that Beth would mention her mother. They resembled each other so much that it stabbed like a knife. Both had dimples, a cute, petite nose, a soft freckled complexion, and black hair flowing down their backs.

I forced my hands to relax. "Yeah. Your mom made a big production of arranging the manger scene beside the Christmas tree."

"Uh-huh. When Tom and I were growing up, we enjoyed how she dramatized the birth of Jesus."

"I know. When I read the story of Jesus' birth from the Gospel of Luke, your mom performed it like a stage play. She was good at those kinds of things."

Memories—so many memories.

Beth drew stick figures on the window of a family around a Christmas tree. "Mom's enactments made it special for Tom and me. I remember her flying the baby Jesus through the air and saying, 'God sent him special from heaven to land in the manger.'"

My breathing picked up speed. "I miss your mother so much that it hurts. The house isn't the same without her. The ranch isn't the same. Nothing's the same without her."

Beth twisted the necklace we'd given her at her high school graduation five years ago. "Dad, I know you miss Mom. We all do. But she's been gone for almost two years. What's it going to take for you to be happy again?"

My jaw tightened. *Here we go again. This must be part of her scheme.* "I don't know." How could I be happy without my wife? Wherever I went in the house, I saw her: the frilly blue curtains in the kitchen, the mountain picture on the living room wall, the bathroom shelf I hadn't cleaned off. The house was an empty tomb without her.

"Dad, I see changes in you since Mom died. Your attitude is different."

I stopped at a crossroads before proceeding on through. "Attitude, like how?"

"You act differently. Today, with the family, you resembled a defeated dog cowering under the porch. You didn't smile and hardly spoke. You need to realize that Mom is gone, and you need to move on with your life."

I swallowed the lump in my throat. "How can I move on? I remember holding her. I roll over at night and find an empty pillow. When she washed dishes, I'd sneak up behind her to kiss her neck, and she'd lean against me like melting butter."

In the glow of the headlights, the mailbox at Shook's farm appeared out of the darkness. I slowly eased around the sharp corner, and the pickup's bouncing air freshener resembled Judith's bobbing earrings. The hollow feeling in my chest made it hard to breathe.

Beth adjusted her seatbelt. "What do you miss the most about Mom?"

Everything. Her question opened a floodgate of memories: the times my wife and I sat together while the kids opened Christmas presents, the summer afternoons we watched them play croquet in the backyard, or when we tried to guess the number of grandkids we'd eventually spoil. "I never realized how much I enjoyed wrapping my arms around her and cuddling."

Beth's fingers almost snapped the necklace. "Cuddling? Do you miss the sex?" Her voice stretched like a rubber band.

The pickup swerved, but I straightened it. "What in tarnation? We taught you better."

"Okaaaaayyyy." Her voice twanged like a plucked piano wire.

"What brought that on?" I glared at my impulsive child. She hadn't gotten her boldness from her mother. It could only have come from me.

Her left hand toyed with the necklace that always became a plaything when she planned a scatterbrained idea. And she'd been twisting it all afternoon. "Dad, why haven't you dated? You're good-looking at forty-two. Women love tall men, and you've got a full head of hair."

My stomach tightened. "What's gotten into you? Are you in need of a new mother? Or do you want a grandma for your boys?"

"Neither. I'm concerned about you. You're grouchy. You're alone. My boys ask why Grandpa is angry when they visit. Sometimes I feel like I don't know you."

The eggnog in my stomach gurgled. "*If* I want to date, I'll consider it. But it's too soon."

"No, it's not. You let the dishes pile up in the sink, you don't wash your clothes, you don't clean the house, and you don't ride the horses. Why did you stop going to the rodeo? You and Mom received the top award at Grand Island three years ago. 'Philip and Judith York, Champion Ropers 2018.'"

"I quit going because your mom isn't here. That's why, and I refuse to date. Just drop the idea. You have two boys and a husband to care for, so quit telling me how to live my life." Would my life ever return to normal without Judith?

"Dad, I miss Mom as much as you do. But she's still anchored in your heart, and you haven't let her go. You should move on with your life."

"Just stop it, Beth. I don't want to talk about her."

"Then I'll change the subject."

Thank God. It's about time. "Do I have a choice? You usually say what you want, anyway."

"See, I'm right. You're in a cranky mood. Anyway, Gene Wilcox stopped me at the supermarket, and he asked when you'd settle the account for his damaged horse trailer."

"Blast it. I'll settle when I get the money."

"You always keep short accounts. How much do you owe?"

"More than I've got. Drop it, because it's none of your business."

I let Beth out in front of her white brick home, and she hugged me, which I assumed was a way of apologizing. Hopefully, she wouldn't mention dating again, but I knew she would.

She said, "In the morning, Kim and I will be over to help clean the house after today's gathering."

Housework was my least favorite activity. I wouldn't do most household chores unless someone helped or forced me. "Thanks for offering. It's appreciated."

She kissed my cheek and pointed to her living room window. "David left a light on and is waiting up. I'll see you in the morning." She climbed the front steps and disappeared inside.

I made the lonely thirty-minute drive back to a dark and empty ranch house.

In my study, I plopped into the chair and looked at the picture of Beth and Kim on my desk. A photographer took the picture at their high school graduation, and the girls looked radiant in their caps and gowns. Kim was Beth's best friend, an orphan who'd lived across the road with Reverend Gerald and Rachel Johnson. When the girls were growing up, it was common to find them at either of the homes.

Their birthdays were in early March, four days apart, and Judith put on a big weekend celebration, inviting all their friends. Kim was more levelheaded and not impulsive, like Beth, who always dreamed up crazy ideas. She'd set Tom up on a blind date, which hadn't ended well when the girl asked to move in with him. *More memories.*

I picked up a picture of Tom. He'd gone to Nebraska University after high school and would receive his degree next May. Why couldn't Beth have been like him? No matter how much Judith cajoled, Beth refused to go to college, even on a scholarship, because she was in a hurry to marry David.

At least my wife and I had one sensible child. How could we have parented such a crazy, problem-causing daughter? Being a mother to two boys hadn't dampened her scheming.

My stomach tightened. If I bet a hundred dollars that she wouldn't drop the idea of me dating, I'd win hands down.

Chapter 2

Saturday, December 26th, morning

I hardly slept and crawled out of bed to do the chores. My mind churned, and I dreaded what Beth might plot. If she planned for me to date someone, it wouldn't end well because she seldom thought through the details. Like trying to repair the faucet in the bathroom and breaking a water line, drowning our bedroom.

The clear sky and brisk fourteen degrees did little to improve my mood, and the hardened crust of last week's six-inch snow crackled underfoot as I tramped to the stables.

Jinx, our five-year-old border collie, bounded out of his doghouse to prance beside me. Judith had surprised me with a wiggling, yipping, and licking ball of fur for my birthday five years ago. The pup's name became fitting when he got stuck in the fence, waking our family with his loud yowling, along with everyone at the Johnsons' house across the road.

I scratched him behind his ears, and he scampered off to squeeze under the white corral fence, barking at the horses I boarded. They eyed him warily.

While I fed the livestock, Beth's gray horse, Isabel, nickered and plucked my coat sleeve.

Memories.

Judith and I had proudly watched Beth ride Isabel in the championship barrel race at the state fair, and we were heartbroken when she missed winning by a hundredth of a second. My wife placed the runner-up silver cup in the den to dominate like a spotlight. Kim had competed in the same event but knocked over a barrel to finish twelfth.

Judith and I had helped the girls practice for the competition, watching them sprint their horses around the barrels while racing against the clock. She proudly aligned the many 4-H ribbons in the den. *There are so many memories.*

I shook my head to clear it. Why did memories mean so much? I saw Judith everywhere: in the vegetable garden, among the rose bushes, in the flower beds, at the bird feeders, and with the calico cat she named Sweetie Pie.

I scratched Isabel's ears and poured her a measure of oats. "Here you go, girl."

The horses in the adjacent corral waited in anticipation for their morning feed. I fed them and stacked the feed buckets in the stables' storage room.

Out on the road, Kim's yellow car waited for a truck to pass before turning into our driveway that was bordered by white wooden fences.

I checked my watch: 7:21 a.m. The ladies had arrived earlier than I expected. A small cloud cast a shadow over the corral as Kim parked beside the fence.

Beth hopped out of the car, and Isabel stuck her nose over the fence and nickered. "Hey, Isabel. Maybe we could go riding today." She stroked the mare's neck.

Kim wore the bright yellow coat that Judith and I had given her at Christmas three years ago. It matched her blonde hair. "Good morning, Phil."

"Good morning, ladies."

Kim looked into the stables. "Where's Marston? Isn't he working today?"

"He and his folks went to visit his grandparents in Arizona. He'll be back after the first of the year."

"Can you handle everything while he's gone, or do you want my help?"

"Thanks for the offer, but I can feed the livestock by myself and am putting off doing the other things." I glanced at her yellow car. "Seeing you and Beth in the same car reminded me of one time you rode to church together. Darrel and Janice Meador were new to the church and thought you were sisters."

She grinned. "They thought I'd dyed my hair and didn't believe we were BFFs."

"You were often together."

She glanced at Beth. "We kind of resemble each other except for our hair."

I didn't think they did.

"Are you finished with the chores?" asked Kim. "Or can I help?"

I tilted my head toward the horses. "Fill the corral hay bunk and open the gate to let the horses stretch their legs in the pasture."

She smiled—the one Judith said could melt an ice cube in ten seconds flat. "I love working with your horses and cattle." She trotted to the shed and tossed several hay bales into the bunk before opening the gate.

Beth approached with a sparkle in her eyes. "Dad, could we go riding today? I'd like to ride Isabel, and Kim wants to ride Lindy."

"I suppose you and Kim could saddle up after we finish cleaning the house."

"Why don't you ride Fargo and join us? You haven't ridden him since Mom—"

"Stop meddling! Why do you press me to do things I don't want to do? If there's time, you girls can go riding." I lowered my chin and growled, "Without me."

Kim appeared at my elbow. "Phil, you're almost done with chores. Beth and I will get the coffee perked while you finish." She turned Beth around and pushed her toward the house.

Kim was a peacemaker, but something just stirred in her eyes, like when she was a teenager, and I caught her daydreaming on the backyard swing. She'd blushed, brushed off her skirt, and went inside to help Judith.

The girls mounted the porch steps and entered the back door, chatting like they hadn't talked in ages. As girls, they helped each other with schoolwork and housework to get everything done before they rode the horses.

Judith and I figured Kim would have a hard time keeping boys from fawning over her. She was a lovely woman. When Beth had gone out with David, Kim stayed at the Johnsons', studying or reading a book. Occasionally, she came to our house to play a board game with Tom or us. She never went on a date, not even in college.

Tom had asked Kim for a date a few times. She said he was too young by two years, and she'd be robbing the cradle. He bantered back, saying that if she didn't go on a date with him, she'd turn into a crotchety old maid for the rest of her life. She stuck out her tongue, and he made a face. Judith laughed at their antics and gave them each a hug.

Memories, more memories.

I closed the corral gate and was heading into the stables when Challenger, Judith's red horse, stuck his nose in my ear. "Hey, big fellow." He was her roping horse, and it was an unwritten rule that only she or I rode him. Whenever we went to the timber on a tryst, I'd ride beside her on Fargo. During those times, we talked about when we'd rattle like loose marbles in the house. She dreamed of making a playroom for the grandkids until the accident shattered her plans.

My chest tightened, and I had trouble breathing. *Would I ever get over losing her?*

Challenger nuzzled my arm. "You miss her too, don't you, boy?" He bobbed his head, as though he understood, and tugged on my coat.

I ran my hand down his withers. "Sorry, big fellow. We can't ride today." Judith should have been here to saddle up for a jaunt.

I trudged to the house, Jinx by my side. Today, I'd enjoy the girls' company, but Beth's conversation from last night echoed in my head. I prayed she wouldn't resurrect it.

Chapter 3

I kicked off my overshoes on the back porch and hung up my coat.

In the kitchen, sunlight streamed through Judith's blue curtains above the sink, shining down on Kim and Beth as they nursed cups of coffee at the walnut table.

I closed my eyes and tried to focus because I imagined Judith sitting at the table, drinking coffee and waiting for me to join her.

Kim said to Beth, "I missed Tom yesterday at the family Christmas. Now I won't see him until Easter."

Beth snickered. "He's been smitten with Bonnie and spent the holidays with her. At least his absence kept him from trashing the house."

"Stop it, Beth. He's not that messy."

"Yes, he is. He never cleaned his room, and Mom was always picking up after him."

As I filled my coffee cup, Kim said, "Phil, we're ready to clean the house."

I plopped down beside her and blew into the cup before taking a sip. "What's today's plan of attack?"

"We'll begin taking down the decorations and start cleaning the rooms if you'll fix breakfast."

"That means less cleaning for me. You've got a deal."

Within a few minutes, they were taking down the tree in the living room while I finished my coffee. After fetching the fixings from the pantry, I fried bacon, scrambled the eggs, and called the girls after buttering the toast.

The ladies joined me at the kitchen table, and I said a quick prayer.

Beth leaned on her elbows. "Dad, when can I get Mom's twelve-place setting of china with the pussywillow pattern?"

"What did I tell you the last time you asked?"

"Come on, Dad."

I lowered my chin. "What did I tell you?"

She huffed. "They'd be mine when you kicked the bucket. But you live alone and will never use them, so why can't I have them?"

"Your grandpa and grandma York gave them to your mother as a special wedding present. They're not yours."

"Mom's not here, and they just sit in the china closet, collecting dust along with the silverware. She said they'd be mine one day."

I raised an eyebrow. "No, she didn't. If she had told you that, she'd have told me the same thing. This subject is off-limits, and there'll be no more talk about it."

Beth glowered and was about to say something, but she didn't.

Kim asked, "Phil, could I ride with you to church tomorrow?"

"I guess. Couldn't you drive yourself? It would be closer."

"I always rode to church with you and Judith at Christmas. It's like a tradition for me."

"Then, to ride with me, you'll have to help with chores before going."

She grinned. "Deal. I'll be here early."

For the rest of the meal, we made small talk and discussed the plans for cleaning the entire house. It needed it.

"I'm grateful you girls are helping put the house back in order," I said.

Beth pushed back from the table. "It's okay. After running off my mouth last night, I owe you."

My stomach knotted.

Kim looked at Beth with a question in her eyes.

"Beth," I said, "let's not go there. Okay?"

"Whatever." She stacked the dishes in the sink.

All three of us dug into cleaning the house, and the hours zipped along. The decorations went back into the boxes, the kitchen shone spotlessly, and we put the living room, dining room, and den back in order. The ladies changed the bedsheets.

Evening arrived, and I was placing a box in the hall closet when they came up behind me. I yawned and asked over my shoulder, "Do you ladies want me to order pizza?"

"Yes," said Beth. "We'll wash the dirty bedsheets and your smelly work clothes while you're doing the chores."

I called Edward's Pizzeria and placed the order before stepping outside to feed the livestock. Our pizza arrived as I placed a big hay bale in the steer's feed bunk.

In the kitchen, I was working on my third piece of pizza when Beth asked, "Dad, are you still mad about last night's question?"

My jaw tightened. *Why couldn't she keep her mouth shut?* "I'm not mad, more like irritated."

"I want to press for an answer." She toyed with her silver necklace.

Inwardly, I groaned.

Kim must have known what Beth's question was because she didn't appear surprised.

"I wish you wouldn't," I said.

Beth set down her slice of pizza. "What you prefer and what you'll tolerate are two separate things."

My lips tightened. "Blast you, girl." Judith and I taught the kids they could discuss any topic, and Beth would push this to the limit. I kept my voice even. "What do you want to know?"

"You need to answer my question about dating someone." Her lips twitched as if she sensed victory because she knew how to dig into forbidden territory and get away with it.

"I'm not interested in dating anyone. It's my choice, not yours. Will you just forget it and leave me alone?"

"No. Why won't you date someone, Dad?"

My hands clenched under the table. She needed to stop this tomfoolery.

Kim must have sensed my tension. "Phil, Judith made this home sing. I saw how her death turned Tom's and Beth's lives upside down. They cried, but they've accepted that their mother was gone. You've never accepted her death, never cried, and never moved on. You're moody, angry, and grouchy. It's like you simply exist and are living alone in this big, empty house."

Mentally, I stepped back. Whenever Kim spoke, it paid to listen, because she was good at judging people. "What do you mean by 'simply exist'?"

"Except for church or going to town for supplies, you never leave the ranch. You're not sociable. You don't visit friends. Folks never see you. I miss you whistling *Back in the Saddle Again*. You used to ride Fargo and practice roping. Why not now?"

Beth said, "The other day, Ian asked, 'Why doesn't Grandpa take me riding anymore? He did with Grandma.'"

I stopped breathing because my chest felt as if a bale of hay had fallen on it. I remember putting Ian in the saddle with me, and Judith would ride Challenger. The sun seemed to shine on her as she laughed at our grandson's attempt to guide Fargo.

She would decorate the house at Christmas for the boys, and together they baked Snickerdoodles. She invited folks over for no reason except to visit with them and play games. Without her, my house had become a dreary fruit cellar.

More memories.

"You're alone and need to be more sociable," said Kim. "You're not the same person. If Judith were here, she'd say the same thing."

"I agree," said Beth. "Without Mom, you're different. It's what I was telling you last night."

Judith and I had talked around this table while sipping our coffee. The girls were doing it, except I was the topic. To have light focused on me was as comforting as sitting on a bronc with a burr under the saddle. "I'll consider your suggestion about getting out more. Let's talk about something else."

"Phil, the New Year's Eve party is at Arena Hall," said Kim. "Will you go with me?" Her soft brown eyes offered a gift-wrapped personal invitation.

Socialization held little interest, but her beautiful smile crumpled my resistance. If I attended the party, I'd be getting away from the ranch, and it might keep Beth off my back.

Before I could answer, Beth said, "David and I found a babysitter and will be going. If you go, I'll introduce you to a wonderful lady, and you could ask her out."

Confound her. She was setting me up. "No," I bellowed and stomped to the living room, flicking on the TV.

An '80s sitcom rerun filled the unwatched screen, and I kept the sound down, listening to the ladies' murmurings from the kitchen.

Darn daughter. She was a crazy, meddling woman who was setting me up.

I slouched lower in the overstuffed chair and propped my feet on the coffee table. My eyes grew heavy. Beth would probably hook me up with a wallflower, someone who wouldn't like horses and hated the ranch, someone who wanted to live in town, someone as ugly as a frog, someone who …

***

Night

In the living room, Beth shook me awake. "Dad, it's almost midnight. Let's get you to bed. Kim and I didn't want to leave you alone and will sleep in my old room."

My eyes wouldn't stay open as she escorted me down the hall. I sank onto the bed, and she tugged off my boots and pulled off my socks. "Dad, you need a woman in your life."

What she said made no sense to my sleep-fogged mind. "What did you say?"

"I want you to meet someone special."

She gave my shoulders a slight push, and I landed on my back. Sleep arrived as I hit the pillow.

Chapter 4

Sunday, December 27th, morning

I awoke to the smell of percolating coffee and checked my watch: 8:47. *Blast it*. I'd forgotten to set the alarm and had overslept by three hours. Who was here? It took a minute to clear my head. Ah, the ladies had stayed overnight.

I pulled on clean clothes and headed to the kitchen.

Beth looked up from buttering the toast. "Good morning. You were sleeping so well that Kim and I didn't want to wake you."

"I wish you had. It's past time to feed the livestock."

"Stop fretting. Kim and I did the chores."

I glanced out the kitchen window at the steers nibbling hay from the bunk. "You did?"

"You were so tired last night that we're skipping church today."

"But I'm supposed to be there. Bill Peterson and I were planning to discuss the claims for Christ's virgin birth with his class."

"I called Bill, and he knows you're not coming. He said it's the holiday season anyway, and there won't be many people. He wants you to call to set up another time."

"Oh, you did? Okay, I'll call him later. I didn't know I was that tired."

"Yeah, you were. Resting up will do you good."

"Beth, it's nice to have you here in the morning. Seeing you in the kitchen reminds me of when you bustled about helping your mom make breakfast. I remember Tom teasing that you should go get prettied up."

Beth shot Kim a glance and winked. "So I'm not pretty, huh?"

"I said nothing of the sort. Seeing you two beautiful ladies always brightens my day." I reached for the coffeepot.

Kim nudged me with her hip, which I took to mean thanks for the compliment. She worked a spatula around the skillet's edge to tumble a mound of scrambled eggs into a serving bowl. "Hungry?" she asked while displaying her melt-all smile.

"I'm famished."

We sat, and I asked Kim to pray for the food.

After the amen, Beth took a bite, fiddled with her silver necklace, looked out the window, sipped her coffee, twisted the necklace again, and forked another bite.

She was unusually quiet, and she had to be plotting something. Normally, she bubbled over with plans of what she'd do and who'd do that.

"Is something eating you, Beth?" I asked. "Spit out your conspiracy."

Her gaze met mine. "Dad, it's necessary to say this. Last evening, you brushed Kim and me aside. Stop mourning for Mom. You've turned into a loner, and being a hermit doesn't suit you. Let go of her and find someone else."

"Crime in Italy!" I roared. "Why won't you forget about it?" I shook my finger. "Stay out of my life. No one can come close to your mom, let alone take her place. She was the best-darned woman around here."

"Yes, she was the best mom." She reached across the table and tapped my chest. "We all miss her, but you're living on memories, and they're tearing you apart. She'd want you to fill this empty-hole."

Judith once said, "Without me, you're an empty old goat. But with me riding by your side, I'll fill your heart." I looked at Kim, then at Beth. Beth wouldn't drop the subject, and Kim would go along with her. My jaw tightened. "What do you have in mind?"

"Get out socially. David and I are going to the New Year's Eve party, and you should go to be more active."

I squinted. "Active? I suppose you want me to meet a woman?"

She dropped her eyes.

"Your silence proves your guilt," I growled.

Kim placed her hand over mine. "Calm down." Her eyes looked straight into my soul. "There's no reason to be upset. We're trying to help you realize how different you've become. We see changes that scare us."

If Beth had said this, I'd have brushed her off. But Kim never had a hidden motive. I closed my eyes and inhaled through my nose, forcing my muscles to relax.

Beth leaned forward and rested her arms on the table. "I'm asking you to meet someone to see if you like her."

The girls were tag-teaming, and it wouldn't stop until ... A lightbulb lit up in my head. "I'll go to this party on one condition."

Beth cocked her head. "What's the condition?"

"I'll go if you quit pushing for me to meet this mystery woman and guarantee I don't meet her at the party. Deal?"

"Daaaaad." Beth extended the word out to four syllables.

For a moment, we stared at each other.

She blinked. "Dad, you need to meet someone."

"No, I don't, and I won't go unless you agree to back off." My gaze didn't waver. From the corner of my eye, Kim motioned for Beth to accept.

Beth pursed her lips and tried to stare me down, but her eyes wouldn't lock. "Come on, Dad. You've got to meet women."

"And I suppose you know the best one for me."

"She's a great person."

"If your plan is for me to meet this mystery woman, then I won't go to this shindig." Whenever I set my mind to something, it took a solid horse kick to knock me loose from my York family stubbornness.

She scowled. "You're being stubborn."

"You bet I am. If you keep pushing, then I'll keep dragging my feet. Back off if you want me to go on New Year's Eve."

"Alright, deal." Her words came out in staccato.

Not for one minute would she quit plotting. I could bet that she'd already connived a sour-faced granny into attending the party and had arranged for her to bump into me.

Chapter 5

Monday, December 28th, morning

After chores, I retreated to my study, and the front doorbell chimed. Who would visit today? If it were the ladies, they'd come in the back door.

I opened the front door and stood face-to-face with Jerry Dunlap. Last week, the police raided his office for suspected illegal activity. He was a known bookie for sporting events and held a reputation as a loan shark. "What do *you* want?"

"You're sure grouchy." He looked past me into the main room. "I thought you'd have family here."

"They were here the other day, and we celebrated Christmas. Then they went home."

He smirked. "Because your wife is dead, I kind of figured you—"

"*Enough*, Mr. Dunlap. My personal life is not your concern. Why are you here?"

He looked toward the corral. "You've got fine stock and have done well with the ranch."

Where was this discussion headed? "Most of the horses aren't mine because I board them for other folks. Do you have one you want to board?"

His eyes narrowed. "Everyone knows you board horses, and no, that isn't why I came. I have a business proposition. Could I come inside?"

Something didn't smell right. "We'll talk on the front stoop. I'll be saying no to whatever you want, and it shouldn't take long."

He raised an eyebrow. "I have an honest proposal."

I wouldn't trust his honesty as far as I could throw him. "You're a bookie and known for dangling a carrot to stack the odds in your favor before taking money from the unwary."

His lips tightened. "Who are you to judge? I help folks improve their finances."

"You earned the reputation of being a cheat. Live with it. Jamie Crouch owes you a mint for his gambling habit. Ed Flynn is in the same boat."

"They wagered more than they could afford. It's not my fault."

"You talked Jamie into making the wager because it was a sure thing. After he lost, you began charging a high rate of interest. He can't pay it off and will be in debt for a long time."

"He placed the bet. It was his choice."

"But you encouraged him, strung him along, and will keep him on the hook until you bleed him dry. You're a swindler."

His jaw tightened. "You'll regret saying that."

"No, I won't. If you treat my friends that way, you'll do the same with me. What do you want?"

"I want to buy one of your horses, a straight-up cash deal. What's to be afraid of?"

Any deal with him smelled rotten.

"I'll pay top dollar for Challenger," he said.

I glared. "He's not for sale, never has been, and never will be."

"Why not? You no longer compete with him in the rodeo."

I straightened to my full height. "I said no. He's not for sale."

"What are you going to do with him? You feed him, and he's just taking up space."

I squinted. "I'll say it again. Challenger is not for sale."

"Why are you keeping him? I hear you haven't ridden him."

How had he heard that? "My wife raised him as a colt. He's *not* for sale."

"I'll pay $12,000 for Challenger."

Yeah, right. Mr. Dunlap had to know he was worth twice the price and was shortchanging me. At the Grand

Island Rodeo, an investor offered twenty-five grand, and I declined.

It took a few seconds to collect my wits.

He said, "I'll pay cash and go to the bank to deposit it in your account. Eazy peazy, lemon squeezy."

"I said no. He's not for sale, not for any amount."

"Come on, it's good money."

"Why would you want him? He's not a Thoroughbred, and you can't race him on the track. No deal."

"It's cash. Surely, you've got debts to pay off."

"My outstanding mortgage for the ranch is $940,000." I held out my hand.

"Not hardly. With my offer, you could put a down payment on a new pickup, a top-of-the-line model like the one you had before your wife's accident."

If he brings up Judith again, I'll slug him. "My old flivver works fine for what I need."

He looked toward the machine shed. "Then a new piece of farm equipment, like a hay bailer?"

"I said no, and that's my final answer."

"Come on, Phil, be reasonable."

"Mr. Dunlap, you drove here unannounced. I gave my firm answer and am asking you to leave. My horse isn't for sale, not to you or anyone."

"Surely you need money for something?"

"Yes, I do, to put a gate across the driveway so unwanted scum like you won't drive in without an invitation. I want you to leave."

"You're not treating a visitor nicely."

"You're right. I'm not. Leave so I can forget someone of your ilk was ever here."

He glared before descending the front steps. He said over his shoulder, "My offer stands. Keep that in mind. I want your horse, and you haven't heard the last from me."

He drove past the corral, out to the highway, and headed toward town.

My tension eased slightly, but my stomach churned. Something wasn't right. If he wanted Challenger, it had to be a scheme to make money, but he could only sell him. A bookie bets on horses and doesn't race them. A well-heeled cowboy might be interested, but those were as scarce as hen's teeth.

I returned to the study. If Judith were here, she'd disown me if I remotely considered his offer.

Chapter 6

In my study, after Mr. Dunlap's departure, I began reading the Bible for my morning devotions. My cell phone chimed. "Hello."

"Phil, this is Gene Wilcox. I trust you had a great Christmas."

Oh great. "Hi, Gene. Yeah, I did. The whole family was here. What do you need?"

"My situation has changed, and I need a horse trailer soon. How soon can you settle the account?"

I set my jaw. "It wasn't my fault the kid unhitched it from my truck, and you know it. He caused the damage. Charge him."

"You borrowed the trailer and had it hooked up to your pickup."

My voice rose. "I was bringing it back and stopped to talk to Pastor James. That crazy kid unhooked it."

"But you're responsible because it was in your possession. It rolled down the hill, and those rocks tore it up pretty bad."

I yelled, "And I didn't cause the accident!"

The call went silent for a moment. His voice quieted. "And I need a trailer."

"And I don't have the money."

"I don't have a trailer, either. What am I supposed to do when the rodeo season starts?"

I took a breath to calm down. "What about fixing it? Is it repairable?"

"Anything is repairable, but it requires money. It'll take ten grand and two months to put it in shape."

Ouch. "Maybe I could get a loan from the bank."

"How many horses do you have?"

"A dozen are mine. The others are boarders. Why?"

"I'll take Challenger as payment. He'd cover your debt."

Why was everyone suddenly interested in Challenger? "Not in your life. He was my wife's rodeo horse, and I had an offer of twenty-five grand. Even at that price, he's not for sale."

"What am I supposed to do, Phil? You ruined my horse trailer, and I need one by April."

"Could you use mine?"

"You borrowed mine because it hauls four horses—yours hauls two. Also, it doesn't have a feeding stall and isn't self-leveling. I need one to transport four horses, has a hay bunk, and can travel distances."

"How soon do you need it? Can you give me time?"

He paused. "If it were anyone else, I'd want it this week. You have until the end of January. Will that work?"

"Hopefully. I'll see if I can get a loan from the bank."

"Phil, I'm not joking. If you don't get the money—"

"Trust me, Gene. After the first of the year, I'll talk to my banker."

"If you don't come up with the money and keep dragging your feet, I'll start legal proceedings to take Challenger. Keep that in mind. We'll talk later." He disconnected.

Not if I could help it. Why was Gene demanding payment when two weeks ago he didn't need the trailer until summer? Why did he and Jerry Dunlap both want Challenger? *Calm down.*

The bank was closed to in-person services until after the first of the year. I could access the ATM or the website, but my accounts were nearly empty.

I flipped open my laptop, pulled up the spreadsheet for the horses I boarded, and scrolled down the page.

Aaron Berkoff was always prompt with his monthly fees. His horses were Morgans and good riding stock. He and his family often went camping with them down by the river.

Ed Barton's account was up-to-date. His girls rode his horses in the barrel races and did well.

Richard Foot's check had arrived in the mail just before Christmas, and later this week I'd drop it in the drive-through deposit box.

Sarah Green's Appaloosa was a standout and caught everyone's attention. Her account was up-to-date.

Juanita Lewis was late with her fees, as always, but she didn't receive her paycheck until after the first of the month.

Candy Murray hadn't paid her October or November fees, and the end of the year was close. Was she having financial difficulties? She'd never been late. Had she over-budgeted for Christmas gifts?

I punched in her number on my cell phone.

A man answered. "Hello?"

"This is Phil York. Could I speak to Candy, please?"

"I'm Harold, her son. She's gone to town and won't be back for a while. May I take a message?"

"Your mom is three months late with her boarding fees. It hasn't happened before."

"I just got home from the army. Let me ask my sisters. Hold on a minute."

I waited, listening to their muffled discussion.

He came back. "Phil, my sisters say that Mom may not continue boarding the horses and has hinted at selling them. They're trying to talk her out of it. With everything happening in our home and with the Christmas holidays, Mom forgot to pay you. She tries to be prompt. If you'll take cash, I'll bring it over this morning. Is that okay?"

"Sure. I accept checks, cash, credit cards, or direct deposit." I gave him Candy's total bill. "Drive up the lane and park by the stables. I'll meet you there."

"Is it okay if my sisters come? They want to ride the horses."

"Sure. It's been a while since anyone from your family has come. I'll be waiting."

***

Harold and his twin sisters, Sharon and Shelly, arrived an hour later. He stood about five feet ten, with cropped brown hair, and strode with an air of well-muscled determination. Army life must have suited him.

"Here's the money for Mom's boarding fees." He shook my hand and handed me an envelope. "This should bring her account up to date, shouldn't it?"

"That's right." I stuffed the envelope into my hip pocket.

The girls were identical and stood about five feet six with curly brown hair. Their faded blue jeans sported holes at the knees. They wore similar blue coats, and I couldn't tell them apart.

I said to his sisters, "I brought the horses into the stables. They're in stalls four and five."

One of them said, "We've been here before. Rather than gallop around the track in the meadow like everyone else, could we go to the timber and ride along the creek?"

"Go through the gate on the far side of the pasture. Be sure to close it. There are trails along the stream to explore."

"How long can we stay?"

"All day, as long as you want, or until your brother says it's time to go."

"Thanks, Mr. York." She asked Harold, "Do you want to come along?"

"No. I'll just hang out until you get back. I brought a few study books."

"You're a spoilsport and will miss the fun." They hurried into the stables, chatting.

I looked at Harold. "I haven't seen your mom or sisters for a while. Is everything all right?"

"You must not have heard. Mom divorced Dad."

"Whoa. No, I hadn't heard. No wonder she hasn't been around."

"She moved to town at the end of October. She's having a hard time financially and needs to reduce expenses."

"Why did she move to town? I thought your family lived on a farm."

"We did. Mom and us kids did all the farm work on the 160 acres, and Dad was always drunk. He left after the divorce. Mom wanted to stay on the farm and tried to renew the lease but couldn't afford it because of low wheat prices."

"If your mom moved into town, where's she living?"

"She's renting a house on Cedar Lane, just down the street from Beth and David."

"Then they're neighbors. What's your dad doing?"

"He took a job on an oil rig in the Gulf of Mexico. Mom found a job in town but isn't receiving regular alimony payments."

Shelly and Sharon came out of the stables, leading their horses. One of them said, "Harold, we're headed to the creek. See you later, alligator." The other sister said, "After a while, crocodile." They cantered their horses down the lane.

I asked Harold, "Are your sisters seniors in high school?"

"No. They're in their first year of college and came home for Christmas."

"Ah. That's why they haven't come to ride lately."

"I'm out of the army, and the girls are going back to school. So it'll just be Mom and me at the house."

"I trust they'll do well in college. If you've finished your tour of duty, what are your plans?"

"To get a job. There's an opening at Abbott Tech for a web programmer. I've applied and have an interview next week."

"It's a good company, and I hope they hire you." I leaned against the board fence. "On the phone, you mentioned your mother might sell the horses."

"Yeah. The girls consider the horses theirs since they competed with them in the barrel races, but they aren't. Mom needs to cut expenses somewhere, and Sharon and Shelly are afraid she'll sell them while they're at school."

"I'm sorry things are tight. Where does she work?"

"Rollo Accounting. Mom mostly answers phones as the receptionist. When I got home from the army, I went there to let her know I was back home and ran into Beth's friend Kim. I hadn't seen her since our school basketball teams played in the district tournament. She wasn't wearing a ring. Has Beth said if she's dating anyone?"

Interesting. "No one I know about."

"Would she go out with me?"

Would she accept? "I don't know. You'd have to ask." In school and in the youth group, Kim had close friends, but she hadn't been on a date with anyone that I knew about.

"Do you have her number, or should I ask Beth?"

I scrolled through my phone's contacts and gave him Kim's phone number. "Could your mom call to discuss what she wants to do about her horses? If she wants to sell, I'm not able to buy them, but I'll ask around for folks wanting a horse."

"Okay, I'll let her know. My sisters won't like it. Sharon wants Mom to keep them to ride until after she gets married."

"Huh? If your sister is working toward a college degree, how does she expect your mom to keep paying boarding fees until she finishes school?"

"No, I meant when Mom gets married. With having moved to town and needing to work, she doesn't have time to ride. Mom loves horses and is a decent breakaway roper. Sharon is pushing for Mom to get married, and the sooner the better."

"I've seen your mom rope, and she's better than decent. Why is Sharon pushing for your mom to get married?"

"Don't ask me. I'm staying out of the argument. But I believe my sister is more interested in something for her own benefit. She's always planning something, like hooking up with a guy at the rodeo."

Beth is always planning something, too. "Is your mom dating anyone?"

"Not at the moment, but I'm pretty sure she's keeping an eye out. She's suddenly single, and at forty-three, she's afraid no one will look at her. She's raised us kids and thinks everyone will consider her over the hill."

Am I over the hill?

"Getting back to the horses," I said, "have your mother call to discuss what she wants to do. Depending on her finances and what she's able to pay, maybe we can work something out."

"Thanks, Mr. York. I'll tell her."

"Thanks for settling her account." *A big thanks.*

If Harold was interested in dating Kim and she went out with him, a relationship might prove interesting.

Chapter 7

Monday, December 28th, afternoon

I attached the bale spear to the tractor and lugged a six-foot round bale into the steers' muddy feedlot. My cell phone chimed, and I fished it from my pocket. The number wasn't familiar and was likely a telemarketer. I let the call go to voice mail and returned the phone to my pocket. It rang again. Same number. I ignored it.

The phone rang a third time from the same number. A telemarketer wouldn't keep calling. I slid the answer button. "Hello?"

"Phil, this is Candy Murray, and I've been trying to call you."

"Sorry for not answering. The number wasn't in my contacts."

"I got a new cell phone this morning because I gave my old one to Harold. He told me what you said about the horses. Are you busy? Could I come and talk?"

"I plan to check the fence down by the oxbow. It's winter, and a section of the creek will dry up soon, making it necessary to open the other pasture for the steers to drink."

"If it's a bad time, when could we talk?"

The cattle pushed forward to get at the hay bale. "Candy, I'm in the middle of feeding the cattle and need to put you on hold for a minute." I muted the phone, maneuvered the tractor through the muddy feedlot, hopped out, and placed the feeder ring over the hay.

After leaving the lot and shutting the galvanized utility gate, I took the phone off mute. "Hey, Candy. Sorry about the delay. It's about half-past one right now. If you get here before three, I'll have time to talk."

"Thank you, thank you, thank you. I'll be there in forty minutes."

I was busy mucking out the horse stalls when Candy drove in and parked by the corral. As a slender, athletic woman, she stood about five feet six with short brown hair, graying at the temples. Wearing blue jeans and a brown corduroy coat, she stepped around the patches of snow and ice in her western boots, carrying herself with grace.

I said, "Candy, I kept your horses in after your girls went riding."

Her horses poked their heads over the gate, and she rubbed their necks. "They're lovely, aren't they?"

"They are. Roan Quarter Horses with white stockings are beautiful. Where did you get them?"

"At the Aksarben auction in Omaha. A girl raised them for a 4-H project. After I bought them, we chatted.

She won a blue ribbon with this one, Pigeon, and wanted to keep him, but her father took a job in Des Moines and said she had to sell them both."

Pigeon stuck his nose in her face, and she pushed it away.

"I bought Pigeon to be my roping horse, and I let the girls race around the barrels. They want me to keep them, but I can't afford to. My job is front-desk clerical at minimum wage. My ex isn't sending alimony as the court ordered, and I have to cut something from the budget."

"Harold said you've considered selling them. Is that what you're thinking?"

"I'd rather not. I came to beg for them to stay at a reduced rate. Is it possible?"

"I have bills to pay, too. If you want to sell them, I could search for someone. Or I could take them to the auction, but I'd have to charge for it."

She fidgeted. "I've still got the rodeo bug, and the girls want to ride whenever they're home. What if I helped you on the ranch to offset the boarding costs?"

Whoa. Where was this going? "Marston McGwin has been helping me. He'll be back after the New Year."

She looked around. "With all this livestock and with folks boarding their horses and coming to ride, surely you could use extra help?"

"You already have a regular job at Rollo."

"I know. I'm in a difficult situation. Is there any way to keep them? Please."

"Marston has talked about going to college. If he did, and Harold was to work for me, I could keep your horses. But I couldn't pay him what he would earn at Abbott Tech."

She wrinkled her mouth. "He wouldn't be interested. My ex berated him if he didn't help with the farm work, and he's had his fill of it. His stint in the army got him hooked on computers, and he wants to be a programmer to build websites."

"Then I don't see how I can help unless you know of another option," I said.

"If I quit my job and worked for you full time, Marston could go to college. I enjoy working on the farm and am a hard worker. You could probably pay better than what I'm currently making."

I leaned against the wall. "You're willing to give up a job with health insurance? I can't offer benefits. The hours would be long and hard."

"Phil, I've worked with horses. You know that. On the farm, I did everything imaginable and relished doing it. I operated tractors and equipment, sowed and harvested wheat, took care of animals, made hay, fixed fences, patched roofs, worked with the vet, everything."

I scratched my chin. Candy was a nice-looking woman, but if she worked for me, it would cause another problem. "There's a bigger reason you shouldn't work for me."

"Please, Phil, give me a chance. You could use the help even if Marston doesn't go to college. If he does, I'd already be working for you. I grew up as a farm girl, and I'm a good one. Ask my kids or anyone. They'll tell you I'm a first-rate farm worker."

"Candy, I'm a widower, and you're a divorcee. If you worked here, our reputations could take a nosedive. I don't want you to develop a reputation as a loose woman."

"Oh. I hadn't thought of that. I'd truly love to work on a farm or find a better job to keep the horses."

"You competed with Pigeon in the rodeo, and he means a lot, doesn't he?"

"Yes, he does. I'll do any kind of farm work to keep them both."

"Okay, here's what I'll do. I'll keep them rent-free for the next couple of weeks, say, until the middle of January. I'll make sure they have water. But I want you to come every day to feed, exercise, and clean up after them."

"Thank you, thank you, thank you. But what happens then?"

"Let me think it over. Maybe after the New Year, I'll come up with an idea. You be thinking too."

"Thanks. Speaking of the New Year, are you going to the New Year's Eve celebration?"

I snorted. "I don't have a choice. Beth corralled me into it."

"Yeah, she asked me too. She's on the planning committee and stopped by my house the other day. She's been knocking on the neighborhood's doors to invite everyone. We talked for a while, and I asked if she knew of another job that paid better. She thought for a bit and said she'd look around. If she found one, she'd introduce me to someone at the party."

Candy could go with me. I sucked air. *Where had that thought come from?* Judith would kill me for even thinking it.

Chapter 8

Monday, December 28th, evening

I finished currying Fargo and put the brush on the shelf as a bright red BMW turned into my driveway. JoAnn wasn't welcome and knew better than to come to the ranch. I leaned against the stable door and folded my arms.

She parked by the corral and watched me through the windshield before getting out, keeping the car door between her and me. "Am I safe, or will you throw me in the creek?"

"You're safe, but not welcome. Whether I let you stay will depend on why you came."

"You've hated me since my sister's funeral, haven't you?"

I easily could. "JoAnn, I don't hate you. If Judith were here, she'd tell you the same."

"I know she would. Is it possible to mend fences between you and me?"

Why would she mend fences after the horrible things she said? "In my book, you caused our trouble."

"That's why I came to apologize and patch up things between us. We could do fun things like when I treated you and your kids to the Kansas City Royals playoff game."

I planted my fists on my hips. "I'm listening." *This better be good.*

"Phil, I was mad that the accident had stolen away my sister, and I was hurting. You're not the mean ogre I called you at Judith's funeral, and you're not to blame for her death."

"You think you're hurting?" I yelled. "I still hurt. The ache never goes away. The love of my life should be here, not in the ground. I still see you berating me and claiming I caused her death. You stuck a knife in me as they lowered her casket. Everyone knew I treated her like a queen and would've died for her."

"I'm sorry for blaming you. How can I convince you I'm sorry?"

I took a breath. "Sorry for yelling. I shouldn't have lost control."

"I accept your apology. Will you accept mine?"

"Why should I? It's been almost two years since Judith's funeral. You could have said you're sorry at any time."

"Arrogance. It's hard to admit I'm wrong or own up to a fault. My conscience has been convicting me lately to patch up things between us."

"You buy and sell expensive real estate and make sure people know you have money. Two years ago, you sold a house to the mayor for about a million dollars." I pointed to her red BMW. "There's exhibit A. You should have apologized months ago. Why didn't you?"

"I read a letter and learned something." She stepped away from the car. "Phil, I'll get down on my knees to apologize."

This was something new. I pointed at her legs. "Are you sure you want to do that? The mud will ruin your expensive pantsuit."

"I'll grovel in the mud just to convince you, even if it means ruining this pantsuit. I came to mend fences, not burn bridges. The past is over, and I'm asking for a fresh start."

"I've never known you to humble yourself."

"Let's make a New Year's resolution or swear on the Bible."

When I hesitated, she dropped to her knees, and the mud splashed. "I mean it, Phil. Can we be friends like before my sister's death?"

Wow. She was very serious. I offered her a hand. "Will you get out of the mud?"

"Will you accept my apology?"

"If you let me know how much your pantsuit cost. It must have cost a mint."

She grasped my hand and struggled to stand. "It cost over twelve hundred. I've ruined these pants, but I had to show that my apology was real. What I said at my sister's funeral was wrong, and I've been too proud to admit it."

I motioned toward the house. "Let's go inside, where you can clean up."

She grabbed her purse from the car.

Inside, she changed into a pair of Judith's pants, and we retired to the den.

I said, "JoAnn, I forgive you, but my feelings may take a while to smooth over."

"It's understandable, and I'll accept it."

"You were always too smug to admit you were wrong. What changed?"

"I read something you wrote to Judith, and it gave me a new perception of you."

"Something I wrote? What was it?"

"Do you remember back when we were at Roosevelt High?" She reached into her purse.

"Yes, but that was ages ago."

She handed me a stack of letters. "You wrote these love letters to my big sister when you were dating her, and I read one."

Chapter 9

I raised my voice in the den as JoAnn handed me a stack of letters. "I wrote those letters to Judith, and they were supposed to be private."

She patted the air. "Calm down. I didn't realize they were your love letters until I read one. I didn't intend to snoop."

My fingers tightened. "I thought Judith burned them. Where did you find them?"

"After you married my sister, Dad stored her dresser in the basement. Last week, I planned to take it to Goodwill, and I removed the drawers to bring it upstairs. Judith had taped these letters to the back of them."

I'd written a letter to Judith every week during our last semester in high school, and she'd saved all fifteen. "Which one did you read?"

"Only the top one. That's when I stopped because they were so personal. What you wrote tells me more about you than anything I've learned in the thirty years I've known you."

Had it been thirty years? JoAnn had been an ornery, skinny girl back then, always hanging around and not leaving us alone. "I wish you hadn't read it."

"Honest, Phil, I didn't read any of the others because of how private they are."

I opened the envelope and removed the letter. "Only this one?"

She nodded. "None of the others."

I unfolded the pages. It had been a long time since I'd written in longhand.

My dearest sweetheart, Judith,

Earlier this week, I asked you to marry me. Your exuberant excitement and hopping up and down thrilled me almost as much as your yes. I can hardly wait until we graduate at the end of the semester and say I do to become partners for life.

Please understand that I don't take marriage lightly. It's a promise we'll make to each other and a covenant before God. I'm willingly binding myself to you for our entire lives. We'll have arguments and disagreements, but because of my love for you and your love for me, we'll steer our marriage through those rough waters.

I promise the idea of divorce will never enter my mind. Never. I'm not naïve about this promise and am well aware that situations may come between us, resulting in emotional tension. Without reservation, I'm determined to accept you as my wife for our entire lives, no matter what happens.

In our vows, I'll repeat, 'From this day forward.' I'll say it with my whole heart, and it'll mean until we're separated by death. In our vows, I'll repeat, 'until death do us part.' I'll not abandon our union, no matter how hard things become. In our vows, I'll repeat, 'in sickness and in health.' If, in the future, you become sick and bedridden, I'll not leave your side. These are my promises to you.

I love you as a sweetheart and will love you as my wife. As a Christian, I'll never act to cheapen our love. This letter is my contract with you and a promise before God.

I can hardly wait until we receive our diplomas at graduation and say our vows on the first of June. I love you, Judith, with a depth greater than the deepest sea.

Abundant love, innumerable kisses, and unconditionally yours forever.

Phil.

My throat tightened. *There were so many memories. Dates to ball games, senior prom, English class, South Pacific stage play, concert and marching band, studying together.* We told Beth and Tom about our promise, so it wasn't a total secret. Judith never told JoAnn.

I'd snuck this letter into Judith's school locker before going to class. In the middle of the period, she burst into the room and gave me a full lip lock, much to the enjoyment of everyone and our teacher's shock. He sent us to the principal's office.

"Phil," said JoAnn, "when I read the letter, you grew in stature. There isn't a superlative high enough for what you wrote. No wonder Judith cherished you. I wish Keith had written something like this while we were dating."

"Didn't he write love notes while you were in school?"

"Not really. Only on Valentine's Day and my birthday."

"Didn't he write while serving in Afghanistan?"

"His emails were about where he was going, what he was seeing, and what he was doing—mostly about his activities but not much else. Before the army shipped him out, I got pregnant and didn't realize it. When I wrote to him about the miscarriage, he wrote back to only say he was sorry. I wanted to scratch his eyes out. Didn't I mean more than an 'I'm sorry?'"

Oh, my word. "I … I never knew about your miscarriage. Judith said nothing about it."

She sighed. "To learn that I was pregnant excited me, but suddenly I wasn't. That was the same time they shipped Keith's coffin home. There was no reason to talk about losing a baby, and I didn't share it with anyone."

"JoAnn, I … I really don't know what to say. To offer condolences would sound trite."

"I suppose it's my fault for being so proud and afraid to say anything."

I sat back in the chair. "At the funeral, why did you vilify me? You embarrassed Beth and Tom. Did you mean any of what you said?"

"No, because I'd been drinking."

I frowned. "You never drank."

"Someone sent a bottle of wine out of kindness. Right before Judith's funeral, I drank it to kill the pain. Death had stolen away my sister, and I was bitter. At the gravesite, my anger boiled over, and the alcohol started talking. You were the scapegoat."

I slowly shook my head. "JoAnn, I never knew this. If you had told me months ago, I'd have forgiven you. The way you maligned me, I honestly thought you equated me with the devil incarnate. Why did you keep it hidden?"

"Because of my stubborn pride. I never drank, not even in high school. Arnold Geisinger said he'd give me two hundred dollars if I publicly got plastered, and I refused. I hate alcohol and didn't want it known that my sister's death made me succumb to its evils. My conscience has been kicking to get our relationship straightened out. It's the main reason I came today. I was horrible to you and feared you wouldn't forgive me."

"Truthfully, I almost didn't. If the main reason for coming was to say you're sorry, is there another reason?"

She covered her mouth and blushed. "Confound it. Me and my big mouth. When will I keep it shut?"

I waited, and when she didn't say more, I asked, "What do you mean?"

"I guess back in high school, I had a huge crush on you. You were dating my big sister and came to the house so often that I became infatuated."

"Judith said you had starry eyes for me."

"All the girls in my class thought you were a prize catch. In Judith's freshman year, when you asked her to go steady, she giggled because you could have asked anyone but chose her. You had eyes only for my sister."

I smiled. "That's true."

JoAnn snickered. "Do you remember when Gloria Atwell asked you to the *Sadie Hawkins Day* dance? The rules required you to go with her, but you didn't."

I shook my head. "No, I don't remember."

"You and Judith spent the evening at our place. Because you didn't show up, it mortified Gloria, and she told everyone you were sick instead of admitting that you stood her up."

"Are you sure she asked me?"

"She thought she'd asked you, and she told everyone you were going to the dance with her."

"I remember nothing about it."

"No one could deny that you and my sister were an item. You never looked at another girl. Maybe Judith wasn't the prettiest, but you belonged to her."

"Thanks for the praise. I'm glad we've gotten things straightened out between us."

"Me too. Because I'd built a wall, I refused to tear it down for fear you'd hate me."

"Not once have I hated you." I glanced toward the kitchen. "Sorry, JoAnn, I'm not very hospitable. Would you like a cup of coffee?"

"That sounds nice. I'll help you perk it."

In the kitchen, I got the cups from the cupboard as she filled the machine with water.

While we waited, I said, "I want to ask something, and it may sound strange."

"What is it?"

"I want to continue to mend fences between us, and I have a special request. It would help me out of an embarrassing situation."

"You said you forgave me. If it's legal, I'll help."

"Beth corralled me into going to the New Year's Eve party, and she had plans to set me up with someone. If my sister-in-law went with me, it would foil her plans."

"At school, I always dreamed of dating you." JoAnn fished her phone out of her purse and checked the calendar. "I've got an appointment in Omaha about a problem with a property. If I can move the meeting to another time, I'll go with you."

Chapter 10

Tuesday, December 29th, morning

I dialed Beth's number. "Hey Princess, how is the family?"

"Hi, Dad. Eddy has a cold, and I'm keeping him inside. Everyone else is okay."

"I'm sorry. Will you take him to the doctor?"

"No, I'm going to wait and see. It could be the weather affecting his sinuses. If it gets worse, I'll take him to the doctor. What did you need?"

"I need to fix the fence down by the oxbow and could use your help. I plan to move the cattle to the other pasture, but a tree fell, knocking over three posts and destroying a section of the fence. Marston is out of town for the holidays. Could you give me a hand?"

"I can't because of Eddy's sniffles, and I don't want to chance it. Since Marston is visiting family, why don't you hire someone temporarily? Do you know anyone?"

"Candy Murray mentioned her son, Harold, but he's interviewing for a job at Abbott Tech. If they hired him, he'd be working with computers. It's web programming, I think."

Her voice rose. "Oh really? That's interesting. When did you talk to Candy?"

"Yesterday. She came to discuss her horses and wants to keep them but can't pay the boarding fees. I worked out something for a couple of weeks until after the New Year. Then we'll talk again."

"I talked with her too and invited her to the New Year's Eve party. She's planning to go. She doesn't like her job and wants to work on a farm. If you hired her, she could keep her horses, couldn't she? And you'd have a woman to keep you company."

"Bethany Lynn, that's enough. You promised to back off. Don't set me up."

"She'd be a big help around the ranch."

"No more of this." A slice of sun peeked above the horizon, but a layer of clouds quickly covered it. "Is David on holiday? Could he help fix the fence?"

"No. His boss called him back to work for an emergency. He isn't sure when he'll be home. What about Kim? She'd help you."

"I thought she was working. With all the year-end accounting, she said she wouldn't be able to get off."

"She's off today. We talked last night, and they're giving the staff a day off on a rolling schedule. Call her."

"Thanks. I will."

When Beth and Tom were growing up, Kim worked alongside them and was a big help around the ranch.

I called her and asked if she could help with my fencing problem.

"I'd be glad to help," she said. "Let me change into work clothes, and I'll be right there."

I got the tractor and trailer ready and loaded the wire, fence posts, and tools from the storage shed.

Kim arrived and jumped out of her car. "I see you have everything ready. Let's go fix your fence."

"The last time I saw you with a long ponytail was when you were in college. You look nice."

"Thanks. I cut my hair after graduation and have been letting it grow again. A ponytail is the simplest, and I was putting it up when you called."

"Well, this person likes it. What does Beth say?"

"She hasn't seen it yet."

Down by the oxbow, we used the chainsaw to clear away the fallen tree. I'd ask Marston to burn the branches when he returned. Kim and I dug the postholes and replaced the broken posts, tamping the surrounding dirt.

We took a breather.

She leaned against the tractor tire and said, "Beth has you feeling anxious about meeting someone. Don't let her get to you. She means well."

"Not hardly because she sticks her nose in where it doesn't belong."

"I don't believe she does."

"I do. Why would you say that?"

"Right after the funeral, you were grieving, and I could understand your sorrow. In your pain, you were irritable. But it's been two years, and you're still short-tempered and grouchy."

"If what you say is true, and I'm not saying it is, what's your answer to my grouchiness?"

"You're lonely. Beth sees it, I see it, and you refuse to admit it. It's why we want you to meet someone. Without a woman, you're not complete."

I sat on the wagon bed. "Don't forget the adage. Before a man marries, he's not complete. After he marries, he's finished."

"Quit that. When you married Judith, she didn't finish you. You formed a good couple, and together, you raised two beautiful children. You should realize you need a woman. If you don't, you'll continue to be a grumpy sourpuss."

"I hear you, but I don't see it. There was no one like Judith. Do you know anyone like her?"

"Yes, I do, and no, I'm not telling. I won't set you up with anyone. You should meet her on your own."

"No matter what you ladies say, I'm not ready for a wife. It's much too soon."

"I don't think two years is too soon, and I believe you should have already found someone."

I swung my arm toward the horizon. "If I wanted to, where would I look? Give me a hint."

"You already know this person. It's the only hint I'll give."

"That's not much help. Is it why you want me to attend the New Year's Eve party, to meet someone?"

"It's Beth's reason."

"If it's not yours, why do you want me to go?"

"I want you to have fun by getting away from the horses and cows. Your life revolves around this ranch, and it's stunting your personality. You need an outlet."

"I love this ranch, and it's my whole life."

"Loving this ranch isn't your problem. Loving it *alone* is. You need someone who'll love it as much as you."

"Who would love this ranch as much as me? This person, what's she like? Would she be like Judith?"

"That's a silly question and doesn't need an answer. Let's finish this fence and move the cows into the pasture. I'm ready for coffee."

While we strung the fence and pulled the wire tight, my mind wouldn't slow down. Kim was logical in her thinking and reasoned well. No matter how hard I tried, I couldn't see what she meant. I didn't see the need to date, but why did she?

Chapter 11

Tuesday, December 29th, late morning

Back at the house, Kim perked the coffee and poured it. As we sat at the kitchen table, she said, "Phil, are you upset that I want you to meet someone?"

"I hear what you're saying, but it doesn't register. It's as if you're saying, 'Phil isn't happy.'"

"That's exactly what I'm saying. You're too involved with your memories of Judith and don't see what others see. Beth and I see it, but we can't get it through your thick skull. Because of your lack of contentment, you need a woman by your side."

I leaned back in my chair. "If what you say is true, am I supposed to follow Beth's suggestion?"

"Don't follow either of us. Follow the Lord. Have you been praying?"

I waggled my head. "A few times."

"You know better. The Lord will lead if you pray as you did with Judith. If you followed him, you'd be happy. Are you?"

"I'm not sure. Maybe."

"See, I rest my case."

"Ouch. Judith scolded me like this."

"Thanks for comparing us, but I'm nothing like her because she was a lot smarter."

Outside, a car drove up to the stables, and Kim looked out the kitchen window. "Who are those people?"

"It's Candy Murray, her two daughters, and her son. They came to take care of their horses. The girls will go riding."

"I didn't recognize her at first. She works at Rollo's front desk."

"She told me the same thing when she came yesterday to discuss her horses. Because of her divorce, she can't pay the boarding fees and asked if I'd hire her full-time. It wouldn't look good for her to work with me."

"I agree. It could be awkward."

"She doesn't want to sell the horses. I'd like to help her, but I don't see how."

Kim touched my arm. "I have an idea, so hear me out. If she can't pay her boarding fees and she sold her horses, you'd be minus the money. Correct?"

I nodded. "That's right."

"Consider this. If she's not paying now, you're still short those funds."

"You're saying, either way, I'm not getting paid."

"That's what I'm saying. Why not give her a break? Reduce what you charge down to what she's able to pay."

"I need money now. I owe Gene Wilcox ten grand for the damaged horse trailer."

She grimaced. "Wow. That's a lot. But if Candy's little bit was coming in, it would be better than nothing. When she got a raise or found a better job, you could adjust her fees."

"If I gave her a break, and she told others, they'd want the same deal."

"Tell Candy not to talk about your generosity, not even to her girls. The Bible says you're not to tell your neighbor to come back tomorrow when you can help today. God put you in the perfect place to help her."

Outside, the girls led the horses out of the stables. They mounted and cantered across the pasture toward the trail leading down to the creek.

Kim nudged me. "If you decide to help Candy, now's a good time."

"Do you figure I should?"

"It's a suggestion. I won't tell you how to run this ranch. It's up to you to decide if you can afford it or not."

I scratched my head. "Yeah, you're right, I can. Let me get my coat."

***

Candy's girls closed the pasture gate and broke into a gallop down the trail as I walked up to the paddock fence.

I said to Candy and Harold, "They look like they're having fun."

She rolled her eyes. "When they knew I'd be feeding the horses every day, they begged to tag along. I told them they had to clean up their messes and brush them, too."

"Harold said your girls are in college. When will they head back?"

"The fourth of January. Then it'll only be me taking care of them." She looked over her shoulder. "Is that Kim's car?"

"I called her to help fix a downed section of the fence. She's staying for supper before heading back to her apartment."

"Could I talk to her?" asked Harold.

"Sure. Knock on the back door."

He sped toward the house and tapped on the door. Kim answered and invited him in.

Candy gestured to the house. "He plans to ask her out. Will she go with him?"

"I don't know. She might. I stay out of her private life, and she doesn't say much."

"I've talked to her a few times at work. She's nice."

"She's smart, too." I leaned against the corral fence. "I assume you're looking for a different job."

"Wish me luck. All I've got are farming skills. I'm not able to move anywhere, and no one will hire a farmgirl with no college education. I'm stuck and don't know what to do."

"What about Harold? Could he help financially?"

"Maybe, but he doesn't have a job yet, and I'm not counting on it. Everything I make goes for rent, utilities, and food. What's an over-the-hill farmgirl supposed to do?"

"What about your alimony? Could the court force your ex to pay regularly?"

"It means lawyers, and they don't come cheap, so I'm stuck." She shrugged. "Maybe I could marry a rich farmer."

"Marrying someone for money is never a good idea."

"I know. It was just a thought that came to mind, and I meant it as a joke."

While leaning against the fence, I said, "I came outside to ask you something."

"That's kind of what I figured."

"I have a proposition, but I want to know how much you can pay for boarding your horses. Anything or nothing?"

"Not much, maybe twenty-five dollars a week. It might cover their feed costs, wouldn't it?"

"It would. Here's what I'll do. I'll board them if you continue to come daily to care for them, and you pay me the twenty-five dollars a week or, if it's easier, monthly."

Her eyes opened wide. "You'll let them stay for that paltry amount? Do you mean it?"

"Only if you promise two things. One, you don't tell anyone about this arrangement, not even your kids.

Second, if you get a raise or a better job, you'll make up the difference. Is that agreeable?"

"Thank you, thank you, thank you. Yes, it's great, and I don't know what else to say. May I hug you?"

I opened my arms.

She squeezed me tight. "Thank you, Phil. You don't know how much this means."

"This arrangement should help for a while until you're able to pay more."

She smiled. "This is a marvelous New Year's present. I won't have a debt hanging over me."

But thanks to Gene Wilcox, I had one. "I'm glad to make the new year brighter."

"Phil, the New Year's Eve party is in two days. I don't want to be forward, but Shelly and Sharon are pushing like bulldozers for me to date you. They want me to ask if you and I could go to the party together."

Whoa. Her girls were aggressive, and Beth was doing the same thing to me. "I can't. I've already asked someone."

Chapter 12

Tuesday, December 29th, night

As I crawled into bed, my cell phone rang. I rolled over and fumbled for it on the nightstand. "Hello."

"Dad, are you awake?"

"I'm talking to you, aren't I, Princess? Why did you call at this time of night?"

"Could you make an emergency trip to town?"

"What's going on? What happened?"

"Someone's Christmas tree caught fire at the Apex Apartments. The building is a total loss, and the fire department is still putting out hot spots."

I sat up. "Oh, my. Was anyone hurt?"

"Jim and Mary Peters and their son went to the hospital for minor burns and smoke inhalation. Everyone else got out. The police asked the Skyway Motel to accept folks for a couple of nights. I'm calling because Elaine

Freeman and her three kids don't have a place to stay. The motel is full."

"They could come to the ranch, I suppose. Is that what you're asking?"

"No, Candy Murray said they could temporarily stay with her, but she doesn't have beds, meaning they'd have to sleep on the floor. Shelly and Sharon said they're willing to sleep double until they go back to college, which will free up one bed. I have an air mattress, but it leaks. You have that old clunker of a bed in the garage. Could you bring it and any spare blankets?"

"Sure. I've got an extra mattress someplace, too. How old are Elaine's kids? Do they need clothes?"

"Three, seven, and eleven. The girls are the older ones. I've got clothes and toys for the boy, but not the girls."

"Let me see what I can scrounge up. What about her husband? I've got clothes he could wear if he's close to my size."

"Don't bother. Elaine divorced him three years ago when he went to prison. She's been existing on welfare. Bring the bed, mattresses, and whatever else you can find to Candy's house. It's two houses down from me."

"I'll be there as soon as I can."

***

Beth and David were waiting in front of Candy's house as I parked the pickup.

David ran his fingers through his thin hair. "Phil, let's get the bed frame and mattresses inside and set them up. Honey, bring the blankets so the kids will have a place to sleep. This may be a long night."

Inside, I lay under the bedframe, assembling it as Candy and Elaine watched. I asked, "Elaine, how are your kids?"

She grimaced. "They're pretty shaken up. They lost their clothes, Christmas toys, and everything. Candy loaned me these clothes."

"They're not a loan," said Candy. "I'm giving them to you. I also have more that you can have. Shelly and Sharon will go through their closet in the morning. Their items might not fit your girls exactly, but they won't be in PJs either."

Beth stuck her head into the room. "Elaine, your boy is the same age as Ian, so don't worry about clothes or shoes for him."

Elaine held back tears. "Everybody, thank you. I don't know what we'd have done."

I tightened the last bolt on the bedframe. "Let's get this bed made up so someone can sleep here."

Beth and David placed a mattress on the frame and covered it with sheets and blankets.

I said, "Candy, this past summer, Kim canned green beans and corn from our garden. I'll bring those over tomorrow to help feed this crew. David, if you still have your old iPhone, I'll buy it and give it to Elaine."

"There's no need to buy it. I'll give it to her."

"Thank you, everyone," said Elaine.

Candy caught my attention. "Phil, when my girls and I come to care for the horses, could Elaine and her kids come too and maybe ride?"

"Sure. I'll bring the horses into the stables. Harold could come and make it an outing."

"Dad," said Beth, "you could take them to Lookout Station. They could see the entire valley. The snow on the heights is beautiful this year."

I shook my head. "No, I can't go. Fargo got feisty and kicked a hole in his stall. Marston isn't here to fix it, so it's up to me. Why don't you take them to the overlook? I'll take care of your boys while you're gone."

"Come on, Dad. You should ride Fargo or Challenger again."

"Beth, we've talked about this before. I'm not going riding, and this is a family matter. Drop it."

Candy asked, "Why won't you go, Phil? We'd enjoy your company."

"Thanks, Princess, for revealing the family's dirty laundry." My voice dripped with sarcasm. "No, I won't go riding."

"Dad, you need to go riding again."

My jaw stiffened. "I said drop it, Beth, *now*."

Everyone's eyes focused on me.

"Why not?" asked Candy.

"Yes," said Elaine. "Why not?"

"Dad refuses to ride," said Beth. "Ever since Mom died, he stopped going to the rodeo and hasn't climbed aboard a saddle or swung a rope. He refuses, and I don't know why."

"Beth. Leave. Me. Alone," I said through clenched teeth. "You're dredging up old laundry and should have kept your mouth shut. I'm going home." I grabbed my coat and slammed the door on my way out.

Chapter 13

Wednesday, December 30th, morning

I opened my eyes as someone tapped on my bedroom door.

"Phil, it's me, Kim. It's time to feed the livestock."

The clock read 5:56 a.m. I turned off the alarm and grumbled, "I'm awake."

She said from the other side of the door, "I'll get the coffee perked, you get dressed, and I'll help with chores."

When I arrived in the kitchen, she handed me a cup of coffee. "Drink this to get awake. After chores, we're coming back to talk."

"Why?"

"Don't argue. Drink your coffee and get out the door."

"Why are you here? You should be at work."

"Beth called last night and said you threw a hissy fit at Candy's house in front of everyone. I called the office to take a personal day and see what's wrong with you."

"There's nothing wrong with me."

"Don't give me that nonsense. You exploded at three women. I've known you for sixteen years, and it's totally out of character. Something is chewing your tail. Let's go feed the animals, then we'll talk, and I'll fix breakfast."

"Confound Beth. She tells you every jot and tittle. Why won't she keep her mouth shut?"

"Because she loves you, that's why. Enough of this. We'll talk after chores."

Crazy daughter, why couldn't she just leave well enough alone?

Kim and I went to the stables and spoke only what was necessary to do the chores.

Back in the kitchen, she pulled out a chair. "Sit and tell me what's going on."

"I'd rather eat first."

"We'll eat after we talk."

"What if I don't want to talk?"

She locked eyes with me. "I asked you to sit and said it nicely. Sit."

"You're sure ordering me around."

"Because you need it. Sit."

"Alright." I plopped into the chair.

She sat across from me. "I won't bite. Talk to me. What's going on?"

"Maybe you don't bite, but Beth does. She thinks she knows what's best for me, but she doesn't."

"Beth has her faults, but I don't believe she is anything like that. Your emotions are making you feel that way."

"She's trying to get me married. It's nonsense for me to get hitched to someone I know nothing about."

"All Beth asked yesterday was for you to go riding. What's wrong with that?"

"I don't want to ride, and she should know it."

"Phil, would you listen to yourself? You're angry over nothing. You better stop this nonsense."

"What if I don't want to?"

"For crying out loud, I give up. You're a stubborn, thickheaded old goat and beyond help." She stood. "Stew in your own beard. Call me when you're ready to talk."

I stuck out my hand and blocked her exit. "Don't go."

She looked down at me. "Then, for goodness' sake, tell me what's going on." She returned to her chair and said, "I'm waiting. Why won't you ride the horses?"

"Because Judith isn't here."

"I know that. Keep talking."

"She rode Challenger, and we were a team in the rodeo."

"I know that, too. So why won't you ride him?"

"If someone else rode him, I'd be blackening her name."

"I don't agree," said Kim. "If it bothers you, why not ride Fargo or Serenity or another horse?"

"I'd be an adulterer."

"No, you wouldn't."

"Yes, I would. Beth keeps pushing and doesn't understand how I feel."

"Leave Beth out of this. We're talking about riding a horse. Help me understand how you'd be an adulterer."

I swallowed and looked down. "When Judith rode with me, it was like we were making love. I can't explain it any better than that. If someone else rode Challenger, it would be like sleeping with another woman. If I rode Fargo without Judith beside me, it would be like divorcing her. I've never been unfaithful."

Kim waited until I was looking at her. "What would it take for you not to feel unfaithful to Judith?"

"For her to come back."

She tapped the table. "That isn't possible. Now, tell me the other way."

"What other way?"

Her voice went up a notch. "Phillip Edward York, you're avoiding the entire issue. You need a woman to share your life so your heart will heal."

"Why does everyone want to set me up with someone? I just want everyone to leave me alone."

"Phil, close your eyes for a minute. Come on, close them."

I did. "What am I supposed to visualize?"

"Imagine you had a wife—not Judith, but someone else. How would you treat her? What would you do for her? You'd have someone by your side, helping and encouraging you. She'd be someone in the house—someone to ride horses with, someone to embrace, and someone to dream with. You'd focus on her, and your attitude would change."

I winced as I opened my eyes. "I'd be an adulterer if I found another woman."

"No one would believe that."

"Judith would. I promised never to cheapen my love for her."

"You promised until death do us part, not until you were both dead. She'd want you to live a full life with someone."

"I find that hard to believe."

"Phil, your heart is bleeding. Judith's death has torn your life into tatters, and you've got a thick head for not realizing it. Have you prayed about it?"

"Yeah, I did last night, and it was a one-way conversation. All I got was silence."

"Then God's not ready to answer. When the time comes, you'll meet the woman that God has for you. Until then, have an open mind. If you build walls, God can't work in your life."

I shifted in the chair. "I wish Beth talked like you."

"What do you mean? She'd say the same things I'm saying."

"I hate the way she pushes and prods."

"She may have problems, but you don't hate her."

"I love my daughter, but I hate the way she treats me. You talk without an ulterior motive."

"Are you sure? I have a strong motive and always have your best interests at heart."

"Well, you don't push."

"I'm strongly nudging you to find a relationship. Are you open to one?"

"No, but out of respect, I'll keep my eyes open."

"Look around," she said. "You'll find someone."

"I've recently been around three ladies near my age. Are you saying I should consider them?"

"It's a starting point. Ask God to lead, but don't close your eyes to anyone else."

"I'll try, but it would feel like cheating."

"Well, you're not. The Bible says that when a man loses his spouse, he's freed from the law of marriage. I know you were close to Judith, but for goodness' sake, don't let it muddle your heart. God has someone for you. Lean on him, and he'll direct your next step."

Chapter 14

Wednesday, December 30th, afternoon

I said to Kim after lunch, "I promised Candy several jars of the vegetables you canned. Could you take them when you go to town?"

"Sure. But shouldn't you apologize to Candy and Elaine?"

"You're right. I will."

"What about apologizing to Beth?"

"Definitely not Beth."

"Would you listen to yourself?" said Kim. "You sound like you're out for revenge."

"Let me simmer down."

"Beth needs an apology. She's not the devil."

"I know she's not. A devil is what I thought of JoAnn before she came to apologize."

"*Wait? What?* She never apologizes. This is huge, earth-shaking news."

I grunted. "Yes, it is. She stopped by two days ago to grovel in the mud, literally, and ask for forgiveness for being idiotic."

"She must have had quite a story. Or did she pull the wool over your eyes?"

"It was an honest apology. If you want the details of why she called me such vile names at Judith's funeral, ask her."

"She's always been a proud woman and doesn't like anyone telling her she's wrong. I can hardly believe she came crawling back."

"She came to mend fences, and I forgave her. We're working to rebuild our relationship."

Kim's melt-all smile filled her face. "Wow, this is fantastic."

"I want to say something so it won't be a surprise. I asked JoAnn to go with me tomorrow evening. It would put a kink in Beth's plans."

Kim's smile faded. "If Beth concerns you, at least tell her you're sorry for yesterday."

"You make it sound important."

"It's what God wants, so it is."

"I assume you're going to the New Year's Eve party. Did Harold ask for a date?"

She frowned. "Did he tell you?"

"No, I didn't know for sure. He came to pay Candy's boarding fees and asked if you were dating. I suspected he'd ask. Tomorrow night would be a good time for a date, wouldn't it?"

"It would. Anyway, getting back to Beth, you need to apologize for your hissy fit."

"I will."

"When?"

"Yesterday. Will that be soon enough?"

"Your sarcasm isn't funny. When?"

"This afternoon."

"Thank you. I'll take the canning jars to Candy. She and Elaine will appreciate it."

***

I returned from town after apologizing to the three ladies. At least they were smiling when I left.

JoAnn was waiting by the stables.

I stepped out of the pickup. "Hi, JoAnn. I hope you didn't wait long."

"I've been waiting for about thirty minutes and was ready to leave when I saw your pickup puttering down the road. Where did you go?"

"I was in town talking to Beth. What did you want?"

"You asked me to go to the party and said something about foiling Beth's plan. Are there problems between you and her?"

"We have our differences. I blew my top yesterday and had to apologize."

"I don't remember you ever exploding at Beth."

"Beth keeps insisting I should start dating and wants to set me up with someone. It's the last thing I want."

"If you don't want to go out with anyone, why did you ask me?"

"I thought going to the party would smooth things out between us and rebuild our relationship."

"Are you using me for an external purpose?"

Lord, help me now. "No, I am not using you. I want to rebuild our friendship. Before Judith died, you went with us to school ball games and sometimes to the rodeo. We had good times at church socials and family picnics. The New Year's Eve party could be another good time."

"Oh, I won't be able to go to the party because I'll be in Omaha. My business client insists we discuss his problem before the New Year. Let me square up this matter, and we'll plan another outing."

"Thanks for letting me know."

Now, what could I do? Without JoAnn to accompany me, I wouldn't have a roadblock to squash Beth's plans. Should I ask Candy? No, I'd be cheating on Judith and exploiting Candy.

Chapter 15

Thursday, December 31st, evening

The New Year's Eve party appeared to be in full swing when I arrived. Beth and David weren't here yet. I spotted Kim, shrugged out of my coat, and settled in beside her. "Where's Harold? I thought you'd be with him."

She wrinkled her nose. "I declined when he asked."

"I thought you agreed to go with him."

"He's nice, but I came alone. Where's JoAnn? Wasn't she coming with you?"

"She had a business problem requiring attention. Meaning she won't be here as a buffer to keep Beth from setting me up."

"Will you stop fretting about her? At least enjoy the evening with me."

"It makes me anxious about what she might do."

"She promised to back off, so forget it. She and David should be here soon, and we'll have a grand time."

"I hope so. Ah, you've kept your ponytail."

"Beth liked it, and so did David."

"It makes you look lovely."

Kim blushed. "Thank you. I'll accept a compliment from you any day."

I glanced around the hall. "It looks like the city council did a marvelous job of decorating."

Streamers, bunting, and multi-colored lights draped from every horizontal surface. A picture of Father Time hung on the far wall as he tottered down a road toward the horizon. Beside him, the bright-eyed infant, New Year, watched him pass. A digital clock counted down the minutes. A glittering ball spun slowly above the floor, splattering showers of light over the dancers.

I nudged Kim. "You must have made a beeline to this table as soon as you arrived. The balloons, tablecloth, and everything are yellow."

"I couldn't resist. Do you remember when Beth and I dressed up for our eighth-grade Halloween party? You called me the Yellow Kid."

I laughed out loud. "You were so bright that we said you glowed. We needed sunglasses to keep our eyes from bleeding."

She laughed with me. "Whatever happened to my yellow cowgirl hat and boots? I can't imagine Goodwill wanting them."

"Judith was sentimental and probably put them in the attic. Remember the look on the clerk's face when you and Beth ordered your yellow costumes? He announced to everyone in the store that you were nuttier than a fruitcake."

Her hands flew to her cheeks. "I'll never live that down." She took a moment to regain her composure. "What do you think of the band?"

I listened for a moment as they played a song I didn't know. "When I came in tonight, they were playing a country song, then they shifted to a jazz tune. They're all right, I guess. I'm too old-fashioned for today's songs."

Jerry Dunlap sauntered up to our table. "Good evening, Phil," he crooned, extending his hand.

I stared at him and ignored his hand. "What do *you* want?"

He withdrew his hand. "Don't forget my offer. It's open and will help with money problems." He grinned. "Even you have money problems. We'll talk more later." He strolled away.

"What was that about?" asked Kim. "Why would you do business with that creep?"

"I'll never do business with him. He offered to buy Challenger, and it sounded crooked. I don't trust him."

"Does he know about your debt to Gene?"

"Probably. He's got his fingers in a lot of finances, and it makes me wonder."

David and Beth entered the hall through the far door.

Kim stood to catch their attention and motioned them toward our table.

I helped Beth remove her coat. "Your dress looks nice. It reminds me of the one I bought your mother for your cousin Esther's wedding."

"It's the same dress. I took it out of your closet to wear tonight."

I took a breath to stay calm. "It belonged to your mother, not you."

"I can't imagine you wearing it, and I know you like the red flowers. It fits me just fine."

"Beth, I don't like it when you intrude into my privacy. Don't do it again."

David removed his hat and ran his fingers through his sparse hair. "I'm starved. Let's head to the buffet."

Food always came first for him. Kim and I followed Beth and David to the buffet line.

Back at the table, after I'd forked the last bit of baked potato into my mouth, Beth tugged on my arm. "Come on, Dad, let's dance."

I hadn't danced since a long-ago wedding when there was no respectable way to decline. "You won't appreciate me stomping on your toes, Princess."

"Da-ad, you can dance."

Was it her plan for me to meet someone by bumping into them on the dance floor? She kept pulling, and several heads turned in our direction. I said, "Okay, you win. But I've warned about your toes." I might as well try to enjoy the evening.

Through the slow dance, I could smell Beth's black hair, and it was like Judith's sun-dried sheets hanging from our clothesline. It had been a long time since I'd wrapped my arms around my wife.

Beth wiggled. "You're proving my point, Dad."

"What point is that?"

"You're holding me like you held Mom."

I dropped my arms.

"She's gone, Dad, and you should find someone else."

"That's enough, Beth. You promised to back off."

"You're right, I did."

The band finished the song, and I was returning to the table when she grabbed my shirt and said, "Oh no, you're not getting away." She kept me on the floor for another dance.

During the next song, I knew she wouldn't give up, so I might as well see who she had in mind. "Who's the woman you want me to meet?"

She looked up at me. "I gave my word to back off."

"Could you give me a hint so I can rigorously avoid her?"

"Quit it. I promised not to push. You'll have to meet her on your own."

"Is this mystery woman here tonight?"

"I'm not saying."

Beth would arrange for me to meet the unknown woman, even if I didn't want to.

The band took a breather, and we returned to our seats.

"Dancing with you was fun," she said.

I made a face. "Not hardly."

"Come on, Dad. Enjoy the evening."

After sitting down, I said to Kim, "Did you see Howard on the other side of the room?"

"I saw him."

"Will you dance if he asks?"

"I'm pretty sure he won't."

"I thought their whole family was coming," said Beth. "Where are Candy and Shelly?"

"They'll probably be here later," said David.

"No, something happened," said Kim. "Sharon and Shelly are always together."

"You're right," said Beth. "They're never apart."

David said to me, "Come on, Phil. Let the ladies talk, and we'll get dessert for everyone."

We stood in the buffet line, and as we inched forward, I spoke to his back, teasing him. "You're sure a short son-in-law. Will you ever grow taller?"

He snickered. "Being a runt makes me more grounded than you, especially with my extra weight—it anchors my feet to the floor. You're so tall that your head floats in the clouds, and you can't see clearly. You're such an airhead that you need me to keep you from floating away."

I rubbed his bald spot. "They say cooler heads are better than hot heads. This is sure warm. Does Beth shine this chrome dome?"

He chortled. "Your head is a weed patch and grows nothing worthwhile. I'm proud of my bald spot. Grass doesn't grow on a busy street. What's your excuse?"

I shook my finger at him. "Grass doesn't grow on a rock, either."

He roared with laughter. "I've never heard that comeback. You got me there."

We moved closer to the dessert table, and I glanced toward the ladies. Beth was talking on her cell phone. "I wish your wife would quit meddling for me to meet someone."

"She's always got a bee in her bonnet about something. I've learned to live with it." He examined the pie selections.

"Well, she's got a swarm of bees buzzing around her head and is playing matchmaker for me to meet a woman." I surveyed the hall for an unattached female about my age. Candy and Elaine might still arrive. Was one of them part of Beth's plan?

David chose the usual apple and pumpkin pies and slathered them with a double portion of whipped cream. "I stay out of my wife's schemes."

Beth approached with a pinched expression and whispered in David's ear.

He blanched.

She said, "Dad, I got a call from the sitter. Ian cut his finger really deep."

I winced. "Oh, my word. How bad is it?"

"Clear to the bone. She got the bleeding stopped, but he's in a lot of pain. It looks like we're visiting the hospital tonight." She kissed my cheek. "Sorry, we won't be here to enjoy the evening with you. Be sociable with all the ladies and don't be a sourpuss like usual. Kim will help you check them out. Try to have a good time with someone. Love you."

I collected the dessert plates from David and said a quick prayer for my grandson. I stopped short. Beth wouldn't be here to enact her monkeyshines. I could enjoy the evening.

Chapter 16

After Beth and David had departed from the New Year's Eve party, the place seemed to brighten as I returned to the table. Kim's smile radiated like a gift from heaven.

I set the plates of pie down. "I assume you heard about Ian."

She grimaced. "The call from the sitter rattled Beth. While the sitter was cutting cheese for a snack, she turned away. Ian snatched up the knife and sliced a finger pretty badly. I hope he'll be okay."

"Yeah, so do I."

Kim selected the pumpkin pie and cut a piece.

"Beth is always protective of her boys." I savored the apple pie and watched the crowd. When Kim stayed quiet, my gaze swung to her.

She twiddled the fork in her fingers while staring at the far wall.

I smiled. "Kim, you often drift off into a world of your own. Penny for your thoughts."

She blushed and put down her fork. "I remembered things I did as a girl—stuff I did, plans I made. It's strange how I ended up being someone different from my dreams."

"I caught you daydreaming on our backyard swing. What was your biggest wish?"

"Oh, I don't know. I suppose every girl fantasizes that a knight in shining armor will come and rescue her. I visualized him riding up on his gallant charger and whisking me away to the church. We'd settle down, have lots of babies, and live happily ever after. You know, the stuff of fairy tales."

"You're twenty-five, and there's still time for you to meet somebody."

"Don't say it like that. It sounds like Tom is teasing that I'm an old maid. Beth and I are the same age—twenty-three."

"I was never good at remembering ages, and I meant it as a compliment."

"I know you did." Kim pushed her pie aside and stood. "You haven't danced with me since our high school graduation party."

I frowned. "Why is everyone wanting me to dance?"

"Come on. You danced pretty well with Beth. Why not with me?" She tugged on my hand.

"Okay." I stood and pointed to the band. "Will you teach me how to dance to their fast song?"

"I'll be glad to."

It took two songs to get the hang of how to fast-dance. A couple of tunes later, I stopped. "Gotta rest. This old man's exhausted."

"You're not old, just a mature forty-two."

"Mature or not, I'm tuckered."

We returned to the table and reminisced about her growing-up years: the ice cream socials at the church with the Johnsons, the evenings of board games, the rodeo competitions, the neighborly Bar-B-Qs, and the horse rides along the creek.

"Back when you were living with the Johnsons and had befriended Beth," I said, "Judith helped you get over your fear of horses. Do you remember?"

"I'd never been close to one. Dad told me horses were mean and would kick my head in. They scared me." She forked a piece of pie into her mouth.

"You never told us that."

She swallowed. "I never shared a lot of the stuff he did, either. I didn't enjoy living with him."

"He may have been your father, but he didn't deserve you. I never saw him sober."

"My life was a mess. He only let me out of the trailer house to go to school, and not always even then."

"You told us your mom skipped town after you were born."

She shrugged. "I don't remember her, and it's what Dad told me."

"You were five or six when he shot himself, weren't you?"

"I was six. My life got better when the court placed me with the Johnsons." Kim smiled. "I can still see Beth excitedly racing across the road to introduce herself."

I smiled. "Beth wanted a friend her age. I'm glad the two of you were so friendly because it helped you make a change for the better."

She put her fork down. "I couldn't believe it when Gerald said I was free to go to your house and be with Beth as long as I helped Rachel in the kitchen and finished my homework. I was super excited to have a friend across the road, and I could visit anytime."

"Beth was too. She wanted you to live with us, but the court wouldn't have allowed it."

"When you invited the Johnsons and me over for your family devotions, I experienced Christian love in action. You put legs to the Bible's teachings."

"The pleasure was all ours. We enjoyed including you in our Bible time."

"When the Johnsons moved into a retirement home, you surprised me."

I frowned. "Oh, how is that?"

"You and Judith let me commute to college from the ranch."

"Judith suggested the idea because supporting yourself would have been a financial hardship for such a beautiful person."

She lowered her lashes, and color crept up her neck.

Her coy look made me smile. "You're a lovely woman, Kim, especially when you blush."

Pink exploded from her cheeks as she grinned. She took a moment to compose herself. "When Beth and I were growing up, we told each other our secrets. But there's one thing I never told her." She looked at her hands. "I don't know if I should tell you this, but I've craved to be a mother, and I envy Beth because she's started her family."

My hand covered hers. "You're still a young woman. There's time to meet someone and start a family. He'll be the luckiest man on earth."

Her fingers intertwined with mine. "But it's taking forever. I want the man of my dreams to sweep me off my feet."

"You could have had a date with Harold."

She shook her head. "Not him. I got to know him when our school teams played against each other. He's good at what he does, but he has an ego complex. When he looks in the mirror, he applauds."

I disentangled our hand. "Keep looking. You'll find the guy of your dreams. Just have faith."

Kim looked over my shoulder. "Hi, Candy. Hi, Shelly. I see you finally made it tonight."

"We came from Urgent Care," said Candy, "and that's why we're late. Shelly had stomach cramps, and we didn't want to chance it. The nurse gave her a prescription to settle her nerves. She's been anxious about keeping up her grades up at school."

"I'm glad it's nothing too serious," I said.

Candy looked from me to Kim. "Phil, I thought you asked someone to come with you."

"I asked JoAnn Allen, but she couldn't make it because of a business appointment. Beth and David were here earlier but left to take Ian to the hospital. Now it's just Kim and me enjoying the evening."

Shelly tugged on Candy's arm. "Let's go, Mom. I want to meet the cute guy talking with Sharon and Harold."

Candy rolled her eyes. "You're always looking at the boys. Okay, let's go." She said to me, "Beth asked me to be sure to say hi. You and Kim have a good evening." They wound their way through the tables toward Harold and Shelly.

Up by the band, Gene Wilcox was talking to an elderly lady. He spotted me and began meandering through the crowd. For a 250-pound man at just over six feet tall, he had a spring to his step. I never understood why someone would completely shave their head. He said he did it because no one commented on his lack of hair, and folks easily noticed him in his rodeo work.

"Hi, Phil. I trust you're having a good evening." He nodded at Kim. "Kim, you look lovely."

She smiled. "Thank you, Mr. Wilcox."

I shook his hand. "You appear to be enjoying yourself."

"I'm having a good time, but I came to ask Kim a question. Do you know Sherry Sue Settle?"

"She was a senior in the church youth group but got pregnant and left. Why do you ask?"

"What do you know about her? What type of person is she?"

"She's a nice girl, but kind of flirty with the boys."

I asked, "Is her father, Chris Settle, the rodeo clown?"

Gene nodded. "Chris is her father." He said to Kim, "Is Sherry Sue truthful? Does she make up stories?"

Kim shook her head. "I've never known her to lie or fabricate anything. Is she all right?"

"As far as I know, she's fine. She said she's working at a place called Hancock Village near Atlantic, Iowa. She sent me an email with a straaaaange request. I'm trying to figure out if I should reply."

"What did she want?"

"To know if I could organize a rodeo for Hancock Village in February."

"What? It's winter," I said. "Nobody holds rodeos until spring."

"I know. It's what makes me wonder if she's pulling a fast one. She didn't give details. If I let her know it's doable, she'll send the details. Here's the kicker. She stated emphatically that the cost wouldn't matter. Mr. Hancock would cover it."

"Whoa," I said. "How big of a rodeo is she thinking? Setting one up could cost a hundred grand or more, plus the event prizes. Would she have workers, or was she thinking you'd supply them? Where would they find participants at this time of the year?"

"Mr. Wilcox," said Kim, "you should write back. It might be real."

"You believe her question is on the up and up?"

"Knowing Sherry Sue, as strange as it may seem, it's probably an honest question."

"Okay, I'll trust that you're right and answer her email."

"If you find out anything, let me know," I said. "This could be interesting."

"I'll do that." Gene dipped his head. "Kim, Phil, I hope you have an enjoyable evening." He disappeared among the crowd.

I said to Kim,. "The email from Sherry Sue sounded odd."

"Not odd. The other kids said her imagination came up with good ideas that often worked out."

For the rest of the evening, Kim and I danced a little and talked a lot. She said she was enjoying herself, and I was too. Most of our conversations revolved around the time she spent at the ranch with Beth and Tom. She told me she liked her apartment and that her accounting job was okay. But I got the feeling she'd rather be working somewhere else.

Before we knew it, midnight drew near.

She flashed her warm smile. "Let's dance in the New Year."

"You're going to wear this old man out. But okay, let's have fun."

The number was fast. I kept pace.

The next song picked up speed, and she said, "You learned quickly."

"I had an excellent teacher."

When the clock displayed two minutes until twelve, the band switched to a slow tune. Kim placed her arms around my neck, and I held her waist as we swayed to the rhythm.

The countdown began. "Ten—nine—eight ..."

The dancing stopped, and folks at the tables stood to face the clock. Kim and I held each other while looking toward the digital display.

"... three—two—one. Happy New Year!" everyone shouted in unison. The year 2021 had officially begun.

Kim stood on her tiptoes, and our lips met in a soft, warm, passionate kiss.

My heart skipped a beat, and my world jerked to a halt like a snubbed calf in a roping tournament.

What had led to this? My mind misfired in its attempt to sort through the evening's events. I drew back to apologize but only stammered, "Hap ... happy New Year."

Her fingers maintained their hold around my neck, and her melting smile seemed meant for no one else.

My knees wobbled. What was going on? I tried to read the expression in her clear, bright brown eyes.

"Happy New Year, Phil."

A few folks began making their way to the exits.

I was about to let go when she gave me another lingering kiss.

She released me, and her eyes searched my face. "Could I come to the ranch for a midnight cup of coffee? We'll talk, and I'll explain."

My mind couldn't think straight, but I said, "You're always welcome." I tried to collect my thoughts. Her gaze didn't waver, and a heavy cloud of confusion bubbled in my head.

She snatched up her coat and purse. "I'll … I'll explain at the ranch." She sped out the door.

Chapter 17

Friday, January 1st, after midnight

Forty-five minutes after leaving the New Year's Eve party, I pulled the truck up to the ranch house, killed the motor, and let my head thump against the steering wheel. The engine pinged and popped as it cooled. Had someone at Kim's office dared her to kiss me?

Inside the house, I got the coffee perking and set out leftover Christmas cookies. When Kim, Tom, and Beth visited last Thanksgiving, the house felt like a home again. Beth and Kim's laughter filled the kitchen while they cooked up a scrumptious meal. David, Tom, and I camped out in the living room to discuss football and play Legos with the grandkids until the ladies called us to eat. Everyone congregated around the table. The ensuing chatter resembled a well-orchestrated symphony.

I leaned against the kitchen counter. When the ladies and Tom weren't here, eating alone seemed like banishment to the basement. I looked forward to their visits. No, that wasn't right. Without Judith, I longed for them.

Tires crunched on gravel, and I peered out the window.

Kim parked her yellow car behind the spirea bushes, and Jinx bounded around the corner from his doghouse, wagging his tail and barking. He planted his dirty paws on her coat, like he always did with Judith. Kim laughed, rubbed his ears, and said something. Judith had a special friendship with my pooch, and since her death, Kim has replaced the friendship. Jinx pranced around her in a dizzying swirl of paws, ears, and tail as she made her way to the door.

She entered the kitchen, set her purse on the table, and took off her gloves. Her cheeks were pink. "Brrrrrr." She shivered. "It's cold out there."

An edginess had crept into her words like tiny icicles, and her posture was tense.

Maybe someone at work knew she'd never had a date and bet her a hundred dollars to kiss a man at the stroke of midnight, and I was handy.

I retrieved a mug from the cupboard. "I'll pour you a cup of coffee."

She hung up her yellow coat and accepted the coffee mug. "Thanks." She wrapped her fingers around it and took a sip. "Mmm. This hits the spot."

"Did you have trouble on the roads? I know you don't like Shook's Corner."

She shook her head. "I took it slow. Every time I go past his farm, I visualize myself going around the corner too fast and sliding into the ditch."

"The temperature is supposed to get up in the mid-forties tomorrow." The clock in the hallway chimed one. "Today, I mean. It should melt most of the snowpack on the corner."

"That's good. The ravine still scares me, though. There are stories of people slipping over the edge even in the summer."

I pulled a chair from under the kitchen table and offered her the seat. "You asked to talk."

Her face blanked. "I ..." She forced a smile. "Let's talk in the den."

"Okay. The den it is." I picked up the cookies along with my mug and sauntered to the other part of the house.

In her bare feet, Kim padded across the carpet with her coffee. The stiffness in her posture had dissipated. She settled into the opposite chair and tucked her pretty legs under her, draping the yellow dress over them.

Her eyes scanned the rows of achievement ribbons Beth and Tom had won in their teens. Her gaze settled on me. "I had fun tonight. You danced pretty well."

Beth's conversations were direct and to the point. Kim could be subtle. I let her take the lead and said, "Except for weddings and graduations, I haven't danced. Judith was never interested, and to be honest, I wasn't either until you gals roped me into it." I gave a mock impression of someone twisting my arm behind my back.

She smiled at my attempt at levity. "Did you have fun?"

"Yeah, I had a great time with beautiful company. Besides, Beth wasn't there to meddle and hook me up with someone."

Kim rolled her eyes. "Forget Beth."

"She's persistent, that's for certain. Do you know who ... what woman ..." I twiddled my finger. "Who does she want me to meet?" I searched Kim's eyes.

Her face relaxed. "Beth asked me not to tell."

Beth would do that, and Kim would keep her word. As the air between us thickened, I said, "Okay. You promised an explanation about our kiss. I'm listening."

Kim sipped her coffee, and something in her eyes changed—a shadow, a flicker, but it was something deep. "I know how to keep Beth from playing matchmaker." She spoke faster than usual, and her voice had softened.

I became cautious. "Oooo-kaaaaay. How?"

She looked down. "If you tell her you're dating someone, she'll leave you alone."

My mind took off like a hat flung over the stables. This wasn't like Kim. "Huh? Why in the world would I say I'm dating someone when I'm not?"

Her hands trembled, and she spilled coffee into the saucer. "Tell Beth ... tell Beth ... tell her you're dating me."

I froze, and an electric shock zapped up my spine. Had I heard right? Date little Kim? She was the same age as Beth, and eighteen years separated us.

Kim swallowed. "Do you remember the riding accident on my sixteenth birthday?"

"I remember you took a tumble from the saddle and couldn't catch your breath. Your face turned blue."

"That's the time. I couldn't breathe, and you did mouth-to-mouth."

My mind spun. "Did you think I was kissing you?"

"Uh-huh. I did. You carried me into the house and called a doctor. No one else had done that before. My dad was usually drunk. You cared and were concerned that I'd be all right."

"I was trying to get you to breathe, that was all."

"But you cared about what happened to me and made sure I got better. For the first time, I saw how a good man treated a woman. I wanted a husband like you, someone who would care for me and love me with his whole heart."

My thoughts spun like a clothes dryer on high speed, and I couldn't speak.

"That time you caught me daydreaming on the swing, I was fantasizing that you fell in love with me. Another time, we cooked hamburgers in the backyard with the Johnsons, and I couldn't take my eyes off you. Beth elbowed me and said, 'He's got a wife, you know.' There was nothing to say, and I stuffed my feelings."

"I ... I never knew."

"You weren't supposed to know. That's why I buried it, but my affection for you never waned. When Judith died, my hopes sprang to life. But you never noticed. I grew bold tonight to get your attention." Her chin quivered as she watched me through uncertain eyes. "Do you hate me for the kiss?"

My heart skipped a beat. In my confusion, I wanted to comfort her. Why would I want to hold and comfort her? What was happening to me?

My mouth worked with nary a sound. Beth, in her plotting, was trying to hook me up with someone. Kim was asking me to develop a relationship with her. I was lonely and crotchety. I'd isolated myself. The truth hit as if upending a calf at the rodeo. The girls were right, despite my protests to the contrary. I'd been fooling myself.

Her gaze flitted over my face, probably noting the struggles rolling across it. "Phil, say something." When I didn't answer, she said, "I don't know your feelings. Could … could you love me … like a woman?"

My mind shifted from a high-speed clothes dryer into a whirling tornado. How could I love her like a woman? She was the next-door neighbor-girl who was the same age as Beth. A yes was out of the question. I tried to say no, but it was impossible to say it. My mind was in such turmoil that I didn't realize I'd opened my arms until Kim propelled herself out of her chair and onto my lap.

Her affection should have repulsed me. But it didn't. Why?

She said in a soft voice, "Is there a chance you could love me as a woman?"

My mind was screaming to say no, but my heart wouldn't let me vocalize it. Kim looked fragile and was letting my arms protect her. From a distance, as if in a tunnel, I heard my answer. "I'm fond of you."

She smiled. "It's a start." She nestled her head against my shoulder, and I stroked her hair.

Why was I stroking her hair? What was going on? This wasn't me, was it? I'd responded to her affection, but it wasn't Judith in my arms. Was I being unfaithful to Judith? It didn't seem like it. What spell had Kim cast over me? This lovely lady, once a spunky rodeo gal who'd lived across the road, was content in my arms, and my actions encouraged her.

I wanted to say everything was all right, but things weren't all right because they'd spun out of control.

The grandfather clock in the hallway chimed twice: two a.m. Chores would come soon, and I needed to sort through this evening's events. Being close to Kim kept my mind confused and my heart racing. "When will you head back to your apartment?"

Her smile disappeared. "You want me to leave?"

I shut my eyes. "You've dumped a load on me, and I've got to mull it over. I don't know what to do."

She was silent for a few seconds. "May I sleep in Beth's old room?"

From habit, I said, "You're welcome to stay."

Without a word, we picked up the dishes and deposited them in the kitchen sink.

I headed down the hall to my bedroom, and she headed for the stairs. "Phil?"

I faced her, my hand on the doorknob. "Yes?"

"Thank you for a wonderful evening."

"The party was fun. It's our chat in the other room that has me befuddled."

She clasped her hands. "I had to ask."

"I didn't say yes."

"I'm petrified you'll say no."

I was terrified that I'd say yes.

Chapter 18

Kim went upstairs to Beth's old room, and I shucked my clothes in my bedroom, burrowing beneath the blankets. My exhausted body couldn't halt my racing thoughts as they galloped full tilt.

Was I ready for another woman? Was it right to be involved with Kim? Or was Beth setting me up with her best friend? What if they'd collaborated? That scared me. Kim wanted children. I'd already raised two. What would the rest of the family say if I dated Kim, especially Tom, who adored her? People would spread rumors, that was certain. What did I want? What would Judith think? Would she shake her head at my folly or approve of me taking another wife? What …

Questions, questions. My thoughts required sorting, but a tired mind made a poor seedbed to grow solutions. Crawling beneath the covers was easy, but sleep refused to come. I tossed and turned, not able to find answers.

At six a.m., the alarm buzzed. My muscles felt as if they'd wrestled a rambunctious steer. In the darkness, I dressed, donned my coat from the back porch, and stepped outside. Jinx's claws tapped on the sidewalk beside me as I shut the door. He looked up, cocked his ears, and whined. Judith said he could sense when things were wrong, and at the moment, things were spinning out of control. I knelt beside him and envisioned Judith's bright eyes on the day she'd presented me with this pup.

I ruffled his ears. "Happy New Year, Jinx."

He licked my face.

At the stables, I grabbed the feed bucket. The recognizable sounds of the horses banging at the door greeted me. The familiar routine allowed my mind to sort through last night's events.

Since my talk with Beth at Christmas, she'd been trying to convince me to share my life with a mystery woman. But holy mackerel, with Kim? There was our age difference, and people gossiped about lesser things. If I developed a relationship with Beth's best friend, she'd make a scene. What would the folks at the church say?

I threw several bales into the corral's hayrack. Challenger nudged me, and I stumbled. "Hey, watch it, big guy." He nuzzled my arm. When I stretched out my hand, he backed up. I took a step and reached for him. He retreated. This curious dance happened three more times. By then, he'd drawn me away from the other horses. After lifting his head high, he whinnied, wheeled, and trotted to the pasture gate leading to the woods. He pawed the ground and stuck his head over the fence.

I envisioned Judith scurrying out the kitchen door, tugging on her coat as she hurried. Her cheeks were pink with the anticipation of another jaunt on Challenger.

Understanding hit me like a line-drive baseball. *Judith wasn't here.*

A lump caught in my chest and exploded into a hundred pieces.

Challenger whinnied.

I struggled to find my voice. "Judith isn't here."

He faced me and snorted. He hung his head and walked closer so I could scratch his ears.

"Another time, big fellow."

He joined the rest of the herd at the hayrack.

I'd give my soul for another ride with Judith. To feel the breeze as we rode stirrup to stirrup and interlaced our fingers. To see her eyes glisten like a reflection off the pond. To protect her in my arms against the silly fear of barn owls. And to hear her say she loved me more than all the roses in Nebraska.

My heart hammered. It skipped a beat. Those events were gone. They'd never exist again. *Oh, Lord, help me.*

Like a hoof striking a stone, realization slammed home. I hadn't let go of Judith, as the ladies had warned, and I'd corralled her in my heart. I'd become a motherless foal, feeding on memories. And I had pitched a permanent tent in the past, refusing to live in the present. It's what the girls were trying to help me understand. My memories had clouded my thinking, and I was an idiot for not realizing it.

I closed my eyes and let the tears flow.

Challenger nickered. Jinx rubbed against my leg and whined.

I began sobbing and stumbled into the stables, collapsing into an empty stall.

Jinx lay at my feet, his head resting on his paws. His eyebrows danced as he followed my every move. He jumped up and barked, nosed my hands, and licked my face. Maybe it's true that tears can wash away pain because, after crying, I felt clean inside. But a wounded heart thumped in my chest, a lonely, broken heart longing for someone to fill it.

In my mind's eye, Judith stood by the corral, watching Challenger. She blew him a kiss and turned to me with sadness in her eyes. She waggled her finger like a parent cautioning a child.

I knew what she was going to do.

Oh, God, I hurt.

She strode away and waved over her shoulder in a permanent goodbye.

I struggled not to run after her and fought to keep from shouting for her to return. But that was living in the past and would entangle me like a tied-up calf. Today was now.

With a deep breath, I composed myself. Judith was gone and couldn't return. Yet a woman waited in the house, whose question deserved an answer. Whenever Kim smiled, my legs wobbled like jelly. I was comfortable around her and enjoyed her company. She was an intelligent woman. But to say the wrong thing would lift her hopes or crush her spirit. The last thing I wanted was to hurt her. What should I do? What did I want?

While finishing the chores, I ticked off the pros and cons of a relationship with Kim.

Chapter 19

I returned to the house after doing chores, kicked off my overshoes on the back porch, and hung up my coat. The smell of frying bacon greeted me as I stepped into the kitchen.

Kim leaned against the stove, watching me. She must have rummaged through Beth's dresser to find a pair of faded jeans. She'd appropriated one of my red-checked flannel shirts from the Goodwill box with the top Barton missing. Where had she found sneakers with yellow shoelaces?

She clasped her hands. Apprehension filled her face like a snowy TV screen. Things had changed between us. Whichever direction we took, we couldn't return to the same relationship. Her declaration of love had altered that possibility.

Kim's gaze followed my every move. "You didn't sleep, did you?"

I stopped four feet away, hesitant to draw closer. "Does it show?"

She shrugged. "I didn't sleep, either. There's a lot on my mind."

I felt sorry for her. "Yeah, I do too."

Kim's eyes radiated the fear that she'd been too forward last night and had damaged our relationship. I'd given no promise of her gaining anything, yet she'd been willing to sever our previous association like a cut lariat.

She bit her lip. "What are you thinking? I'm guessing you'll tell me a relationship between us shouldn't happen."

"What makes you say that?"

She studied me for a moment, her eyes watching my every expression. "One, folks may say a relationship between us is inappropriate, since I was at the ranch so much. It was almost like I lived here. Two, you're cautious about our ages because I was Beth's best friend while growing up. Three, you're concerned about gossip from friends at the church." She inhaled. "And fourth, you know I want lots of children, and you've already raised yours."

Kim had gotten to the essence of my thinking. "Those questions crossed my mind. Let's talk about them later."

From deep within her eyes, the curtain of fear parted, revealing a flicker of hope. "Is there something I haven't thought about?"

I kept my voice low. "There are things I want to know. If we developed a relationship, what about the stories that would circulate? I don't want to ruin your reputation."

She gripped the edge of the stove with both hands, and her knuckles turned white. "I don't believe the gossip would ruin my reputation, and I would gladly endure the chin-wagging because you'd fulfill my grandest dream. But I don't believe there'd be much negative talk."

"Why wouldn't there be?"

"I'm sure our ages will raise eyebrows, but nothing more."

"If you're sure, I'll move on to my next question." My muscles tightened. "Does Beth know how you feel about me?"

She took a moment to consider, and her fingers loosened their hold. "No, not really. When we were in high school, she thought it was teenage infatuation. I've hidden it pretty much since Judith died."

"That's good." I plunged ahead. "In Beth's thinking, she wants me to meet another woman. Is that correct?"

Kim searched my face and nodded. "Uh-huh, she does."

She wouldn't tell me who, but everything hinged on the last question. "Are you the woman she's paired me with?"

She blinked, and her lips slowly curved upward into her engaging smile. "No."

I took a deep breath. There was no collusion. Kim wasn't the woman in Beth's plan.

Kim's tension melted, and she must have thought she'd passed a test because anticipation radiated from her face.

I ran my tongue over my lips. "This morning, during chores, I did a truckload of thinking. One question kept coming back. If we were closer in age, would I be interested in dating you?" For a second, I closed my eyes. *Lord, I pray this isn't a mistake.* "Yes, I'm interested. If you're willing, I want to see where courting might lead us."

Her eyes glistened like moonbeams on a rippling stream. The corners of her mouth seemed fixed in a permanent upward curve. No smile could illuminate a face more than hers. She cocked her head. "Are you serious? Please don't mess with me because I've waited too long to hear those words."

"If you and I date, Bethany Lynn might fear you'll end up as her new mom."

Kim laughed. "If she thinks that, she'll have a cow."

My knees grew shaky, yet a warm glow filled my heart—a glow that had been absent for far too long. At this moment, I tumbled over the edge and, given enough time, believed I could learn to love this woman. We had details to discuss, and there would be rough patches as we sorted through our changing relationship.

"You're a piece of work, Philip York. It's why I love you."

I already knew the answer to my next question. "After breakfast, if I saddle Fargo, do you want to ride with me down to the creek on Lindy?"

Chapter 20

Friday, January 1st, afternoon

Kim said, "Thank you, Phil. Our fantastic ride down to the creek will be our first date."

"It was a great ride. I enjoyed it, too." I loosened Fargo's saddle and set it astride the stall partition.

A cool wind puffed through the stable door, fluffing the strands of her blonde hair as she hefted her saddle from Lindy. Her foot caught in the straw, and she took a stuttering step to stay balanced.

"Easy there." I retrieved the saddle from her and set it alongside mine. "I've missed this type of ... outing." *Whew, I almost said tryst.* Had it honestly been two years since my last ride? I'd forgotten how much I enjoyed sitting astride a horse.

Kim brushed aside a wayward strand of hair. "A few days ago, you wouldn't have ridden a horse. Why today?"

I removed my gloves and tweaked her nose. "Because I'm with a beautiful woman whose company is mighty enjoyable."

Red flushed her cheeks. "You say the nicest things. Could we ride again soon?"

We'd had a marvelous time. I cleared my throat to imitate Clark Gable, the actor. "Frankly, my dear, that's mighty tempting."

"You're silly, and I like it." In the breeze, a blonde tendril swung past her ear. "Down by the stream, when we gave the horses a rest, we sat on a tree stump, and you put your arm around me. You were going to say something but stopped. What was it?"

"It's nothing important."

Kim's smile filled her face, and she playfully slapped my arm. "You're supposed to tell because we're dating."

I closed my eyes for a second. "Well, I was thinking about our enjoyable time last night and our ride today and hoped we'd have more like them."

"How sweet. You're not a grouch anymore. You whistled and laughed, and you're different."

Had I been that much of a billy goat? The girls were right. Female companionship had altered my outlook. "Don't take this wrong, but those changes are because of you."

"I'm glad they're because of me."

"Kim, last night you said you've loved me since Judith's death. Since I hadn't perceived it, you kissed me at the party. Have you been dropping hints, hoping that I'd notice?"

She grinned. "Uh-huh, all the time. They were subtle hints."

I snorted. "I'm not good at catching subtlety and never have."

"It's why I had to get your attention. Today, at the tree stump, you kissed me. I wasn't expecting it."

"Except for last night, I've not kissed anyone since Judith. Kissing you seemed right."

"I liked it and wanted more."

"If I had, we'd have been kissing like teenagers at Lookout Station."

Something changed in her eyes, like a curtain opening wide. She stuffed her gloves in the hip pocket of her blue jeans. "Phil, what I'm going to say may sound wrong, but it's not. When you took care of me after my horse accident, I wanted a husband like you. Since Judith's death, I've imagined a relationship between us and dreamed that you asked me to be your wife. I think we should get married."

I blinked. "Whoa. Marriage this soon would be much too fast."

She stepped closer. "You're not the grouchy troll from last month or even the other day. If my presence makes this much of a change, shouldn't we get married?"

I put a finger on her lips, and she kissed it. I said, "Please don't repeat it." My heart skipped a beat as her large brown eyes filled my world. Not only could her smile melt an ice cube in ten seconds flat, but her beautiful eyes could soften my flinty heart into pudding.

"Why not?" she asked. "Didn't our ride mean anything? You said you had a fabulous evening. I certainly did. Today, you laughed and enjoyed yourself. I did, too."

"Even though I had a wonderful time, it doesn't lead to marriage."

"I believe it does. It's not like we just met because we've known each other for years."

"I don't believe so. At least I don't see it." I was fond of Kim and enjoyed her friendship. The feelings I felt for Kim differed from those I had for Judith. Kim was the spirited neighbor girl who played with Beth and teased Tom. When I was working in the stables and she came in with Beth to ride the horses, she plied me with questions and bubbled over with excitement. She helped the family repaint the white pasture fence.

She said, "Am I pushing?"

"Uh-huh. Marriage means a different level of relationship—a different level of everything. Although we agreed to date, I'm not ready for a deeper commitment."

Back when our kids were growing up, she pestered Tom while he tinkered on his car in the machine shed. She and Beth spent hours with the horses. When we cleaned the horse stalls, I whistled a tune, and Kim would poke her head over the partition to sing the lyrics.

"Phil, my love for you is strong. I want you to know what I see in your heart."

I stepped back. "It hasn't been twenty-four hours since you declared your love, and it has befuddled my mind. Our relationship feels like a new pair of Western boots. They fit but aren't quite comfortable, making it necessary to walk in them. No, it's much too soon for you to suddenly become my wife. Let's give it time and see what develops."

"I believe deep down you love me, and it scares you."

"You're wrong. I don't."

"Do you remember the winter when Beth and I were helping load hay on the flatbed trailer? I tickled you, and you wouldn't fight back because I was a young woman."

"Was that when the snow was three feet deep and we were taking hay to the stranded cattle?"

She giggled. "That was the time."

"You often teased me, and I had to get even. Beth helped me toss you in the manure pile."

"You got even, alright. When I pushed myself out of the manure, my hands sank deeper into the mess. A bunch got on my face and in my hair. Judith wouldn't let me shower until I stripped to my undies on the back porch. I stank and was shivering and mad."

"All of you kids found time to joke with each other, but you worked hard and had fun. None of you were afraid to get your hands dirty."

"We had good times back then with you and Judith," said Kim. "I'm the same fun-loving girl. This ranch is the most magnificent place on earth, and I want to be part of it with you. I love the land and animals. I want to be beside you while you whistle as you work."

"Do you smell the manure pile over there? Would you love me if I threw you in?"

She looked at me with her beautiful brown eyes. "Even if you did, I'd love you. But you wouldn't dare, would you?" Her eyes twinkled. "If you tried, I'd tickle you."

"Go take a shower. I'll do the evening chores, and then we'll fix supper and talk."

She headed for the door and turned. "I believe deep down you love me."

I lowered my chin. "Dating means I can kiss you. Or would you rather I toss you in the manure pile?"

"I dare you."

"You're on," I said as I took two quick steps.

She squealed, shoved open the door to skedaddle outside, and stuck out her tongue as I leaned against the doorframe. She breathed deeply from her exertion. "I love you, Phil."

"I know you do. You've told me."

"I want you to love me."

"I know that too. But it might take a while." How long was she prepared to wait?

She blew me a kiss before heading to the house.

How do I handle her? Her smile and soft touch made my stomach queasy. What if she knew her smile made my knees wobble like a newborn colt?

Chapter 21

Kim disappeared into the house after our horse ride, and it took me ten minutes to brush the horses. They'd already cooled down and were eager to join the rest of the herd. I let them out and started the chores, asking myself a bunch of questions.

Why not end the relationship with Kim and be done with the whole thing? A simple answer—because, more than I realized, I liked her a lot and, for the first time in a long time, I was happy. Not once had I thought of Judith since early this morning. My thoughts had become squarely cemented on Kimberly Ann.

I opened the feed chute and let the grain flow into the horse trough.

I wasn't ready to commit to marriage, despite her urgings. Why was I reluctant? A simple answer—she might be the wrong woman. I needed time to sort through everything, and events were already speeding at a full gallop. They needed to slow down.

If she was the wrong woman, then who else was there? That was the million-dollar question. No one was on the horizon, and Beth would be persistent in getting me married to a mystery woman. Whoever the lady was could be someone I wouldn't like.

Kim said she loved me. Could I love her? The question tightened my muscles, and I couldn't answer it with a yes.

Isabel came up to the feed trough, clicking with each step. I checked her hooves. "Hey, girl, you've got a loose shoe. I'll fix it next week."

If I set aside my doubts and Kim and I married, what about the children she wanted? I'd be in retirement and have kids in school.

What if Kim and I argued a lot? Had Judith and I always gotten along? That was a big no. During the early years of our marriage, we squabbled about money until we learned to be sensitive to each other. Having two toddlers helped us get through that tough time.

All the horses had come in from the pasture, and I closed the corral gate for the night.

A few gray clouds peppered the evening sky, partially covering the setting sun. Rivulets of water seeped out from under the edges of the snow by the corral. The warmer temperature had turned the open ground into a soggy mess.

Lord, what am I supposed to do? Kim is a wonderful woman, but with eighteen years between us, are we meant to be together? Honestly, I don't know and fear where it might lead. Help me understand. Please don't be silent.

My cell phone buzzed in my pocket, and I fished it out. "Hello."

"Dad, where have you been? I've been calling all day and was ready to call the police."

Beth sounded like I'd died. "Sorry, Princess. I'm doing chores right now, but earlier I enjoyed a ride through the timber. I'd set my phone on vibrate and forgot about it."

"You rode *Fargo? Today?* In your hissy fit, you said you wouldn't ride him." The workings of my daughter's mind rattled like nails in a tin cup. "It's been months since you went riding. You refused to ride the other day, so what lassoed you to bring this miracle on?"

"Dunno. I decided it was time to do something different. It's a new year, isn't it?"

"Speaking of the new year, when did you get home last night?"

"Oh, about one o'clock. Why?"

"Did you meet anyone special at the party?"

Oh, good, Lord. I should have known that she'd ask. "Yes, I met a fabulously beautiful European duchess. We kissed passionately, and she agreed to marry me. Does that make you happy?"

"Don't be sarcastic."

I raised my voice. "Then don't ask personal questions. It's none of your business."

"I'm curious, that's all."

Not just curious. My daughter would pester me until she knew every bit of information. It was time to change the subject. "How's Ian's finger?"

Beth's motherly sigh resembled Judith's. "It needed six stitches, and the doctor wrapped it in a splint. He'll carry a nasty scar."

"Did he cut any tendons?"

"No. David was worried about that, too. The nurse said he'll have almost 100 percent dexterity."

"At least it's not severe. How long will it take to heal?"

"About a month. We're supposed to keep it dry. You know how he loves to play in the snow. I hope he's learned a lesson about using a knife."

"I remember a little girl almost whacking off her toe while attacking a garter snake."

"Daaaaad. Don't remind me of that."

Beth wanted that long-ago incident eradicated from history. Slithering reptiles are, in her estimation, the vilest creatures in God's creation. She'd hacked at a fencerow with a corn knife, demolished five feet of fence, shortened a cat's tail, and ruined one of Judith's rosebushes, not to mention frightening the livestock. Beth didn't realize the seriousness of her injured toe until after the carnage. The snake got away.

I chuckled. "Give Ian's finger a big kiss from Grandpa."

"You can give it to him. I talked David into coming to check on you, and we'll be at the ranch in five minutes." She hung up before I could reply.

Blast it. She'd keep Kim and me from talking this evening.

I finished the chores. In the corral, Lindy and Fargo gamboled about like yearling colts. The ride had done them good, and me too.

By the time I stowed the saddles and bridles in the tack room, Beth and her family drove up the lane. I stood at the door, whistling, as David parked the van by the corral fence.

Ian came running, his unbuttoned coat flopping as he stepped into every patch of snow and mud between the car and the stables. "Grandpa. Grandpa."

I swung him up into my arms, and his wet boots left muddy streaks on my pants. "How's my big boy?"

He held his bandaged finger in my face like a badge of honor. "I got a owie, Grandpa."

"I see. Does it hurt?"

"Um hum."

I kissed the bandage. "Does that make it better?"

"Um hum."

He gave me a quick hug before wiggling to be let down, and he scampered off to look at Serenity's new foal. He stuck his arm through the gate to pet it.

Beth took time to step around the patches of slush and mud.

I said, "Ian looks like he's doing pretty good."

Her gloved hand rested on my arm as she stretched to kiss my cheek. "The doc gave him pain pills, and that's what keeps him comfortable." She cocked her head. "You seem happy, Dad."

I tossed a feed bucket into the storeroom. "Shouldn't I be?"

She set a pitchfork behind the door. "You were whistling, too."

I puckered up and blew a few bars of *Jesus Loves Me*. "There's no law against it, is there?"

"You haven't whistled in ages. You're not grumpy, either."

I hunched my shoulders and growled. "Grrrrrr. Want me to be a grouchy old bear?"

She playfully punched my arm. "No. It's nice to see you in good spirits. The ride did you good."

From outside, David Buttoned Eddy's coat and hefted him into his arms. "Your daughter," David said with a crooked smile, "forced the family to cram into the van and drive out here to check on you in the hopes you'd let us spend the rest of the day at your place." There was mock disgust in his tone.

Beth glowered at him.

"I don't have enough food to feed this hungry crew, and I only have a few Christmas cookies and leftovers," I said. "We'll have to warm something up."

"We came prepared," said Beth. "I made a tuna and macaroni casserole and a tossed salad. If you scrounge up potato chips and soda, we'll have a pretty good meal." She turned to exit the stables.

Ian ran past me and his mom. Outside, he scuffed his boots through the slushy snow, kicking showers of ice crystals into the air.

I waited until everyone had left the stables before closing the door.

Together, we walked to the house.

"There are two bags of chips in the pantry," I said, "one plain and the other Bar-B-Q. We could probably locate a couple of six-packs of cola there, too." I glanced at my watch: 5:17 p.m. The sun had set, and it would be fully dark soon. "By the way, Kim is here."

David didn't break stride. Beth did. She stumble-stepped to catch up. "Where's her car?"

"Behind the spirea bushes."

"Why's she here?"

"Why are you here? You came to provide company. Kim's doing the same thing."

"But ... she didn't tell me."

"I suppose you informed Kim you were coming?"

"No, I didn't. But she tells me everything."

No, Kim didn't. "Regardless, I'll let you ladies set the table and get the food ready while I shower and change into clean duds."

Beth conceded the point, but her squint said her inquisitive mind smelled something fishy.

Chapter 22

Friday, January 1st, evening

I showered and emerged from the bathroom, steam rolling out the door and along the hallway ceiling. The shower had washed away the barnyard smell, and my skin was tingly clean. I tossed my smelly work clothes down the laundry chute to land in the basement on top of the other clothes I hadn't washed in a week.

I halted at the doorway to the den.

Ian and Eddy had scattered Lego blocks across the brown carpeted floor in their effort to build an airplane from a picture on the box.

Ian looked up. "Can you help us, Grandpa?"

"Sure can." I scooted the tan, overstuffed chair out of the way and leaned against it with my legs outstretched.

In a flash, Ian and Eddy crawled into my lap and hindered my attempts to straighten out their construction project.

With an arm around each boy, I sorted through the pile of blocks. "Let's see now. This wing should be stronger." The insertion of a blue block and a red block provided added support. I pointed to where the pilot sat. "This doesn't look right. What do you boys think?"

"We don't know, Grandpa," said Ian.

I compared it to the picture and dug through the stack in search of a tiny angle piece to repair my grandsons' masterpiece.

A shadow fell across our work.

Kim smiled down at us from the doorway and flicked her ponytail off her shoulder. "I came to find three little kids who are playing with Legos. Sorry to interrupt your play time, boys, but supper is almost ready."

From the look in her eyes, she was disappointed that we wouldn't be alone this evening.

As my grandsons wriggled in my lap, eager to see their project completed, Kim's expression changed and the look on her face stung like an attack of hornets. Her deep desire for children flowed from her eyes, and she had me pegged as the father.

Oh boy. I adjusted Ian and Eddy so they could see my face. I winked. "Boys, Aunt Kim could use some hugs and kisses. Could you give her a bunch?"

In the manner of young boys, they dropped everything, scrambled upright, bolted straight for Kim, and plowed through Lego blocks, scattering them in all directions for me to retrieve from under various pieces of furniture.

Kim's beautiful smile broadened as she squatted to receive two energetic bundles of love. In the mad rush of arms and legs and hugs and kisses, tears welled in her eyes.

In their competition to see who could love Kim the most, the boys forgot about their creative construction project.

I collected the Lego blocks and deposited them in the tattered cardboard container.

They kept kissing Kim, and she soaked up their attention as if they'd never done it before and would never do it again.

I stood. "Hey, guys, Aunt Kim and Grandpa are hungry. Run and tell your mommy we want to eat. We'll be there shortly."

They disentangled themselves and sped to the kitchen on their important errand.

I took Kim's hands and helped her stand. "Sorry, I didn't know the family was coming."

"I know you didn't. I'm just disappointed we won't have the evening to ourselves." She flowed into my arms like warm honey.

Our embrace was soft and gentle. I kissed her. "We can't keep it from them."

"I'm scared Beth will explode."

"I am too. She didn't know beforehand that you were here, and it caught her off guard. Her curiosity shifted into overdrive when she found out. We can't avoid telling her."

She kissed me. "I love you so much."

I touched her nose. "By saying those words, are you hoping they'll rub off on me?"

She giggled. "A little. I can wish, can't I?"

I kissed her again. "Come on. We better go to the other room."

Kim and I entered the dining room.

I stopped short. "Bethany Lynn, put your mom's pussywillow dishes back in the china closet. We'll use paper plates and plasticware."

"Come on, Dad. I want to use them."

"I know you'd dearly love to claim them, but they're not yours. They belonged to your mother. Put them back. Kim, get the paper plates."

Beth scowled. "Today is a holiday. We should use them."

"No, we'll not use them. Put them away. Now."

"Alright." She did as I requested and then said with sarcasm, "Is the winter tablecloth okay to use, or do I have to put it away too?"

"It looks pretty. We can use it."

Kim set the paper plates out for everyone, and I sat at the head of the solid walnut dining table.

David and Beth seated my grandsons on either side in booster chairs, with a parent next to each one. Kim sat at the far end, and her smile radiated like a beacon of light. Our family held hands for prayer.

After the amen and after everyone's plates were full, general chitchat erupted around the table. David and I debated whether Nebraska University's basketball team could be the conference champions with this year's infusion of new players. He said they might. I knew they wouldn't. Beth and Kim conversed about something Helen Smith said in church concerning Pastor James' sermon the other Sunday.

Ian and Eddy inhaled their potato chips, asked for more, and devoured those. They ate a bite or two of the casserole and picked at their salad. They ignored Beth's encouragement to eat more, so David said they could get down. Both boys scurried to the living room to watch an episode of VeggieTales, their favorite cartoon show from my DVD library.

After several minutes, the adult conversation lulled. Beth pivoted toward me. "Dad?"

If Beth wore an antenna, she'd have it raised for full broadcast. I could feel the question coming like a fifty-thousand-watt transmission. My stomach tightened. "Yes, Princess?"

She fingered her silver necklace. "Did you meet anyone at the New Year's Eve party?"

Kim maintained a neutral expression as her eyes flicked from face to face.

"Beth, you've already asked that question, and I answered. Is it your crusade to snoop into my romantic life, or are you inconsiderate of my feelings?"

She blinked twice. "You're my father, and I should know who you meet."

Not hardly. She was interested in my romantic life and hoped a certain unknown female would catch my attention. "I'm tired of your prying into my personal life."

"But you're my father. Why can't I know?"

"I'll give you as much input into my romantic life as you had when I dated your mother. That turned out pretty good, and I didn't do too badly for myself. And I did it without you, too. If I tell you, then you might gossip."

"Dad, I don't gossip."

That wasn't quite correct. She might not share it, but she collected it and soaked it up to use in her plans. "Why do you have a continued interest in my personal relationships?"

"Because you're my father. Please tell me if you met someone."

All my avoidance would prolong her prodding and prying, and she'd eventually find out anyway. Kim and I might as well get it over with, and I hoped Beth wouldn't explode. "All right, the only way to quench your infernal meddling is to share details. What do you want to know?"

Beth tightened the grip on her necklace as her attention shifted into high gear. "So you *actually* met someone. Who is she?"

"I already told you. I met a fabulously beautiful European duchess, and we kissed. She agreed to marry me, and we'll live happily ever after."

Kim quickly covered her mouth to keep from laughing out loud.

"You're being sarcastic," said Beth. "Tell me the truth."

"Kim," I asked, "should I reveal the woman's name?"

She shook her head. "Make a game of it and string Beth along."

Beth gave Kim a hard look. "Butt out of this. If you know who she is, I should, too." Beth turned back to me. "Do you like her, Dad?"

I smiled. "She's a gracious lady, and we've known each other for several years."

"You have? That's great."

"Do you plan on dating her?" asked David.

I nodded. "She's willing, so yes, we'll be going out." I gave no hint that we'd had our first date—a horse ride down to the timber and along the creek.

Beth focused on my every word. "What does she look like?"

"She's about five feet, six inches tall, with blond hair down her back. She's pretty and has a job in town."

Beth's eyes wavered as if scrolling through viable candidates. "Does she go to our church?"

Five widows attended our congregation. Two were in their seventies, and Beth wouldn't consider them. Neither would she consider Minnie Marshall, who came infrequently. Tiffany Greer's husband died in the Afghan War, and Sandra Reed's husband died in a tractor accident. Tiff and Sandy were in their early forties and worked in town to support their children. Both had light-colored hair.

"Yes, she does."

Beth went silent as she stared at the wall.

Kim's wry smile said my answer was a dirty trick.

Maybe it was, but I wanted Beth to receive a dose of her own medicine.

David's expression was non-committal. "Do you think you'll get serious with her, Phil?"

Beth jerked back to the present and scooted forward. She folded her arms on the table and looked straight at me.

Kim took a breath and held it.

"On a scale of one to ten, this lady is," I said, while keeping my eyes off Kim and counting each finger, wiggling the tenth digit. "She's tops."

Beth gasped. "Oh my. You're very serious with each other."

"Not really. We've just known each other for several years."

"Phil?" David measured his voice. "Does she like you?"

Kim fiddled with a fork.

I focused on her. "She's told me she likes me a great deal."

Beth let go of her necklace. "When will we meet her?"

After considering the impact of my answer, I said, "You've already met her."

Beth's eyes bugged. "Why won't you tell us?"

"Dear daughter," I said, letting my gaze drift away from Kim. "We don't know what you'll think."

"What can I think? I don't know who she is."

"What if she's several years younger than me?"

Beth's slack jaw said every name that she'd considered no longer matched. "Dad ..." She worked to find words. "An age gap shouldn't be the most important thing."

I raised an eyebrow. "You know how people will talk if the woman is younger."

"Mrs. Jensen at church said she's eight years younger than her husband. There are couples in town with large age gaps. If you like the woman, I want you to be happy."

"Really? How much of an age gap would you say is okay for me to date someone?" The deciding moment was fast approaching.

Beth looked at everyone around the table.

Kim's face remained passive, although her anxiety level had probably risen.

David shrugged. "A few extra years shouldn't matter." He grabbed a handful of Bar-B-Q potato chips.

Beth said, "Sure, Dad. As David just said, an age gap isn't important."

He nodded his agreement while stuffing his mouth full of chips.

Kim gave a tiny nod that only I witnessed.

"Are you agreeing," I asked, "that it's okay for me to date Kimberly Ann Ryan?"

Chapter 23

Beth's eyes grew enormous, and she screamed, "No! You can't date Kim."

David spluttered in mid-chew. He swallowed and pointed at Kim. "You … you mean you want to date our Kim? This Kim?"

Beth asked, "You're joking, right? You couldn't mean you'd date Kim." She turned to Kim. "This is one of your gags, right?"

She shook her head. "Your dad and I want to date."

Beth hit the table, and the plasticware jumped. "Don't you dare date my father. It's wrong."

Kim folded her hands. "You said age didn't matter."

David found his voice. "She's like family, so you shouldn't date each other."

"We have different names," I said, "Ryan and York. There's no family conflict."

Kim's voice flowed as softly as cotton. "I'm of age and can choose who I want to date."

"Age has nothing to do with it," said Beth. She turned to me. "Don't you dare date Kim. It's not right."

I stretched my hands out to Beth and David. "Kim and I have discussed dating plans. We see only social obstacles and believe we can overcome them. We're not asking you to like it, but only accept for us to date."

The TV speakers in the living room played a theme song to a different cartoon movie.

Beth glared at me. "Dating each other is totally wrong."

"You keep saying it's wrong," I said. "What's the law that makes it wrong?"

"The court placed me with the Johnsons," said Kim. "Gerald said that because they didn't have children, it was okay to spend a lot of time here because you were just across the road."

Beth's eyes locked with David's in a silent conversation. She rubbed her hands. "David and I won't accept a dating relationship between you and Kim. If you dated, you'd be cheating on Mom."

I exhaled, not knowing I'd held my breath. "Dating Kim isn't cheating on your mother because she's deceased."

"Why don't you want us to date?" asked Kim.

Beth spun on her and waggled her finger. "It's wrong. It's wrong. It's wrong."

"Beth, don't be like that," I said. "Why would it be wrong to date Kim, and how would it be cheating on your mother? You said it was okay for the woman to be younger than me. So why are you upset?"

Beth's voice turned brittle. "If it's not wrong, then go ahead, get married, and see what'll happen."

Kim jerked.

So did I. "What did you say? Nothing will happen if we date."

My daughter glared at me. "You heard me. Ruin your lives, for all I care. Go ahead. Cut out the in-between stuff and say I do. Destroy our family. Destroy your reputation. My boys won't know what to think because they'll be so confused." Her words were loud and clipped.

"Enough," I said. "That's not funny. You promised not to interfere in my relationships."

"I promised to quit pushing, but you've messed it up. It should be Candy."

So Candy was the woman my daughter planned for me to marry.

As if to hold us apart, Beth spread her hands between Kim and me. "You've both gone off the deep end where sharks swim, and you haven't any idea how to fight them off."

David said nothing and let Beth take the lead.

"You've put me in the middle," said Beth. "It's bizarre and totally wrong."

Kim returned Beth's stare. "You keep saying that it's wrong to date your father, but you haven't told us why. Dating should be a decision between Phil and me."

Beth glowered at Kim. "You don't know Dad well enough, and it's not possible for you to develop a romantic relationship with him."

Kim planted her hands on the table, and she half stood. "That's what dating is for—to find out about each other."

The air crackled with electricity.

"Do you want to find out if you love Dad enough to marry him?" Venom dripped from Beth's voice as she took control of the conversation.

Kim probably didn't see the trap.

"Yes," Kim said. "I want to find out if he loves me enough to marry me."

"There's no way he could love you enough. You're letting your feelings do the talking."

"Beth, you're being hateful," I said.

She folded her arms. "Dad, Kim is half the equation. If she were younger, she'd be jailbait, and they'd lock you up."

Beth's tongue had never been this sharp. She'd been eighteen when she married David, right out of high school. Kim was currently twenty-three and more mature than Beth had ever been. "Stop it, Beth. Your words are hurtful."

"I'm being truthful, and the truth hurts, doesn't it?" Her voice softened as she pointed to her sons. "This will mess up my boys' lives as well as yours."

"My relationship with Kim won't mess up anything," I said. "We're not related."

My daughter squinted. "Ooooh," she crooned in a singsong tone. "Do you love her?"

This had to stop. "What I feel for Kim isn't anything like what I had with your mom."

Beth leaned so far forward that she blocked my view of Kim. "Well, duh, Dad. They're different women. What do you expect—peaches and cream? What you're doing is mixing vinegar and soda."

Her words struck like a kick to my chest. "Beth, stop being hostile. Drop it."

"Intervention is necessary. If you date Kim, the rumors will ruin the family's reputation." She sat back in her chair with a scowl so deep it resembled a furrow in the dirt.

Confound my daughter. Where was her common sense? My lips tightened. "I said drop it, Beth, and I meant it. This should be a pleasant family evening. Instead, you're attempting to push us into what you think is best."

If this conversation continued, it would be with Beth.

Beth's eyes didn't shift away from me. "I see it now. My boys will think their grandfather married Aunt Kim."

"I'm not their real aunt," said Kim.

"You might as well be because that's what they think. You asked them to call you Aunt Kim." She faced me. "Dad, if you date Kim, she'll be the biggest mistake you ever made."

Kim stood and glared at Beth. "Did my best friend call me a mistake?"

"If you dated Dad, you'd be a mistake. If you married him, you'd be a huge mistake."

"We're supposed to be friends. You can't say things like that."

"Yes, I can. If you date Dad, that's what you'd be—a dreadful mistake."

I planted my hands on the table. "Bethany Lynn, you know better. If you reject our relationship for selfish reasons, then you're not welcome in this house." I balled my fists. "I'm going to my study, and I want you and David to leave this house immediately."

David's jaw dropped open.

"This is my home, too," said Beth.

"Not anymore. If you talk like that, you have no claim to this home."

Kim's gaze followed me as I stomped past her.

I strode to the back of the house, passing the boys, who glanced at me before returning to their cartoon show. In the study, I dropped into my chair and left the door half-open with my jaw clenched.

Chapter 24

Only one other time had I lost my temper with Beth. Tonight, I left the table for her protection because I was ready to swing. Her comments went over the top.

Muffled voices filtered from the living room. A door closed as someone went outside, probably David, to warm up the van. Kim would help the boys put on their coats, making a game of it, and Beth would clear the table and put away the food.

Why had Beth been so hostile? To say Kim was a mistake went far beyond an insult and was callous to a lovely woman.

I flexed my work-swollen fingers. What kind of daughter had Judith and I raised? I'd expected resistance, but nothing like her explosion.

With my elbows on the cluttered desk and my head in my hands, I closed my eyes. Our announcement had ruined the evening. Kim didn't deserve this type of treatment, not from Beth, not from anyone.

Lord, what should Kim and I do? Please show us if we're wrong. If we are, I'll put a stop to the relationship. You know I don't want to hurt her. I'm asking for wisdom and guidance. If we date, will it be wrong? Please don't be silent.

On the bookshelf above the desk, Judith's red and well-worn Bible drew my gaze. I pulled it down. The volume plopped open of its own accord to a New Testament passage. Judith read the scriptures every day, often underlining, marking passages, and putting comments in the margin.

A solid block of red ink surrounded one verse. "*The aim of our charge is love that issues from a pure heart and a good conscience and a sincere faith.*"

Words swam in my head, spinning me until I was almost dizzy. *Oh my.* My throat went dry. I licked my lips and swallowed.

Another photo at the edge of the desk included Kim standing to my left and Judith to my right. Beth, David, and Tom squatted in front. The photographer had positioned Kim beside me as if she belonged there. A month later, Beth married David, and in the fall, Kim entered college while commuting from the ranch.

Outside, a car door slammed, and the engine's noise faded as the vehicle traveled past the stables, down the lane, and out to the road.

Footsteps clipped along the hallway toward my study.

My heart picked up speed.

Kim tapped three times on the half-open door and stepped into the room.

I scooted around to face her. "I figured you might have left because of what happened." She sat in the chair by the door, and I said, "I'm glad you haven't."

She sat forward, her spine rigid, and her legs together. "This mess is totally my fault." She gave no hint of a smile. Her golden ponytail flicked back and forth and caught on her shoulder. She flicked it away.

The movement of her hand, the cute, petite nose, the straight, and perfect legs—she looked stunning. "When did you become so beautiful?"

"Don't butter me up. Beth's tirade made it too late for compliments."

"I recall a young blonde woman flitting around the house with Beth and who helped Judith. She loved horses as much as my daughter." I swallowed because my throat was still dry. "Right now, I see an attractive woman who's special."

She huffed. "Not hardly. I'm the woman who created a major rift between you and Beth. If I hadn't kissed you last night, none of this would have happened."

"And you would tie up your heart like a roped calf to become drier and sadder until it shriveled into a prune."

She closed her eyes. "Don't make it worse. I don't want to hurt anyone, especially you, because I love you so much." She took a breath. "Beth and I promised to be best friends forever. When she called me a mistake, she broke that bond. She's petrified her best friend will become her stepmother, and it's tearing me apart."

Beth's tantrum had gone deeper than Kim knew. "Yes," I said. "It's partly why she's scared."

Kim blinked. "Are there other reasons?"

"Um hum. Imagine for a minute that you're her. If I were to marry a younger woman and have children, she'd be at least twenty-five years older than her siblings, propelling her into the age of ancientness. Her boys would have been born before their aunts or uncles, confusing the generational gap."

"She's married and has children. It's been one of her goals."

I nodded. "Those are perks for someone who thinks she's a teenager. Beth wants to remain a cowgirl who was, or still thinks she is, a barrel racing champion."

"I guess. I hadn't thought of it like that."

"Why does Beth try to get her own way?"

"I don't know. She just does."

I leaned on my elbows. "It makes her feel important, like she's in control of everything. By her estimation, it makes her seem like she's worth more. When her planning doesn't work, what does she do?"

"She pouts. But tonight, she exploded like Mount Saint Helens. That's different."

"It may take a while to get over it, but she will."

Kim shook her head. "No, she won't. I came between you and her and caused this family quarrel. Things should go back to the way they were between you and me."

"It's not possible for our relationship to go back. If we did, it would hurt like a knife to the heart and rip me apart."

A tear rolled down her cheek. "It's best if I leave and don't come back." She dropped her face into her hands.

"Oh my gosh, you don't know how much it hurts to say those words."

She bolted upright without looking at me, stepped toward the door, and spoke over her shoulder. "I'm leaving. I love you too much to come between you and Beth."

"Kim, don't go." How could I stop her? I raised my voice as she disappeared into the hallway with only her hand clutching the doorframe. "There's another answer to this mess."

Her white-knuckled fingers gripped the door's molding like she'd glued them there.

My legs tensed, ready to sprint. "Kim, please? Come back. We need to talk."

Her face reappeared with moist cheeks, and she leaned against the frame. "We've already talked about everything."

"No, we haven't. There's another way."

She sniffed. "I hope it's good."

My skills are deficient in finding unique words, so I plunged ahead. "Kimberly Ann Ryan, will you marry me?"

Her eyes fluttered, her chin quivered, and her lips twitched. She took a hesitant step and collapsed in the chair she'd just vacated. Her mouth opened, then closed. "What ... what did you ask? Did ... did I hear right?"

After she dropped her guard, she looked more beautiful.

I locked eyes with her. "For honest to goodness, and real truth, will you marry me and become my wife?"

She gulped. "This can't be real."

"It's very real. Will you marry me?"

Her smile slowly appeared. "Yes, I will."

"Are you prepared to upset Beth? You know it will."

"I know, but I wish it wouldn't. Will it bother Tom?"

"It won't upset him," I said. "He'll probably tease you about it, and I'm fairly certain of that. One of Beth's concerns was how our marriage would affect her children. Do you think it will?"

"It may surprise her boys, but that's all. They're young and will still accept me as their Aunt Kim."

"If you're willing to accept how Beth reacts, when do we get married? Would tomorrow morning be too soon?"

She double-blinked. "Was this planned all along as a surprise?"

"I've planned nothing and have been winging it for the past several minutes. In the morning, after chores, we'll go to your place for you to change into something more appropriate and pick up a few necessities. Then we'll hit the jewelry stores in town to select matching rings before going to the courthouse to get our license and to visit a judge. Next week, we'll clean out your apartment, close out the lease, and report to your boss about your marriage. But there's no rush with those."

During my spiel, she glided toward me, a lovely and beautiful woman. Not the beauty of a magazine model or a movie star. Kim possessed a charm of character, a loveliness of heart, and an inner beauty displayed by the lift of her shoulders, the tilt of her chin, and the sparkle of her eyes. She possessed a poise no one could doubt, and her golden hair highlighted her glowing face.

I scooted back.

She slid into my lap and draped her arms around my neck. "Those plans are amazing."

"Should we invite anyone, maybe from the church?"

Her smile faded, and she vigorously shook her head. "Definitely not Beth. Let's not tell anyone and enjoy the time by ourselves. We'll tell everyone afterward."

"Are you absolutely sure you want to elope with me?"

"I'm absolutely sure. I'm still angry with Beth because she called me a mistake, and it hurt more than anything."

"She pries and prods, and I'm sick of it. I meant what I said. If she mentions our relationship in that vile manner, she won't be welcome in this house. Could you agree?"

"As the woman of your house, you and I will set the rules."

I took Kim's face in my hands and kissed her. "Mmm, you taste delicious."

She laid her head against my shoulder. "You know I want children. Do you?"

I pulled her tight and curled my fingers through her blonde strands. "I've set my heart on twenty or thirty, all boys."

She giggled. "You're silly." She was quiet for a moment. "Phil, why did you ask me to marry you? You didn't want to this afternoon when we came back from our ride. There has to be another reason besides Beth's tirade."

It surprised me that Kim waited this long to ask. I stroked her arm. "You and Judith are different women. Why couldn't my affections be different for each of you?"

Kim placed her hands on my cheeks. "And? What's the real reason?"

I wrinkled my nose. "You know me too well."

"I ought to after all these years."

I pointed to the Bible. "Read the highlighted verse."

She scooted the book around and quietly read the passage. "What does it mean?"

"Earlier, I read this and was thinking about you. God spoke, not out loud, but in my head. He said, *'I've given you love for her.'* In an instant, all my objections, doubts, and fears vanished. If the Lord gave me love for you, my arguments were empty, and Beth's protests were not important. Though she said it as sarcasm, she said we should marry."

Kim placed her forehead against mine, and our noses touched. "You are a wonderful man. Your faith in God is another reason I love you."

I gave her a peck on the lips.

She looked around. "It seems strange that this home has become mine."

I waggled a finger in front of her nose. "It'll be your home tomorrow."

She kissed the finger. "I know. My grandest dreams are coming true so amazingly fast."

"This is the Lord's doing. Only he could have made it happen."

Our eyes locked, and time seemed to disappear. Somehow, I knew her thoughts, and she appeared to know mine. I said, "We have to tell Beth and David."

She shifted to sit up straight. "Beth will hate the news. Could it dampen her explosion if you called a family meeting and included Tom?"

"It might. I don't want to be mean to her. But she'll have to live with our marriage."

"Better call her. It's not too late."

I scrunched around to fish out my cell phone and punched in Beth's number.

It rang four times before she answered and said, "Hi, Dad. Are you calling to apologize since you and Kim have called it quits? You better say you're sorry, you know."

She should be apologizing. "I'm inviting you, David, and the boys over for a York family meal. How about Monday evening around six o'clock after David gets off work?"

"I hope you straighten out the mess you created tonight."

"We'll be talking, and I'll straighten everything out. It's a promise."

"Great. Hold on. Let me ask David."

A muffled discussion carried over the line from the other end of as she talked with her husband. A minute passed before she came back on. "Okay. He had something planned at work, but he changed his schedule. Should we bring anything?"

"Just your appetites. I'm cooking, and everything is on me. After the meal, we'll have a family meeting."

"We can't have a family meeting. Tom won't be there."

"I'll arrange for your brother to be on speakerphone. Kim will be there. What you said tonight really hurt her. You better smooth things over."

"I meant no harm. She'll understand."

"Princess, maybe you didn't mean to hurt her with your words, but they wounded her deeply." I dropped my voice. "You better mend fences. Don't destroy years of friendship."

"I hear you. Is the family meeting intended to straighten out tonight's mess?"

"It's what I said earlier."

"You better make it the right way."

My grip tightened. "I promise it will be." Though not to my daughter's satisfaction.

Chapter 25

Saturday, January 2nd, morning

Kim and I went to town and stopped by her apartment. I helped her pack two suitcases to take back to the ranch. While I waited in the other room, she changed into different clothes.

She came out and twirled before me. "Do I look pretty in this?"

"Wow. You look stunning in that dress. The blue dress contrasts with your blonde hair and highlights your smile."

"Thank you. At work, Edith knows I love yellow but thought blue would be a delightful change and gave me a web link. When I saw this, I fell in love with it and splurged."

"Why didn't you wear it to the New Year's Eve party? You'd have gotten a ton of attention."

"I thought about it, but I didn't want to be too flashy."

"But you want to be flashy today?"

She smiled. "For my husband-to-be, yes. I want today to be special for us."

"By wearing this dress, you'll be my gracious and lovely bride. Even though it's Saturday, the courthouse is open this morning, and we'll be able to get our marriage license. Nebraska doesn't have a waiting period, so we can stand before a judge right away. We'll need to find witnesses, although I'm sure there'll be folks who we can ask to stand in."

I helped her put on her coat, and we rolled the suitcases to the car. In a few minutes, we were cruising down Main Street toward the center of town.

Kim asked, "We haven't talked about this, but could we have Gerald Johnson perform the ceremony? It would be something special for him and a way of saying thanks for having raised me."

"That sounds like a great idea. Where's he staying?"

"Cedar Ridge Healthcare on Fifteenth Street. We talk by phone every week, and I visit him once a month."

Kim and I stopped at White Star Jewelers to select our rings, and, at the courthouse, we got our marriage license.

Arriving at Cedar Ridge, we entered the lobby.

A nurse looked up from her computer. "Hi, Kim. You're visiting early this month."

"Hi, Amy. Is Gerald Johnson in the lounge, or is he reading in his room? Phil and I want to ask an important question."

"He's in bed. Yesterday, he took a fall in the shower. He didn't break any bones, but he bruised his legs and hips pretty badly."

I winced. "Is he able to accept visitors?"

"We don't want him walking, but he can sit in bed. Follow me to his room."

We walked behind her into Pastor Johnson's room. She said, "Gerald, you have visitors. Let me help you sit up." She raised his bed and put a pillow behind him.

When Kim and I went in, he held out his arms. "Oh my. My darling Kimberly came to see me. Give me a hug."

She sat on the edge of the bed and hugged him.

He touched her arm. "This dress looks pretty on you, but you've always been a beautiful girl."

"Thank you. How are you feeling? Amy told us you fell."

Nurse Amy turned off the TV and left the room.

He touched his legs under the blanket. "I bruised up pretty badly, but I plan to stick around another year until I turn ninety, Lord willing. If the Lord doesn't return in the rapture, maybe I'll reach a hundred." He spotted me. "Wonderful. Wonderful. Phil, it's great to see you again."

I shook his hand. "Hi, Gerald."

"I'm sorry Judith couldn't come with you," he said. "I miss her lovely laugh. How are Bethany and Thomas?"

"They're doing well. Tom will graduate this spring, and Beth is busy with her two boys."

"Tell Thomas to visit sometime, because this old man doesn't get many visitors. Have Bethany bring her boys. I'll play dominoes with them. They'll like the game."

"I'll let them know."

"Gerald," said Kim, "Phil and I have a special request. We want you to marry us. Could you perform the ceremony right now?"

His eyes opened wide. "Oh, you beautiful, darling girl, yes, I will. Your precious dream has come true. Phil, my little Kimberly is a sweet girl. You couldn't have found a better wife."

"She is an amazing woman," I said.

Gerald picked up the picture from beside his bed. "My Rachel would have loved to be here today. But she'll have a better view, watching from heaven."

I handed him the marriage license.

He examined it. "This is perfect. We'll need witnesses." He pushed the call button.

A ding, ding sounded in the hallway, and a female aide entered. "Yes, Gerald, what do you need?"

He held up three fingers. "I need two people for fifteen minutes, but three would be better. Kimberly and Phil are getting married right now, and we'll need witnesses. See if Nurse Amy can be one of them."

The aid's eyes grew large. "A wedding? Right here?"

"Yes," I said. "Kim and I have asked Pastor Johnson to perform the ceremony. We'd like witnesses if you could find a few folks to join us."

Her face lit up. "Give me a few minutes to round them up."

While we waited, Kim shared the events of the past few days. "I couldn't get Phil's attention and had to take matters into my own hands."

"Phil, didn't you know she wanted to marry you after Judith's passing?" asked Gerald.

I winked at Kim. "No, I didn't. When I found out, she turned my world upside down. I've been trying to get rid of her ever since, but she won't leave me alone."

She grinned and lightheartedly slapped my shoulder. "Enough of your silly jokes."

Pastor Johnson laughed. "It's good you have a sense of humor. It'll help when things get tough."

"Kim's already tough with me." I laughed.

"No more of your jokes," said Kim, "because we're getting married."

Outside the room, a crowd of about twenty people congregated as Nurse Amy entered with four balloons. "There should be a room full of people for a wedding. When we heard about the ceremony, the residents wanted to celebrate with you."

More folks began showing up in the doorway.

Pastor Johnson motioned to his bookshelf. "Someone, please get me my Bible. Kimberly and Phil stand at the foot of the bed. Everyone else, come in, and let's celebrate their union."

After everyone was in the room, I held Kim's hands, and Reverend Johnson read from the 'Love Chapter' in his Bible. He spoke a few words about God ordaining marriage and the importance of joining a man and woman into a family.

He said, "Kimberly, please recite your vows before God and these witnesses."

Kim locked eyes with me. "I, Kimberly Ann Ryan, choose you, Philip Edward York, to be my lawfully wedded husband, to have and to hold, from this day forward, for richer or for poorer, in sickness and in health, until we should be parted by death."

I followed Kim with my vows, and we slipped the rings on each other's fingers.

Pastor Johnson said, "By the authority vested in me by the state of Nebraska as a preacher of the Gospel of Jesus Christ, I now pronounce you husband and wife. You may kiss the bride."

I took Kim in my arms, but we immediately broke apart as several people showered us with bird seed. Handfuls fell around us and got into our hair and clothes.

Everyone cheered and whistled. Someone tooted a party horn.

I brushed birdseed out of Kim's hair, and she dusted my shirt.

Someone shouted, "Where's the cake? We want a party."

Kim grinned. "I don't think they'll let us leave unless we have a reception."

I laughed. "Okay, and we shall." I said to Amy, "If someone has a car and will go to the discount store, I'll give them fifty dollars to buy a cake and ice cream. Then we'll have a proper celebration."

She pointed to a tall, slender girl whose nametag read Natalie. I handed her the money, and she sped off while the rest of us moved to the dining room. Amy commandeered a wheelchair for Pastor Johnson.

For the next couple of hours, everyone congratulated Kim and me. Marlin, a male resident, took photos with his Nikon and promised to give us copies. He asked Kim and me to stuff cake in each other's mouths, which we did to the cheers of everyone while he snapped pictures.

The entire staff and residents at Cedar Ridge Healthcare gave us a rollicking, grand, and unplanned wedding reception. Seeing their enjoyment was the greatest wedding present any of them could have given to Kim and me.

Chapter 26

Saturday, January 2nd, afternoon

Kim and I returned to the ranch after our wedding reception at Cedar Ridge Healthcare. Candy and her daughters had arrived earlier and were in the stables with their horses.

JoAnn met us with her hands on her hips. "I've been calling all day, and I get shunted to voicemail. What's going on, Phil?" She noticed Kim. "You have a lovely blue dress." She turned back to me. "Where have you been for crying out loud?"

"Kim and I took care of personal business. I turned off my phone so no one would disturb us. What do you need?"

"I need help."

"What's the problem? I'll help if I can."

"You know I couldn't come to the New Year's Eve party because of a business problem. The client planned to purchase an apartment building in Omaha and was using a local farm as collateral. I don't know what happened at their end of the deal, but they literally walked away. They dusted their hands and said the farm was mine. They don't want it."

"And? What's the problem?"

"It's the Stephens farm, five miles south of town. I looked over the property today. It's one hundred sixty acres of weedy ground, forty-seven head of Angus feeder calves, two horses, thirty-six pigs, a henhouse full of chickens, a Ford tractor with its equipment, and five bins of last year's wheat. But there's no one around. Someone locked the house and deserted the place. I know nothing about farming or caring for animals."

I said to Kim, "Get Candy. She'll want to hear this."

She slipped into the stables and brought Candy to the door.

I asked JoAnn, "Was the electricity on at the Stephens farm?"

"It was off."

"Then the livestock will need water soon and someone to feed them. Were there any engines or motors running when you visited?"

"The place was silent except for the animals."

"Then the dryers for the grain bins are shut down."

Kim returned to my side.

Candy stepped beside JoAnn and said, "If you're talking about the Stephens farm, it was a half-mile from where I used to live."

"What do you know about the place?"

"It was mainly a wheat farm with a beef operation. They grew spring wheat on most of the land, but thistle, foxtail, and milkweed covered the rest. Everyone nearby considered the farm a nursery for weeds and was constantly battling the seeds from infesting their land."

"What do you know about the livestock?"

"I visited the farm once. Someone had purchased culled beef steers from other farms to fatten them, but they weren't doing a good job. If they intended the pigs for slaughter, they hadn't fed them well. I could hear chickens squawking from the henhouse but didn't see them."

"Who worked there?"

"A retired man and his young grandson. He puttered around and mainly took care of the livestock. I only saw them that one time. They kept to themselves."

JoAnn said to me, "Well, the man wasn't there." She spread her hands. "The farm needs a lot of work if I'm to recoup my investment. Help me out. I don't know what to do."

"Get the electricity turned on. It's too late today, so make sure it's on by tomorrow."

"Could you take care of the livestock until I decide what to do with the farm?"

"There's no way I could work my ranch and the Stephens farm. You better find someone else."

"I know nothing about a farm. If you can't help, who would you recommend?"

I glanced at Candy. Her lips twitched as she gave a tiny nod. I said, "JoAnn, I know someone who might be interested. They've worked on a wheat farm, are good workers, and have cared for livestock. But they're not cheap."

JoAnn raised her eyebrows. "How much is not cheap?"

"Eighty thousand for the first year, and they stay in the house rent-free. If they prove themselves, and I'm sure they will, the second year will be ninety thousand. Thereafter, negotiate with them."

"Wait a minute. That's highway robbery."

I shook my head. "No, it's not. The salary may be a bit on the high side, but you're in a desperate situation, and this person is immediately available."

She glared. "How soon is 'immediately available?' I hope it isn't next week because I need someone right now, not in the morning."

I said to Candy, "You know who I'm talking about. Would they help JoAnn out and take care of the farm?"

"They would be interested. If JoAnn offered them the job as her farm manager, they could travel back and forth for a few days until they moved to the farm."

I turned back to JoAnn. "If you hire this person and you later sell the farm, you'll find them another job at equal pay. Do we have a deal?"

"I don't like to haggle under these circumstances."

I smiled. "When you buy, sell, and lease property, you haggle. I'm haggling for this person's benefit. Do we have a deal?"

"When will I meet this person? I want to evaluate them."

"You have my evaluation, and they're a great farm worker. I'll tell you who this person is after we have a deal."

She hesitated. "I don't like this."

"You don't have to like it. If you want someone to help immediately, you need to agree to hire this person."

She winced. "Could they go this evening? I need someone now."

Without looking at Candy, I saw her nod. "Yes, the person can be there in an hour."

"Do I know this person?"

"You know them." I folded my arms. "I'll add honey to the pot. If this person needs help for any reason, Kim and I are available."

"I don't have a choice because I'm in a tight spot. We have a deal. Who is this man?"

I gestured to Candy. "JoAnn, you already know Candy Murray. Shake hands with your new farm manager."

JoAnn squinted at Candy. "I was expecting a man."

"But you gave your word," I said.

She closed her eyes. "You're right, I did." She shook Candy's hand. "How soon can you check the livestock?"

"Let me finish with the horses first. I need your cell number if something isn't right."

JoAnn fished her phone from her purse and gave Candy the number. "Call Phil if the problem is farm-related." She turned to me. "Could you go with her?"

"Not today. I'm occupied."

Kim squeezed my hand.

"Occupied with what? I trust your judgment with livestock. Kim is here. She could take care of your animals while you help Candy."

"JoAnn, you hired Candy and are trusting her. If she has questions about the animals, she can call me. I'm not going anywhere today." I held out Kim's left hand and displayed my ring beside hers. "We were married this afternoon."

Chapter 27

Sunday, January 3rd, morning and afternoon

Kim and I finished the morning chores and stayed home from church. We perked a pot of coffee, cooked breakfast, and ate at the kitchen table.

"This is the second straight Sunday I've missed services," I said. "Will Pastor James say anything?"

"It's the holiday season, and you're visiting with family."

I smiled. "I'm having a marvelous time with my new family."

Kim grinned. "Is JoAnn upset with how you tricked her yesterday?"

"I don't think so. If I'd revealed Candy beforehand, she would have refused. JoAnn is a businessperson, and I was conducting a transaction. Maybe it wasn't what she expected and cost her more than she'd have liked, but she can't complain about the result. She got a good worker in Candy, and I'm sure she knows it's a great deal."

"Can Candy handle the job?"

"I believe so. She knew what I was doing before I revealed who she was. It gave her a chance to decline. Since she didn't back away, she accepted everything and the responsibility that goes with it."

"Has she ever been a farm manager?"

"She managed a farm without her husband's help, and I'm sure she's a fast learner. If she has questions, she can ask. She'll be here this afternoon to take care of the horses, and we'll talk. I want you beside me when she comes—no secrets between us."

Except for chores, Kim and I spent the day in the house talking and getting to know each other. Mentally, I needed to shift my image to view her as my wife and woman of the house. Hopefully, it wouldn't take long.

Candy and her girls arrived at the stables in the late afternoon, and Kim and I waited for them. Candy said to her girls, "Take care of the horses. I'll be talking to Kim and Phil."

The girls disappeared inside the stables.

"Candy, how was your first day on the job?" I asked.

She rolled her eyes. "The farm is a disaster. No one left feed for the animals, and they hadn't repaired the leaking water tanks or fences. Nor had they cleaned out the two feet of manure in the barn. The electricity came on about noon, and the water pump and blowers to the grain bins began working. But those problems don't bother me."

"Does JoAnn bother you?"

"No, JoAnn was helpful. She set up accounts at Huber Implement Company and the Farmer's Co-op. They deliver, which is good because nobody licensed the farm's truck."

Candy looked down at her hands. "You won't like this. Beth troubles me. She visited my home last evening."

Uh oh. "What did she want?"

"I told her about my new job but said nothing about you and Kim, as you asked. She became super excited because I'd be working with you regularly. Then she started saying crazy stuff like you weren't married and needed a wife, or you were handsome with thick hair, or would I be interested in dating you? She mentioned me marrying you in a roundabout way. Phil, you've got to rein her in and tell her you're already married. I almost blurted it out. What's Beth trying to pull?"

Kim gasped. "Oh, good gravy. I never dreamed she'd be like this. Beth and I have been friends for years, and she thinks of me as the sister she never had. When she heard Phil and I had started a relationship, she blew her stack. She's been finagling for Phil to ask if you would marry him."

"Well, I'm not available just because she thinks I am. Eventually, I want to meet someone, but it has to be on my terms."

"Kim and I will straighten her out," I said. "We've said nothing because she thinks a relationship between Kim and me is wrong. We'll tell her tomorrow evening that we're married."

"What am I supposed to do? She urged me to ask for a date, but all I promised was to talk to you. She's planning to come to my house to find out what you said."

"Wow," said Kim.

"Let me take the pressure off," I said. "Come to the house."

"What for?" asked Candy.

"Trust me, you'll see."

In the kitchen, I said to Candy, "Go ahead. Ask me for a date."

"What's going on?"

"When Beth talks to you this evening," said Kim, "it's something to keep her satisfied." "

"Okay. Phil, may I have a date?"

"Sure." I removed a package of sun-sweetened pitted dates from the shelf and handed them to her. "Tell Beth you asked, and I said sure."

Candy stuck the package in her coat pocket. "What if she asks for details?"

"Tell her I said sure, and everything else is personal. She'll accept it."

"I hope she will. I don't want to lie outright. She was aggressive, like a logger cutting down a big tree."

"I'm sorry," said Kim. "Tell her what we told you and nothing more. To change the subject, are you able to handle everything on the Stephens farm?"

"Not alone. At least not until I get the farm in order. My kids were super excited that I got a great job. We talked together, and Harold reluctantly said he'd help until he found work. After I bribed the girls, they agreed to not go back to college for one semester. I had to promise them two weeks of vacation to visit Pikes Peak and the Garden of the Gods after we sowed the spring wheat."

"It's good they'll be able to help," I said.

"JoAnn was helpful, too, more than I expected from the way she acted yesterday. Which surprised me."

"That's good to hear," said Kim.

"Phil, could you use your trailer to bring JoAnn's horses over here? One is a Morgan, and the other is a mixed breed. They're not in the best shape because they lack pasture, and someone left them in the barn without space to move around. JoAnn agreed to have a vet give them shots, get them dewormed, and do anything else. They don't wear horseshoes and will need their hooves trimmed."

"No problem. I'll set up an account with JoAnn and ensure her horses get good care."

We talked for a while longer. Candy was smart and had good ideas about how she wanted to get the farm in shape.

After she and her girls left, Kim said, "You were right about Beth. I thought she just wanted you to be friends with Candy and hope something developed. I was wrong because she's been plotting to get you married to her against everyone's wishes. What do we do about her?"

"I don't know for sure, but she needs her tail trimmed."

Chapter 28

Monday, January 4th, evening

Before Beth and her family arrived for the family meal, I said to Kim, "Are you okay with what we planned?"

"What else can we do? We're using the good china dishes, which will surprise her."

"It's part of the plan. Let's finish cooking the food. They should be here shortly."

I broiled steaks in the oven while Kim whipped up her famous rice pudding with raisins, which the entire family loved. Buttered peas, mashed potatoes, and a cherry pie finished out the menu.

I said to Kim, "We have to remove our wedding rings to prevent questions."

"Shucks, I want to show it off, but I understand." She slipped it off, and we put them in my pocket.

She watched through the kitchen window as David drove in and parked the van. "Beth doesn't appear relaxed," said Kim, "but she isn't tense. David is David, as always. The boys are excited."

"Let me finish broiling the steaks. You answer the door and just be yourself."

At the door, the chatter between Kim and Beth sounded normal. The boys thundered through the house like a cattle stampede to the toybox in the den.

Beth came up behind me in the kitchen as I removed the last steak from the broiler. "Hey, Dad, it's great you're finally using Mom's china dishes."

I didn't face her and kept my voice even. "I figured we'd use them at least once before I sold them. There's no need to let them take up space."

"What? No. Don't sell Mom's dishes."

"Sure, I can. You said that I'm not using them, so why keep them?"

"If you're not using them, then let me have them."

With my back to her, I said, "I told you I'd leave them to you when I kicked the bucket, but that hasn't happened. Therefore, I'm selling them."

Kim and David appeared in the kitchen doorway.

Beth squeezed between me and the kitchen counter until we stood toe to toe. "You better not sell Mom's dishes. I forbid it."

"Beth, I'm selling them, and it's final."

"Name your price. We'll buy them." She looked over her shoulder. "Won't we, David?"

He nodded.

"The food's getting cold," Kim said to Beth. "Help me set it on the table, and Phil will call your boys. You and he can discuss the china dishes while we eat."

"Dad, I mean it," said Beth. "They were Mom's dishes and should stay in the family."

I handed David the plate of steaks. "Put those on the table. Beth, grab the buttered peas, and I'll call your boys. We'll sit and talk about the dishes." I stepped around her and handed Kim the bowl of rice pudding before going to the den for the boys.

In a few minutes, we all held hands, and I said a prayer of thanks for the food.

David and Beth helped Ian and Eddy with their plates before filling their own.

Beth folded her arms. "Dad, the china dishes were Mom's and should stay in the family. Name your price."

"I doubt you could afford the price."

"How much, Dad? I'll clean out our savings. I'll sell my piano."

"The dishes are worth more. I'm sure you won't have what it takes to buy them."

"Anything, Dad, anything. Name your price. I'll come up with the money. They were Mom's and should stay in the family."

"I said nothing about money. I said you couldn't afford the price."

Beth frowned. "What are you talking about?"

"For you to buy them, I want three things. If you meet my price, then they're yours."

Beth leaned forward. "Really? What are the three things?"

I gestured to Kim. "You tell her the first one."

Kim straightened. "Three days ago, we sat around this table, and you said hurtful words. You called me a mistake and broke our friendship, which was supposed to last forever. I'm asking for an apology … tonight."

Before Beth could say anything, I said to her, "Do you remember when I called you the other night? I asked you to apologize to Kim and thought you would. You didn't."

"But—"

I held up a second finger. "Next, you owe me an apology. You called Kim a mistake and said if I were to have a relationship with her, it would be wrong. But you know it's not. Jesus says that what comes out of the mouth originates from the heart and defiles a person. What you said was harsh."

Beth tightened her lips.

I held up a third finger. "You owe an apology to Candy. You tried to set her up with me, and it distressed her. Your responsibilities don't include Candy's relationships, mine, or anyone else's."

"Do you have a romantic relationship with Kim, or did you end it?" asked Beth.

"Stop changing the subject. I'm talking to you about buying your mom's china."

"Phil," said David, "you're being pretty harsh with Beth."

"No, I'm not. I love my daughter. But I can't forget the harm she's done with her tongue. Or do you think I should?"

He hemmed and hawed. "No, I guess not."

"David, you went along with Beth's criticism of us the other night."

"But a relationship between you and her wouldn't be good."

"Don't change the subject. I'm asking how Beth treated Kim and me. Do you think it was Christian or not?"

He nodded. "Yeah. It wasn't."

Ian said, "Daddy, I want more of that." He pointed to the bowl of rice pudding.

David and Beth took a moment to help the boys with their food.

Beth wiped Eddy's chin and faced me.

She opened her mouth, but I held up my hand. "I'm asking about the words you said to Kim and me the other day. Were they kind?"

Her voice rose. "It's wrong to date Kim."

"Beth, don't change the subject. The words you said to Kim and me, were they kind? This is my focus at the moment, and it's why I'm asking for apologies."

"You hurt us, Beth," said Kim. "You didn't care about our friendship. You didn't care about your father's feelings. You just pushed to get what you wanted."

"Okay, I apologize," Beth griped.

"Not good enough," said Kim. "The words must come from your heart."

"What am I supposed to do? Get down on my knees in the mud like Aunt JoAnn?"

"If that's what's necessary for an honest apology, yes," I said. "And I want you to promise not to interfere with people's relationships. I apologized the other day for blowing my stack. I was wrong, and I admitted it. We're asking you to admit you were wrong and say you're sorry."

"You're mean to me."

"We may be hard on you, but we're not mean," said Kim. "We're trying to help you."

I said, "You were mean to us by the words you said, and that's why I'm selling your mom's china. Or if you want it bad enough, it'll cost you three public apologies. I said the price wouldn't be cheap."

"Let's go outside," said Beth. "And I'll get down in the mud if that's what it takes."

Kim said, "If your boys witness you humbling yourself in front of them and their father, I'll accept it. You won't need to grovel outside."

"I'll accept it, too," I said.

"You're mean if you expect me to do that in front of my boys."

"No," said Kim, "you have it backward. You were mean to us the other night."

When Beth remained quiet, I held up my empty plate. "If you refuse to say you're sorry in front of your family, then tomorrow I'm putting an ad in the newspaper.

If you give us the three apologies we're asking for, then they're yours. What'll it be?"

Beth scowled. "Alright, alright, if that's what it takes. Ian, Eddy, watch your mother apologize to Grandpa and Aunt Kim." She pushed back from the table and knelt beside Kim. "I'm truly sorry for what I said. It was wrong to hurt you. Will you forgive me?"

Kim pulled Beth into an embrace. "Yes, I forgive you." While they held each other, Kim said, "I want us to be best friends forever, like we promised each other."

Beth came around the table and knelt beside me. "Forgive me, Dad. I won't say those things again. I'm sorry."

"You're forgiven, but don't forget to apologize to Candy, too."

"I won't. I promise to say I'm sorry tomorrow."

For the rest of the meal, Beth remained polite, though subdued.

We'd see if her apologies were honest. But I figured they were because she'd humbled herself in front of her husband and boys. If Kim and I had waited a few more days, we might have come up with a different plan. But we needed to settle this problem before we revealed our marriage. We'd see how she reacted tonight, and hopefully she wouldn't have an explosion.

Chapter 29

Kim and Beth cleared the table after the family meal, stacking the dishes in the kitchen sink.

My grandsons made a beeline for the DVD cabinet while I set up the phone in the middle of the table.

Beth and Kim returned to their seats. I dialed Tom and placed the phone on speaker.

"Hi everyone," said Tom. "I'm glad Dad called this meeting because I've got great news. I asked Bonnie to marry me yesterday. She got super excited and said yes. We plan to have the wedding in June after we graduate, but we haven't set a date. I'm bringing her home at Easter to meet the family. You're going to love her."

Kim smiled. "All right, little Tommy Boy. We sort of figured that from the way you've been mooning over her and weren't home for Christmas."

Everyone knew Tom and Kim teased each other.

Tom quipped back, "Hey, pretty Kimmy girl. It should be you and me that get hitched. You know I've still got this thing for you. Maybe we could get something going between us."

"Nah, I'm already taken."

Beth's brows narrowed as she looked at Kim before slowly facing me and frowning.

"Really?" said Tom. "Who's the boyfriend?"

"You know him, but he's not a boyfriend." She looked at me and must have realized she was about to divulge the reason for this family gathering.

I nodded for her to go ahead. By including Tom in the banter, perhaps Beth's objections wouldn't be as severe.

Tom continued. "If he's not a boyfriend, then I still have a chance. I could tell Bonnie how much I adore you. She'd give the ring back, and I could put it on your finger this Easter."

"Be careful, baby boy," said Kim. "The whole family is listening, and I'd be robbing the cradle."

Tom chuckled. "You always raze me about that, but the family won't care. They know how much we love each other."

"What about Bonnie? Won't she be upset?"

"Nah, nobody holds a candle to you. She'll understand."

"Well, I'm turning you down," said Kim. "Bonnie can keep her hooks in you."

"That cuts to the quick. I'm hurt that my favorite girl is saying no. You said this guy wasn't your boyfriend. What have I done to earn your refusal?"

"You're much too young. Besides, I'm already married."

David spun toward me, his eyes wide.

Beth clasped her hands and tightened her lips. Her black hair dangled over her eyes.

"Say what?" said Tom. "Married? When did this happen?"

"Saturday morning. I married a guy twice my age. I'm letting go of your leash, and you're free to pursue Bonnie."

"You're teasing, right?"

"I would never tease you, little Tommy Boy," Kim said in a singsong cadence.

David stood abruptly. "Holy cow, Tom." He spoke directly into the phone. "Kim's not joking. She and your father eloped."

Beth's face tilted toward me, and her black hair half covered her eyes. I couldn't read her expression, and a silent Beth was a huge anomaly.

"Kim, is it true?" asked Tom. "Is this a joke, or did you honestly marry Dad?"

I stepped beside my wife, replaced the ring on her finger, and slipped mine on.

Kim leaned over the phone. "It's true, and I've got the ring to prove it. It makes me your stepmom, and you must *always* obey your momma or I'll get out the wooden spoon."

"Aw, man," said Tom, laughter in his voice. "It means I can't rag on you anymore and have to be good."

He chuckled. "This is so cool. Kim is a permanent member of our family. Waaaaaahooooo! Wait until I tell Bonnie. This is so great. Hey Beth, your best friend is our stepmom."

I leaned toward the phone with my arm around Kim. "Tom, your sister is speechless. Can you imagine her with nothing to say? You have a stepmom, and both of you must toe the line."

Chapter 30

Wednesday, January 6th, late afternoon

A sudden blast of cold winter wind, carrying snowflakes, whipped around the corner of the stables as I tossed my lariat. The rope sailed high in a wabbling arc toward the fencepost and caught on the top edge.

Kim unhooked the rope. "You forgot to compensate for the wind. You should practice before entering the rodeo this summer."

"I have no plans to enter." I turned up my coat collar. "Right now, my hands are stiff, and I'm getting old."

"My husband is not old. Shouldn't you defend the roping record that you and Judith hold? Your ten-second score still stands on top."

I shrugged. "The younger guys can give it a shot. Fargo is nine years old, and we've had a good run."

"You should enter. Fargo is also the best cutting horse in half the state."

"I have no intention of signing up for the rodeo."

"Why not? Lots of people respect you as one of the best."

"I don't care what others say. It's time to call it quits."

"Phil, stop being reluctant. Your reputation put the York Riding Ranch on the map. Why are you quitting?" Her breath rose in the air, and the wind whisked it away.

"Because I lost my roping partner."

"Then find someone else."

"Are you volunteering?"

She huffed. "Not hardly. I don't know what it takes to be a good roper."

"Then there's no reason for me to enter. I'm hanging up my spurs."

Kim planted her hands on her hips. "Philip York, you've never been a quitter. You were always gung-ho to show everyone you could compete with *and beat* them. What's the real reason?"

I turned my back while coiling the rope.

She grabbed my arm and turned me around. "There aren't supposed to be secrets between us, remember? What's the reason?"

I brushed her hand away and entered the stables.

She followed. "Philip York, I'm your wife. You better tell me what's going on."

Challenger stuck his head over the stall gate.

"I'm waiting," said Kim. "We're not going anywhere, and I'll keep asking until you tell me."

I rubbed Challenger's neck. "Because Judith isn't here. Every time I see this horse, I see her."

"What else?"

"When she roped from Challenger, she'd nod to the chute handler, race after the calf, and pull it around so I could lasso its hind legs. My memories have welded her together with this horse. I can't separate her from him. That's my problem."

"Don't I mean anything since we married?"

"You're my wife, and I'm glad. But when I see this horse, he tangles Judith in my head, and I can't get away from her."

"Are you relegating me to a second-place wife?"

I touched her cheek. "No, I'm not. God gave me love for you, and you're the finest woman around. But I have constant memories of Judith riding beside me on Challenger and of us team roping in the rodeo. They doggedly follow and are stuck on with superglue."

Challenger nuzzled me, and I rubbed his nose. "In my head, she's bound to this horse. Every time I look at him, I see her riding him and roping from him. I can't get away from those memories."

"Do you want to erase her from your memory?"

"No. But I don't want to live in the past either, and that's what's happening. If I went to a rodeo, my memories would … I don't know, make me a mess."

"Is there anything I can do?"

"Yes, ride him instead of Lindy. He's yours. Maybe then I'll connect you with him."

She touched Challenger's nose. "Are you sure it'll help?"

"On our ride to the timber, not once did I think of Judith. If you could do that, maybe by riding Challenger, you could create fresh memories. I want to live in the present with you." I opened my arms. "Come here."

She entered my embrace and laid her head against my chest.

"Kim, this is where you belong. I struggle with a knock-down, drag-out war in my head and don't want to push you aside. But that's what's happening."

She looked up at me. "Your heart hasn't healed. It's still wounded from losing Judith."

"God hit me on the head to bring you into my life. Maybe he did it so you could heal me."

"Do you believe I can? I don't know how."

"If given enough time, maybe you can. I'm glad God brought us together. You bring a breath of fresh air to my heart. But my memories of Judith on Challenger and me riding beside her …" I shook my head. "They're etched in stone, which is why I won't enter a rodeo."

"I'll keep praying for you."

We stepped outside and closed the stable door. In the strong wind, the mottled gray clouds dashed across the sky as if in a sprint to reach the eastern horizon.

I pointed to the western skyline. "There's a weather front moving in, and the forecast calls for a drop in temperature with a chance of light snow."

Kim pulled on her gloves. "Thankfully, it won't be heavy. I used to enjoy tossing snowballs at Beth and Tom, but not so much anymore."

A car turned into the lane and parked by the corral. Shelly, Sharon, and Candy hopped out. "Phil, what's the meeting about?" asked Candy.

I frowned. "What meeting?"

"JoAnn called. The girls and I are to meet here with you."

"A meeting with me or with her? I know nothing about it."

"She said it was important for us to be here by 5:30 p.m."

"This is news to us," said Kim.

"It must be with JoAnn, then. We'll take care of the horses while we wait." They entered the stables.

I said to Kim, "A meeting about what? Does she need help at the Stephens farm?"

"If it's a business meeting, should I be present?"

"Any problem Candy can't handle will involve both of us."

Kim pointed toward the road. "Here comes JoAnn. Is Gene Wilcox in the car behind her?"

"If it includes both of them, the meeting won't be about the Stephens farm."

I hollered into the stables, "Candy, JoAnn just got here. Come on out."

The two cars stopped by the corral fence, and JoAnn and Gene got out.

It's freezing. He should wear a hat on his bald head.

He shook my hand. "I hear you and Kim got married. You're rather old for her, aren't you?" He winked.

Kim latched onto my arm. "Thank you for implying I'm young, Gene, but our love is real."

Candy joined the group.

"Phil, could we go to the house?" asked JoAnn. "This meeting will take a while."

"What's so important for you to come to the ranch with Gene?"

"You won't believe this. Let's go inside."

"Believe what?"

"You'll see." She said to Candy, "Have your girls finish with the horses, then join us. They will want to hear this, too."

In the house, I put the coffee on, and the four of us sat around the dining room table.

"This meeting is about the strange email I received from Sherry Sue Settle," said Gene. "Kim, I've verified it's on the up and up."

"How can she put on a rodeo in February?" I asked. "It's not possible."

"Not her. Woodrow Hancock is organizing it. I talked to both of them over the past couple of days, and Sherry Sue is my primary contact." I was about to say something, and he held up his hand. "Phil, let me explain what I know. We'll discuss the details before deciding what to do."

Kim retrieved a legal pad and began taking notes.

"Woodrow Hancock inherited a farm near Atlantic, Iowa, from his uncle," said Gene, "along with a bunch of money. The will allowed Mr. Hancock to build two homes for single pregnant girls to get their lives straightened out. He calls them *The Meadows*. But he cannot use the inherited money for administrative or day-to-day expenses."

He rested his arms on the table. "To operate the homes, he must develop other sources of funds. Sherry Sue Settle was pregnant, and after giving birth, she joined the staff. She's helping others in the same situation and suggested that Mr. Hancock hold a charity rodeo to raise the money he needs. He latched onto the idea like a pit bull."

"Wow," said Kim.

JoAnn said, "Mr. Hancock is sprinting toward the goal line with Sherry Sue's idea. He's in an all-fired hurry to fund *The Meadows*."

"Because Sherry Sue's father is a rodeo clown," said Gene. "She knows I organize rodeos and suggested I supply everything to put one on for Mr. Hancock. It would include the livestock, fencing, food stands, bleachers, restrooms, medical equipment, and the workers to set it up, run it, and clean it up."

"Whoa," I said. "I see problems. If they plan to transport the livestock and all the equipment from here to Atlantic." I rubbed my thumb over my fingers, signifying a lot of money. "There's a cost to putting one on, including getting rodeo permits. If he wants a rodeo in February, he'll need an indoor arena."

"Don't worry about transportation," said JoAnn. "I contacted a Christian man I know from Sagely, Iowa. We talked on the phone, and he's willing to donate his trucks, drivers, fuel, whatever."

"Okay, assuming the transportation is as good as you say, Gene, what about the costs?"

"Don't worry about costs. This man has a bunch of money, and I mean a huge bunch. He's planning this rodeo as a charity and wants as much as possible to be donated. Any costs the rodeo incurs, he'll foot the bill personally."

Kim tapped her pencil against the notepad. "Gene, Phil asked about an indoor arena. There's no way to have an outdoor rodeo in the winter because of inclement weather."

"Mr. Hancock has a crew of construction workers who've already built an indoor arena. Sherry Sue sent me pictures. It's a completely enclosed shell without heating. He asked me to set up everything."

Shelly and Sharon entered, and Kim got chairs for them.

Gene said, "Girls, we're planning a rodeo for February. Are you interested in competing?"

"Yes!" They pumped their fists.

Chapter 31

At my dining room table, Gene Wilcox raised his voice and said, "Everyone, settle down. I called Sherry Sue yesterday, and we discussed the rodeo. She and I talked about logistics, details, requirements, and everything. With all that I'd have to put together, by my estimation and with a lot of luck, it's doable in February, but only in the last half of the month."

"What about rodeo contestants?" asked Kim. "It's winter. How many would be available?"

"It's why we're here. After talking to Sherry Sue, I called Mr. Hancock, and he named five specific participants he wanted in his rodeo. They're at this table."

I stiffened.

Kim placed her hand on my arm and whispered, "Just listen."

I whispered back, "It better not include me."

Candy's finger bounced as she counted everyone. "It's all of us except Gene and JoAnn. How did he know our names?"

"From Sherry Sue," said Gene. "She traveled with her father from rodeo to rodeo and saw all of you compete." He pointed at Candy. "You were one of the best breakaway ropers." He turned to Kim. "And young lady, you and Beth took the top awards in barrel racing for several years and went to the state fair. When you quit racing, Shelly and Sharon became strong competitors." He looked at me. "Phil, you and Judith were team ropers and hold the standing record."

Kim squeezed my hand. "Gene, Phil hasn't roped since Judith's death. He's not interested in going to the rodeo."

He thought for a moment. "Mr. Hancock specifically asked for Phil."

"No, Gene," I said. "I'm a rancher, not a rodeo cowboy. I won't go."

"A rodeo will last for a week or more," said Kim. "Phil and I just got married and can't leave the ranch for that long."

"Harold could do your chores," said JoAnn. "If everyone at this table went, he and Marston could take care of the livestock for both places."

"This is a crazy idea," I said. "Where will you find bull riders, steer wrestlers, and bronc riders? What about the mountain of behind-the-scenes people like stock handlers, gatekeepers, judges, timers, and more?"

"Finding rodeo workers won't be a problem," said Gene. "I know many who'd jump at the chance because they're often out of a job during winter. Mr. Hancock promised five thousand dollars to the first-place winners of each event."

I whistled. "That much for a no-name startup rodeo? You must be joking."

"Not at all. He's planning to advertise. I suggested he contact the United Rodeo Association, the URA. If they put their stamp of approval on it, it would be a huge drawing card."

"Gene, I haven't roped in ages. Count me out. Kim can go as a barrel racer if she wants."

"Phil, if you won both the team roping and cutting events, it would equal the ten grand you owe me. I'll move the due date back a few weeks to allow for it."

I sat up straighter. "You're using outright bribery."

"You bet I am." He held out his hand. "If you pay now, I'll back off. Otherwise, you'll be at the rodeo."

"I'm not going."

He said to Kim, "Will you knock sense into this thickheaded numskull?"

She put her arm around mine. "No, I won't. He's his own man and can do what he wants. If he doesn't want to be in this rodeo, as his wife, I agree with him."

"Knowing Phil," said Gene, "to get him to marry you, you must have had a handful of aces."

"I played a queen to cover his jack and became the queen of his heart."

"That sounds romantic," said Sharon.

"Yeah," said Shelly. "Tell me your secret so I can catch someone."

"Let's get back to the rodeo," said Gene. "Phil, I want you to go."

"No," I said. "I have my reasons."

"If you refuse to go, then I'm demanding full payment right now."

I locked eyes with him and snarled, "I'll see you in court."

Kim yanked my arm. "Shut your mouth. We're talking in private."

With her hand on my back, she pushed me into the bedroom. I sat on the bed as she closed the door.

"Phil, I support your decision not to go, but did you hear what Gene said? Get your head screwed on straight."

"I am talking straight, and it's not nonsense."

"If you hang on to your pride, you'll lose your horses." She pointed toward the other room. "You threatened to take Gene to court, and lawyers don't come cheap. You owe him a valid debt, and if you stood before a judge, you'd lose. He'd take the horses, and to pay the lawyers, you could kiss this ranch goodbye."

"I already told you why I won't compete."

"You'd throw away everything because of memories of Judith? Hogwash. You're smart at running this ranch, but you make terrible decisions when you're thinking with your heart."

My mind jerked to a halt. "Was I like that with Judith?"

"She mellowed you out and forced you to think, and that's what I'm trying to do. You should go to the rodeo, even if you don't want to. If you take legal action against Gene, you'll be in debt so deep that York Riding Ranch won't be a memory."

She sat and held my hand. "Phil, I understand that you have memories of Judith and how they tear you up. Maybe God wants you to go to this rodeo to heal your wounded heart. Don't fight him to the point of hurting yourself and everyone else."

I closed my eyes. "I keep remembering Judith and me competing at rodeos, and everything about Mr. Hancock's rodeo feels wrong because she won't be there."

"It's not wrong because I'll be with you. Trust me."

"If I went, I'd need a roping partner. Would you do it?"

"I wouldn't be much good and don't have what it takes. Candy would be an excellent partner."

"Beth planned for me to meet up with her, so it wouldn't be good."

"Forget what Beth wanted. You're safe. Candy and I talked the other day. I'm your wife, and she has no desire to intrude. Ask her."

"I wish you roped like Judith."

"That's a pipe dream. But if it's okay, I'll ride Challenger in the barrel race."

"I'm okay with it."

She put a hand on my knee. "Will you go?"

"Not willingly."

"Will you go if I'm there?"

"Grudgingly, but only if you're with me and someone takes care of our livestock."

"Thank you. Let's tell Gene."

Back at the dining room table, Gene said, "Kim, did you twist his arm? Will he go or not?"

"I'll enter the team roping and calf cutting events," I said. "But you have to accept my winnings as full payment for the trailer debt."

He eyed me. "You drive a hard bargain. If you're good enough to win both of them, I'll agree. JoAnn, put his name down." He shifted his attention to the ladies. "Sharon and Shelly said they were interested. Candy? Kim? What about you? Should we put your names down?"

Kim looked up from jotting down the meeting's details. "Phil agreed to go. If someone takes care of our livestock, I'll go. Candy, are you sure Harold will help Marston with chores while we're gone?"

"Probably, but only if you pay him. I'll verify it after getting home. JoAnn, if Harold agrees, put me on the list."

JoAnn wrote our names down. "I talked to Trish and Tracy, Ed Barton's girls, last night. They were excited. Getting away won't be a problem because they homeschool and can keep up with assignments at odd times. I chatted with Aaron Berkoff. He's unable to adjust his schedule, but will call back if something changes."

"Phil, would Beth go?" asked Gene.

"Ask her. She'd be interested, but she has to consider her two boys." I glanced at JoAnn. "Could you provide details for the transportation? Does this company have experience hauling livestock, or is it a regular trucking firm?"

"Spence Edwards is the owner of the company," said JoAnn. "He has trailers to transport cattle, horses, and equipment. A good part of his business is hauling livestock."

"If he's hauling Gene's livestock and equipment," I asked, "can he transport my horses? I don't have a trailer large enough."

"I'm sure he has a trailer to haul them. He'll need a head count of how many you have."

"JoAnn, how did you meet Spence Edwards?"

"I was in Des Moines for a real estate conference last year during the Iowa State Fair. We bumped into each other. He'd transported 4-H animals for the judging competitions and was waiting for the fair to be over. We spent an afternoon talking. He's a Christian and prides his company on quality service. When his father passed away, he took over the business."

"Gene," I asked, "are you okay with Mr. Edwards hauling my horses?"

"If he's able, and it doesn't interfere with what I need, I don't have a problem."

"JoAnn, I'd like to chat with Mr. Edwards to iron out the details."

"Sure. I don't have his contact information right now, but I'll email it to you."

Kim whispered, "See. Everything has worked out."

"You know how I feel."

"Pray about it, Phil."

For the next hour, the group discussed plans, ideas, and problems. JoAnn would contact the local folks who'd been in last year's rodeos to see if they were interested.

Gene said, "If they all respond favorably, we'll have the start of a good-sized event."

I wasn't so certain. For a winter no-name startup rodeo with no backing to be successful, it would take a miracle.

Chapter 32

Gene pulled me aside after the meeting at my house. "Phil, it's necessary for us to talk in private."

"No. Kim will come with me and hear whatever you say."

"This is private. We should talk alone."

"Gene, I don't keep secrets from my wife. Whether she hears now or I tell her later, she'll know everything you say."

"You're a stubborn cuss and don't give an inch."

"I made a promise not to keep secrets from her. Wait in the den, and we'll be right back. There's a question I need to ask Candy before she leaves."

Outside, from the back step, I swallowed before saying, "Candy, wait up a minute." I tensed at what I was about to ask.

The wind whipped her hair in the glow from the yard light. "What's up, Phil?"

I took two breaths to ease the tension. "I need a partner for the rodeo team roping event. Would you rope with me?"

She frowned. "I've never done it before. Is there enough time?"

"For you, roping should be easy. To train Pigeon to pull the calf rather than let it run may take some time, but there should be enough."

"I like the idea. Let's talk tomorrow when I take care of the horses."

I flexed and reflexed my hands. "I'll be waiting."

After Candy had gotten in her car, Kim said, "It really bothered you to ask, didn't it?"

"More than you know. I struggled at remembering Judith and wished Candy were her."

"Take one step at a time."

Kim and I said goodbye to the others before returning to the den. We settled into the chairs across from Gene.

"What's so important that you don't want the others to hear?" I asked.

"Phil, how well do you know Sherry Sue Settle?"

"I've seen her at church and greeted her at the rodeo, but nothing more."

"Are you sure you never talked to her at the rodeo?"

I thought for a moment. "I don't recall ever chatting with her. We said hi a few times, but that's all."

"Kim," said Gene, "tell me what you know about Sherry Sue."

"When I helped in the church youth group, she was a sweet girl and friendly. Mostly, she flirted with the boys. She never caused trouble and joined in the lesson discussions."

He scratched his chin. "When I replied to her email, she called me so quickly that I hadn't had time to turn off my computer. She couldn't answer all my questions and said I needed to talk to Mr. Hancock. Before hanging up, she recited a list of people she wanted to take part in the rodeo. Phil, you were on the list, and she was resolute that you be there."

"You said I was on Mr. Hancock's list, not one Sherry Sue had created."

"I lied so the others wouldn't be suspicious."

Could we trust him?

"Suspicious about what?" asked Kim.

"Why was Phil's name at the top of her list?" He looked at me. "Have you visited her home?"

"Never. Chris Settle lives near Lincoln, but I don't know his address."

"Did you have an intimate relationship with Sherry Sue?"

I jerked. "*Absolutely not.* I talked to her father at the rodeo, but never to her."

"Brandon McCloud said she planned to meet up with you."

"That's preposterous. We've never had an actual conversation. Are you implying we slept together?"

He counted on his fingers. "One, Sherry Sue was friendly with boys. Two, I've seen her flirt at different rodeos. Three, Brandon said she wanted to meet up with you. Four, she asked for you to be at Hancock's rodeo. Five, she got pregnant out of wedlock. Connect the dots."

I waved a finger at Gene. "I never met up with Sherry Sue, and it's been two years since I was in a rodeo, so how could I have been around her?"

Kim put her hand on my arm. "Calm down." She said to Gene, "Don't you ever accuse my husband of unfaithfulness."

He huffed. "Everybody lies when they're suspected of intimate activity."

Kim's voice rose. "My husband *doesn't lie*. He's had no affair with Sherry Sue."

"Back off, Gene," I said. "You've got no proof and are treating rumors as if they're true."

"There's no way I can forget it. You and Sherry Sue will be at the rodeo."

I squinted. "If I'm a liability, then I won't go."

"Don't you dare back out. You owe me money and said you'd compete for it. When I talked to Mr. Hancock about Sherry Sue's list, he said, and I quote, 'I definitely want Phil York at the rodeo. Make sure he's there.'"

"That sounds suspicious," said Kim.

"Yes, it does." Gene looked at me. "But you owe me for a trailer, and you'll compete, or I'll start legal proceedings to get Challenger."

"There's no way I'll give him up."

"Either you compete or I'm coming for Challenger, and it's not an empty threat."

I glared. "You sound like the devil. I'll be at this charity rodeo and will avoid Sherry Sue. Don't broadcast a word about her and me, because it's a lie."

Gene wouldn't stay quiet, and his accusation would slander Kim and my reputation.

Chapter 33

Wednesday, January 6th, night

Kim lay next to me in bed. "I heard an ugly rumor that you have a harem."

"That's not funny. You know I've never been near Sherry Sue."

"I know you haven't, but what Gene said made you grumpy. I'm trying to lighten the mood."

"Yeah, I'm cranky. No one ever accused me of infidelity. Have you heard of anyone saying I've been unfaithful?"

"No, I haven't. Where did Gene hear it?"

"That's a good question. He said he lied about the list, so maybe he made up this rumor."

"We should think twice before trusting him," she said. "Who's Brandon McCloud?"

"He's a novice steer wrestler I saw at Grand Island two years ago. He's cocky, thinks he's super good, and believes the world owes him a living. Chris Settle spotted him kissing Sherry Sue."

"Then Brandon could know what Sherry Sue had said."

"Unless Gene is lying about that, too. I've never known him to lie to me, but folks in town say that he bends the truth."

"Phil, was Gene blowing off steam about coming after Challenger?"

"No, and that's another strange thing. He's recently developed an acute interest in him. Since I can't pay the debt, he's using him as a threat."

"If he's interested in Challenger, will you use him or Fargo when you compete?"

I touched her cheek. "Fargo. I told you earlier, Challenger is yours."

"Thank you, but I'd never be a good roper."

"Don't underestimate yourself."

"I'm *not* underestimating myself. You're a roper. I'm a barrel racer."

"Will you ride Challenger or Lindy?" I asked.

"I'm thinking Challenger. When I called Beth, she grumbled about our marriage before I told her about the rodeo. After I mentioned it, she seemed excited. If David is okay with her competing, she'll need to practice here."

"Tomorrow, I'll move the steers out of the lot and set up the portable fence to form a practice area."

"The Stephens farm doesn't have a place to train. Candy will probably ask if she and her girls could train here, too."

"That makes six. Since Ed Barton's horses are here, I figure his girls will want to train, too."

"Then we'll have our own mini-rodeo," she said. "With everyone coming, it scares you, doesn't it?"

"Not scared, only anxious. With you and the girls practicing barrel racing, will I be able to practice roping?"

"You could set aside certain days for us girls to practice, and then on alternate days, you and Candy could help each other with roping."

"Hmmm. Why didn't I think of something so simple? It must be why I married you—for your smarts."

She placed a hand on my chest. "Is that the only reason you married me? I can't see your face in the dark, and I hope you're teasing."

I smiled. "Well, let's see. You're a superb cook, can clean the house, are good with horses, and are mighty pretty. Those are good reasons."

She tapped my nose. "You're being sarcastic. I know two important reasons we married."

My smile faded. "Because the Lord told me to marry you, and you want to be a mother."

"Uh-huh. We've talked about starting a family, and you were willing."

"My focus is on other things at the moment. Today has been hectic."

"Can we discuss it tomorrow?"

"Mrs. York, you're in an all-fired hurry to have a family."

"Yes, I am. Could we make love tonight?"

I kissed her. "Okay. I'll make love to my beautiful wife."

"You say the nicest things."

Chapter 34

Thursday, January 7th, morning

Kim and I came in from the morning chores, and her cell phone rang. "It's Beth," said Kim. She held out her phone for me to hear.

Beth said, "Good morning, Kim. Are you sorry yet that you married Dad? He's old enough to be your father, too."

"Stop it, Beth. You may not like it, but you'll have to get used to it."

"I don't like it, but I don't have a choice."

"Are you interested in the rodeo?"

"I am, but it seems unbelievable that they asked for us personally."

"It's true," said Kim.

"And February is an odd month."

"If you're interested, is David okay with it?"

"David is fine with it. Ian found a photograph of me barrel racing. When I explained, he asked to see me race. I'll have to bring the boys when I come. Could Dad help with them?"

"Bring the boys," I said. "Kim and I will put together the fencing for a practice area in the feedlot."

"I'll be there shortly."

An hour later, Beth arrived. "Dad, keep the boys out of trouble. Kim, let's get Isabel and Lindy saddled up."

Kim shook her head. "I'm riding Challenger."

"He's not a barrel racer. He's Mom's roping horse."

"Challenger is a Quarter Horse and he should do fine."

"Can you train him in time?"

"I guess we'll see. Anyway, red horses are faster than gray ones."

"In your dreams," said Beth. "Isabel is white, like the Lone Ranger's horse."

"Nope. If I held a picture of Native Dancer beside her, they'd be the same gray color."

I hefted Eddy onto my shoulders and took Ian's hand. "Boys, let's get out of the wind. I'll bring Fargo into the stables, and you can brush Serenity's new filly."

I started the boys brushing the foal and heard the ladies talking in the next stall.

Beth said to Kim, "I wish you hadn't married Dad. It feels like someone made a mistake."

"Are you calling me a mistake again?"

"No, I'm not. I just don't see how you can love him."

"I love your father. You married David because you love him."

"It's not the same. It doesn't feel right with you and Dad. I don't like it."

"Beth, your best friend married your father. That's what you don't like—because it makes me your stepmother."

"Yuck. It's even weirder that my best friend is my stepmom. It gives me the creeps."

"We're still best friends," said Kim. "That won't change."

"But being my stepmother is crazy. Does Dad truly love you?"

"He's the one who asked."

"He better love you. I hope you never have children."

I almost bolted around the corner to say it was none of her business.

"Beth, it's not for you to say," said Kim. "Your father and I have talked about it, but we haven't made plans. If we decide to have children, what does it matter?"

"Yuck. For my best friend to have sex with my father, it's disgusting."

"Is having sex with David repulsive?"

"It's different."

"No, it's not. David is your husband. Phil is mine. Procreation and raising children are a natural result of a marriage union."

"For my best friend to have sex with Dad sounds vulgar."

"I'm your best friend, who's the wife of your father."

"But that makes you my stepmother, which feels really weird. Anyway, there's another reason I don't like it."

"I'm guessing you're pregnant," said Kim.

"How did you know?"

"Ian told me his mommy was sick."

Beth smiled. "We could never keep secrets. I'm about two months along. I was going to tell everyone, but after your announcement, it wasn't important."

"Should you be racing on Isabel?"

"The rodeo is six weeks away or more, and I should be fine."

"You better check with your doctor."

"I will. He'll probably say it's okay until I'm five months along. Anyway, let's race. I want to prove Isabel is faster than Challenger."

"No, she isn't," said Kim. "Challenger was fast when coming out of the box for Judith."

"Roping doesn't involve turning corners around a barrel. Anyway, I got second place at the state fair. You got twelfth."

"Only because I knocked over a barrel. If they hadn't added five seconds to my score, Lindy would have been faster."

"You're not riding Lindy. I want you to prove Challenger is faster."

"You're on." Kim stuck her head around the corner of Fargo's stall. "Phil, could you get your stopwatch to time us? We want to see whether Challenger or Isabel is faster around the barrels."

"Sure." I got the watch off the cabinet shelf. "Hey, Ian and Eddy, let's watch your mommy and Aunt Kim race their horses."

They dropped their brushes and joined their mother by the stable's door.

After retrieving their brushes from the straw, I whispered to Kim, "I heard your conversation about being her stepmother."

"I figured you did. She's working through our changed relationship. Give her time. Did you hear she's pregnant?"

"I did, and I'm thinking we should start our family right away."

Her eyes opened wide. "Are you serious?"

"Uh-huh. After our discussion last night, I've been thinking. I don't want to be too old to not see my children graduate or get married."

Kim's smile filled her face. "I love you, Phil."

"I know you do."

Beth exited the stables with Isabel, and I said to Kim, "Go beat the socks off of her."

Chapter 35

Friday, January 8th, morning

The wind had died down, but the temperature had dropped to zero, and a beautiful layer of hoarfrost covered the trees and ground. A few patches of blue sky peeked through the low-hanging clouds.

Kim and I did the chores and returned to the house for breakfast.

I punched in the bank's number on my cell. "This is Phil York. Could I speak with Craig Jones?"

He came on the line. "Hey, Phil, what can I do for you?"

"If I come to the bank, is it possible to get a loan for $10,000?"

"Let me check your credit." He clicked a few keys on a computer. "Hmmm. Your score is excellent, but you froze your credit. I'm not able to do anything until you unfreeze it."

"I didn't lock it and haven't defaulted on my mortgage payments. What caused it?"

"I don't know. With your good credit, normally, you should be able to get a loan."

"Could you give me a loan, anyway?"

"No, I can't approve one until you unlock your credit," said Craig. "If someone else has frozen it, they'll have to remove the lock."

"I need the money fairly soon. Could you look into it?"

"I'll do that. It may take a few days before I get back to you."

"Okay. Call me when you find out what's going on. You've got my number." I disconnected.

"I heard," said Kim. "What are we going to do?"

"We can only wait. I know Craig will get it straightened out. He's good and always helpful. In the meantime, we keep working with the horses."

Back at the stables, she saddled Challenger, and I timed her around the barrels. After knocking over two of them, she wrinkled her nose. "What am I doing wrong? Should I switch to Lindy?"

"You're going too fast."

"I'm supposed to go fast to beat the clock."

"Sometimes it's necessary to slow down a bit. Make certain Challenger is used to your style of changing leads by cantering him around the cloverleaf a dozen times. It'll teach him what to expect. Follow up with another dozen at a faster pace. He's longer-legged than Lindy, so on the turns, don't lengthen his stride. Keep it short. After you circle the last barrel, pour it on."

"I thought that's what I was doing."

"No," I said. "When you're going around each barrel, Challenger's stride is long, making it difficult to navigate the turn. Too much speed isn't always the best. Sometimes slowing down a bit to maneuver a turn will give you a shorter time."

"I'll try it. Beth brags about winning the silver cup. I want to beat her."

"You can. Just keep practicing, and you'll do better."

***

Candy arrived in the afternoon to train for breakaway roping and to team rope with me.

With her arms resting on the board fence, Kim said, "Candy, you and Phil make a great team." She checked the stopwatch. "You caught the last calf in fourteen and a half seconds."

"That's not fast enough," I said.

"You did good," said Kim. "It was slow, but you're relearning."

"I didn't want to risk missing it and waited to make sure the calf hopped a second time."

Candy coiled her rope. "I sort of figured that was why you were slower. You should try to remember how you did it with Judith."

I froze and slowly turned away. "I remember too well. Remembering is my problem."

"Huh? What do you mean that remembering is your problem?"

"Phil remembers his skills," said Kim, "but they're rusty. Having missed the rodeo means he has to relearn and put them into practice."

Thank you, Kim, for saving me from my big mouth.

"I watched you two years ago," said Candy. "You've got the skill and should work on regaining the competitive edge."

A car turned into the lane. "Here comes Harold," said Candy.

I coiled my rope. "I'll be back after showing him how to do the chores."

Together, he and I went through the chore routine. I showed him the location of the supplies in the feed room. "Keep Serenity in the stall with her filly. Don't let her out. Marston knows this, but I want to make sure you know it."

"Okay, I will."

"My steers are in the south pasture and range-fed. Because it's winter, all you need to do is fill their bunk with hay."

"What about the horses? Should I let any of them into the stables?"

"No. Feed them in the corral, but keep the north pasture gate open and let them run."

"Okay. That's straightforward."

"Harold, I wanted to ask, will you get the job at Abbott Tech?"

"Nah. My website training in the army was with HTML and CSS. Abbott needed someone with Java experience. They told me, 'Thanks, but no thanks.' I'm still looking."

"I'm sorry to hear that. Are you just helping your mom, or is she paying you?"

"I don't like farm work, and she's paying to ensure I help. She's paying my sisters, too."

"Your mom is a natural at working on a farm."

"Mom is super grateful you got her the job as JoAnn's farm manager. She's never been this excited."

"Glad to help. The two problems dovetailed. I only brought them together."

"You couldn't have done anything better for her."

"Thanks."

Now, I had to do well in the rodeo or secure a loan to pay off Gene.

Chapter 36

Monday, January 11th, morning

Kim and Beth were in the stables, preparing the horses for the day, when my cell phone rang. The caller ID read Hancock Village. I stepped outside to answer. "Hello."

"Hi," said the voice. "This is Woody Hancock. Am I talking to Phil York?"

"This is Phil speaking."

"I meant to call earlier, but didn't have your number. I asked Sherry Sue to get it from JoAnn Allen."

"What do you need, Mr. Hancock?"

"You know Gene Wilcox is organizing my rodeo, but he isn't being cooperative. Sherry Sue said I should ask for your help. I want my rodeo to be a top event."

"Gene usually does a good job. What's the problem?"

"I don't know for sure. He got angry and uttered a string of expletives. Is Gene a Christian?"

"I can't say about his relationship with the Lord, but he doesn't attend church."

"Gene keeps swearing that I should have given him more time. I can't. It has to be the last half of February, not in March, because I've already placed ads."

"What can I do to help?"

"Sherry Sue said you're an honest Christian, and that's why I'm calling. I need someone to act as a point man."

"Point man, for what? Gene is usually dependable. What's he not doing?"

"He's doing a fantastic job at organizing the physical side of the rodeo. He sent a diagram of the arena, holding pens, chutes, gates, timers, and the announcer's booth. That's great, and he says he'll get the items and workers to set it up. What he's not doing is contacting folks to compete."

"Mr. Hancock, that's what Gene is supposed to do. Your rodeo is an off-season startup with no recognition. You're the sponsor, and it's your responsibility to advertise."

"Oh, great. That means he won't help find competitors. I called you because I don't want things to slide."

"I'll offer a few suggestions. Have you been promoting it?"

"Yes, radio, newspapers, and TV."

"I assume it's local advertising. Because it's a charity rodeo, you should also advertise to reach a different audience."

"What do you mean, different audience?"

"I'm guessing you have people with social media accounts. Have them put up pages to advertise your event and tell their friends. If the local radio and TV stations are advertising, see if they'll broadcast the rodeo live. That will create a lot of excitement. Also, contact every public school, Christian school, and homeschool students in the area and offer free rodeo tickets to those with the best essays or drawings of a rodeo. If the children become excited, they'll beg their parents to take them. Be sure to distribute posters at retail stores in your area."

"Okay, I like the TV and social media ideas. But contacting schools and putting up posters will only bring in an audience. What about competitors? That's where I need help."

"Help to do what?" I asked.

"Contact folks who've competed in past rodeos."

"That will be a ton of work, and I don't have the time. Can't your people there do it?"

"The staff at *The Meadows* knows nothing about rodeos. Nor do my farm workers. I need someone who understands those things."

"I've never advertised."

"But you know what's needed to bring in competitors. Surely you see the need?"

"I see the need because *The Meadows* is a good Christian ministry. But you're asking me to drop everything and do something I've never done."

"Sherry Sue said you were good at organizing and were the go-to person at church. The pastor depended on you."

"But Mr. Hancock—"

"Please call me Woody."

"Okay, Woody. That much work would swamp a person. It'll take several people."

"How many would it take?"

I thought for a moment. "I don't know for sure. Three or four might do it, but they'd be busy."

"What would they be doing?"

"They'd contact other rodeos and ask for their list of participants. Then phone, text, and email everyone on the list. There will be over a thousand names. It's a ton of work."

"I'll permit you to get three or four helpers," said Woody. "I'm asking you to be the point man. I'll pay you and anyone else who helps, plus all the costs incurred. This is important."

"I've got a ranch to run and have to practice my roping. Isn't there someone else?"

"Maybe, but there isn't time to look for someone. Sherry Sue said you could reach out to people. From what I've heard, you're the best person."

"I'm not the person." *Give him more suggestions.* "As the sponsor, contact the United Rodeo Association. Find out what they need for your event to gain accreditation. If they give an endorsement, it'll attract competitors. Your first-prize purses are five thousand dollars. It's par for most rodeos, but yours is a startup. Consider increasing the purses to garner more interest."

"Okaaayyy, I'll consider it. Do you have other recommendations?"

"A rodeo audience should be family-oriented. Folks will bring their children, youngsters of all ages. You should provide kid-oriented side activities like a petting area and a playground, not just the main events in the arena. Find young ladies who'll act as rodeo queens to talk to folks and give out information about the contestants and the history of a rodeo. For the high schoolers, set up a calf scramble."

"What's a calf scramble?"

"Turn young calves loose in the arena with high schoolers. They must catch a calf, halter it, and bring it to the center to win a prize. It's a lot of fun for the youngsters, and the crowd enjoys rooting for their kids."

"This is all great. I wish I'd known it earlier, and it's why I need help."

"Who is helping currently?"

"Sherry Sue, Gene, and my crew of workers here in Atlantic. But I need help to bring in competitors."

Two verses from this morning's devotions popped into my head. *Do nothing from selfish ambition or conceit, but in humility count others more significant than yourselves. Let each of you look not only to his own interests, but also to the interests of others.* Was God telling me to do this?

Woody asked again, "Please, Phil. I really need your help."

Was God nudging me to set aside my plans? *Lord, I need wisdom.* "Woody, my ranch hand is off for the holidays, so I'm pretty busy. And I must practice roping. There's not enough time to do what you're asking."

"If you get three or four others, it should free you up and be doable."

"I don't know. You'd be dumping a load of responsibility on me."

"You said it would take people. Recruit up to four, and I'll pay them what they're worth. I've gotten myself into a bind and need your support."

Lord, I hope this isn't a mistake. "Because your rodeo is for a good cause ..." I sighed. "I'll help by asking around for competitors. But don't ask me to do anything else."

"Fantastic. If you have questions, call me or shoot me an email."

"It looks like I've buried myself under a mountain of work. Could you answer a couple of personal questions?"

"Sure, shoot. What are they?"

"Gene said you asked for me to be at the rodeo, and he was to make sure of it. Why is that?"

"No, I didn't. Your name was one amongst others on Sherry Sue's list. I told Gene to find out if the people on the list would come. I didn't specifically ask for you or anyone."

Then Gene lied. "It's what Gene told me."

"Maybe you misunderstood. I didn't ask for anyone explicitly."

"Okay, thanks. That clears that up. Next, Sherry Sue was pregnant, gave birth at *The Meadows*, and started working for you afterward, correct?"

"That's right. She works for my wife now. Why?"

"There's a rumor floating around that I fathered her child. It's not true. Have you heard anything about it?"

"Whoa. I've heard nothing and can see why the rumor needs to be squashed." He was quiet for a moment. "Let me ask my wife. She might know something."

He muted his phone. After several minutes, he unmuted. "Phil, the rumor is categorically false. When my wife interviewed Sherry Sue, she said Brandon McCloud is the father of her child, and he's refused to accept responsibility. Her father hates Brandon because he got her pregnant, and he pressured her to get an abortion. She refused and came to *The Meadows* to give birth. You can bury the rumor."

Gene lied again. "It's great to hear. Thank you."

"I can understand how a rumor like that would ruin a man's reputation. Concerning the rodeo, you said you'd help find competitors. Is that right?"

"Grudgingly. Send me copies of the advertisements you've already put out and where you're running them. I'll call around to the rodeo associations. Once people learn that it's a charity event, they may be more interested."

"Thanks, Phil. It's appreciated." He disconnected.

Gene was a big, fat liar. How often had he not told me the truth?

Chapter 37

I disconnected from Woody's call and stuck the phone in my pocket. Had I bitten off more than I could chew to find cowboys who'd compete in a startup rodeo? It would be a ton of work.

In the stables, Beth asked, "What was the call about?"

"It was Woody Hancock. He asked me to round up folks to compete in his rodeo. He'd been thinking Gene would do it, but it isn't Gene's responsibility."

"It's not yours either. Why should the responsibility fall on you?"

I removed Fargo's saddle from the wall rack. "Because I said I would."

"It's more than you can do." She placed her hands on my saddle. "Contacting people shouldn't be your responsibility."

I stepped around her and went into Fargo's stall. "I told Mr. Hancock I'd do it."

She spoke to my back. "Call him and say you've changed your mind."

Fargo snorted as I cinched his saddle. "No. I'll follow through."

"Kim, will you talk sense into Dad? He's your husband, and he's acting crazy."

Kim poked her head around the corner. "Honey, think. It would be an awful lot of work."

I set my jaw. "I know it will, but I agreed to help. Will you ladies stop pushing?"

"What about studying for Bill Peterson's Sunday school class? You promised to help Pastor James replace the church water heaters. What about Mr. and Mrs. Mack's toilet? It'll be way too much if you add to what Mr. Hancock is asking."

"Are you ladies going to race around the barrels or criticize me?"

"Kim's right, Dad," said Beth. "You'd have your hands full."

My voice rose. "I'm not a worn-out old man, not yet anyway. His rodeo will be a flop if I don't help, and the way he talked, there was no one else." I pointed at Challenger. "Kim, are you going to ride him? If not, take off the saddle."

"Call him back," said Kim. "If you don't win in the rodeo, Gene will come after Challenger."

"How would he take Challenger?" asked Beth.

"When Phil was returning the trailer to Gene, he stopped to talk to Pastor James. A boy unhooked the trailer on a dare, and it rolled down the hill and onto the rocks. Gene is demanding reimbursement."

Beth faced me. "Dad, he can't take Challenger. He was Mom's horse. Tell Mr. Hancock you're not able to help."

I turned my back. "I told him I would, and that's what I'm going to do."

Kim jockeyed around to stand in front of me. "No. You have more important things to do."

"It's settled," I yelled, "and I'll follow through!"

Kim grabbed my arm. "What's wrong with you?"

Beth asked, "Why are you yelling?"

"I'm angry."

"Then you need to cool off." Kim led me outside.

The wind whistled around the corner as she marched me into the machine shed and backed me up against the tractor. "You keep insisting you won't back away from helping Mr. Hancock. Why?"

My voice went up. "Because I said I would."

"Don't raise your voice at me. You still haven't told me why."

"Because I promised him, that's why."

"What do you mean, you *promised* him? You didn't tell me that."

"When I say I'll do something, I've given my word. It's a promise. What kind of person would I be if I didn't?"

"Okay, now I understand, but I believe you made a terrible promise."

"You ladies kept insisting I should break it, and I got angry."

She pinched her lips. "I was angry, too."

I took a couple of breaths. "A lot is going on. Sorry."

"I forgive you and am sorry for being pushy."

"We have a problem. We lost our tempers and argued."

"It wasn't good for us to argue in front of Beth."

"I'm not talking about Beth," I said. "I'm talking about us arguing with each other. We should set ground rules for when we disagree."

"What did you and Judith do?"

"We never raised our voices. We lowered them and discussed it for a half hour. If we hadn't resolved it, we set it aside and slept on it until morning."

"I like those rules," said Kim. "I don't remember you and Judith ever arguing."

"We had our disagreements, but kept them private. You and I shouldn't let ours get out of control. Thanks for pulling me aside."

"If either of us says count to ten, it's a sign for us to back off."

"Good idea." I stepped away from the tractor. "From talking to Mr. Hancock, I think Gene is a liar." I told her what Woody had said.

"You should be careful. I don't know him very well."

"I will."

"Phil, getting back to Mr. Hancock, do you see the problem that helping him will cause?"

"Yes, but I agreed and will follow through."

"You won't have enough time to do much of anything else."

"Mr. Hancock said I could find helpers, and he'd pay them."

"Pay them? Who do you have in mind?"

I grinned. "I'm told my wife is a capable woman. If she helped, maybe we could apply her earnings to Gene's debt."

"Are you sure your wife will agree to this plan?"

I winked. "I'm sure she will."

"Who else were you thinking?"

"Harold. He could build a website, and it would give him extra income."

"True. He'd love the project, but his mom would expect him to work for her."

Beth screamed, and Kim and I spun to face the stables.

"Grandpa! Grandpa!" Ian ran up to us. "Mommy got hurt."

I snatched Ian into my arms as Kim and I sprinted toward the stables.

Chapter 38

Kim and I raced to the stables as I carried Ian bouncing in my arms.

Beth lay on the aisle floor, moaning.

Kim knelt beside her. "Where do you hurt?"

"My leg. I think it's broken. I was tightening Isabel's cinch, and she kicked."

"Ian," I said, "you and Eddy stand over there while we check your mommy's leg."

They did as I asked.

I knelt beside Beth and put my hand on her right leg. Slowly, I straightened it.

She winced.

"Kim, hand me the shears hanging on the wall."

She retrieved them.

"What are you going to do?" asked Beth.

"Cut your pants to look at the leg." I eased the shears under the cloth and snipped up past her knee. Gently, I felt the bone.

Beth flinched and said, "What does it look like?"

"The bone is still aligned. If it's broken, it's a fracture, and not a clean break. A bruise is forming, and you'll need to see a doctor to have it X-rayed. Kim, there's a broken broom handle about three feet long in the feed room. Please get it."

While she fetched it, I cut the twine from two hay bales.

Within a few minutes, Kim and I created a makeshift splint for Beth's leg. We helped her hobble to the van and got her seated in the cargo area.

Kim said, "I'll stay with the boys and unsaddle the horses while you drive to the hospital. Text me whatever the doctor says."

"Thanks, I will."

On the way to the hospital, Beth said from the back of the van, "Dad, you were pretty angry with Kim and me."

I said over my shoulder, "I know, Princess, I was. Kim and I got it straightened out. I'm sorry for my outburst."

"Then you'll call Mr. Hancock back?"

"I gave him my word, which makes it a promise. I'll keep roping as much as I can."

"You need to win at the rodeo."

"I'm aware of it."

She was quiet for a while. "Dad, do you honestly love Kim?"

I jerked at the unexpected question, but kept the van on the correct side of the road.

While I was figuring out what to say, Beth asked again, "Dad, did you hear me? Do you love Kim?"

"Yes, I heard you, and yes, I love her."

"You better, or I'll wring your neck. I mean it. You better treat her like you did Mom."

"I will. Are you okay with us being married?"

"You eloped, and I don't have a choice."

"It wasn't your choice to make, just like when I married your mom. Kim and I are adults, not children."

"Are you going to have children?"

"It's none of your business, Princess."

"Kim is my best friend, and I want to know if Tom and I will have siblings. Answer the question."

How do I answer and not upset her?

"Dad, I'll find out anyway. Kim will tell me if you don't."

I took a breath. "Yes, we plan to have children."

"I thought so. How many?"

"I don't know, maybe two dozen."

"Yikes. You've got to be kidding."

"It bothers you for us to have children, doesn't it?"

"You know it does. I'll have siblings two and a half decades younger than me, and Ian and Eddy will have baby uncles and aunts. Double yuck."

Would Judith be upset as much as Beth?

Help me, Lord. I forced the unwelcome thought aside. Why did memories of Judith always intrude? Kim was right. The past had wounded my heart and wouldn't leave me alone. Would I ever heal?

We arrived at the hospital, and Beth had a series of X-rays taken. We waited in a cubicle for over an hour for the doctor to arrive.

He entered and said, "I'm Dr. Embry." He stuck Beth's X-rays into a wall viewer and pointed to a spot. "You have a hairline fracture. It's not a clean break, but it will take just as long to heal."

"How long will it be?" asked Beth.

"Six to eight weeks. Do you have children?"

"Yes, two boys."

"Then I'm putting you in a full cast instead of a walking cast. With children, you won't be able to stay off the leg. Use crutches for the first two weeks, followed by limited activity. Sponge baths only. No showers and no driving."

I texted Kim the details.

The nurses fitted Beth with a cast, and she and I headed back to the ranch.

"This will knock you out of the rodeo," I said.

"I know. It's a bummer. I wanted to prove Isabel could beat Kim, even on Challenger." She began toying with her necklace.

I slowed at a stop sign. "Beth, you're twisting your necklace. What are you plotting?"

"I don't know. It's just an idea."

"Let's hear it. Does it involve me or Kim?"

"Sort of. Could the boys and I stay at the ranch? Kim will need pointers when she races Challenger."

"You're welcome to stay, and I don't have a problem with it. But you need to ask your husband and Kim. He's the man of your home, and she's the woman of mine."

"You're the man of the house. You could tell her I'd be staying."

"Yes, I am, and yes, I could, but no, I won't. I'm giving Kim equal say."

"You always let Mom have a say. I should have figured you'd do the same with Kim. It's weird, but I'll ask her."

"Not weird, just different. What about David?"

"He's a fan of Micky D's and can come to the ranch on weekends."

"Is the ranch a hotel for everyone in the family?"

"Why not? You rattle around in it."

"No, I don't. Kim lives with me."

"With me staying at the house," said Beth, "the boys will be part of the family and play with Jinx and Legos."

"Let's discuss this with Kim when we get back to the ranch."

"Okay." She looked out the side window and continued to finger her necklace.

As I turned into the driveway, Kim and the boys came from the stables, and Jinx pranced beside them.

I pulled to a stop by the back door.

The clouds had thinned, and occasionally the sun shone long enough to temper the freezing air. The puddles from the melted snow had refrozen, and my boot tracks from the other day looked fresh.

I helped Beth out of the car and supported her until she got balanced on the crutches.

Eddy said with a smile, "Ian hit me, Mommy."

"What? Ian, did you hit your brother?"

"Relax," said Kim. "We were cleaning up a horse mess, and the handle of Ian's pitchfork banged Eddy's leg. He's fine." She turned to the boys. "Your mother is here. Let's go inside and get warmed up."

Inside, the boys tossed their coats and mittens on the floor and made a beeline for the DVD cabinet to watch a cartoon video.

Kim and I helped Beth get seated in the den with her leg resting on the coffee table. She and I settled on the couch.

Kim said, "Beth, I called David about your accident and told him what the doctor said. He's glad you're in good hands. He loves you and knows you're disappointed about the rodeo."

"Did he say anything else?"

"He'll call during his break to learn what's needed to get the house ready for when you come home. I was wondering, since you can't go to the rodeo, would you let Shelly ride Isabel in the competition?"

"She'd be able to prove Isabel is faster than Challenger, wouldn't she?"

"I was thinking more of Pigeon. Candy could train him to only rope and not double up with barrel racing."

Beth wobbled her head. "Sure. It's okay."

"It's nice of you," I said. "I'll let Candy know."

"Kim, I have a question for you," said Beth. "Dad and I were talking on the way home. I asked if the boys and I could stay here while my leg healed. He said that I should ask you."

"What would David say about you being gone?"

"I don't believe he'll mind. He could come on weekends if it's alright with you."

"Honey, did you say she could stay with us?" asked Kim.

"I don't have a problem with it," I said, "but she'd need your approval, provided David is okay with it."

"Beth, what would you and the boys do?"

"I could spot problems when you barrel race. I'll make sure the boys stay out of the way."

"It means you'll have lots of free …" Kim developed an evil smile. "Time, won't she?"

I could read her mind. "Uh-huh. She would."

"What's going on?" asked Beth.

Kim said, "We'll let you stay, but you have to work for us."

"Work? I can't do much because of my leg. What would I be doing?"

Chapter 39

In our den, Beth asked, "Come on, Kim. If I stayed here while my leg heals, what type of *work* would I be doing?"

"You'd be helping your dad and me."

Beth twirled her finger. "I'm waiting. What evil activity would I be involved in? Rob a bank? Shoot someone?"

I grinned. "Now that you mention it …" I said with a singsong voice.

"Aw, come on. That's enough of your teasing. What am I supposed to do?"

"Collect names for the rodeo," said Kim. "Mr. Hancock would pay you."

"Pay me?" Beth turned to me. "Dad, honestly, or is this a joke?"

"It's no joke. He'll pay us to call rodeo associations and collect names. Then we're to call, text, and email them to sign up for the rodeo."

"How much would he pay me?"

"Are you interested?" asked Kim.

"It depends. How much would he pay me? Just a pittance?"

"No," said Kim. "How does the top rate for secretaries sound?"

I hadn't cleared the amount with Mr. Hancock, but he wouldn't object. "If the rodeo isn't well attended, it won't matter if you help Kim in barrel racing. That's why we need your help."

"How many hours would I work?"

I shrugged. "I don't know. Maybe eighteen or twenty every day."

"Yikes. You're joking again."

I smiled. "I am."

"You're always sarcastic, Dad."

"There'll be lots of calling and emailing," said Kim. "We'll work together as much as possible in between taking care of other stuff."

"Would it only be the three of us?"

"Mostly," I said. "I want Harold Murray to build a website."

"If you promise that all of us will work together, I'll help."

"I promise." I fished my cell phone out of my pocket. "Let me call Candy to see if Harold is available." I punched in her number. "Hey, Candy, how's everything at the Stephens' farm?"

"The general operations have smoothed out, and the livestock look better. JoAnn had me sell the stored wheat, so she'd have money for improvements. What did you need?"

"How much is Harold helping you?"

"Not as much as I want. He keeps asking for time off to find another job. He wants to buy a computer and hone his web skills."

"I've got a part-time job for him if you'll give him time off."

Candy snickered. "Doing what? He'd never agree to more farm work."

"Nothing like that. I want him to build a website for Mr. Hancock's rodeo, secure it, administrate it, and monitor the web traffic. He'll pay him."

"Are you serious?"

"Mr. Hancock asked me to invite folks to take part in his rodeo. A website, if handled well, could draw lots of people. If Harold does a good job, he could put it on his resume. Mr. Hancock might give a recommendation."

"Wow. He'd be interested. When would you need him?"

"Yesterday, or as soon as you give him time off."

"Hold on. He just came into the feed room. Let me ask."

She muted the phone for a minute. She unmuted. "He's not interested—he's over-the-top excited. He'll be there in twenty minutes. Phil, he has to help me, too."

"After I've talked with him, I'll call back, and we'll work out a schedule for him to work between us."

***

I waited at the stables for Harold while Kim helped Beth rearrange her old bedroom for her and the boys.

Harold pulled his car to a stop and raced up to me. "Phil, if I'm to build a website, what type of computer do you have?"

"My laptop is mainly for email and accounting and is five years old. The PC in the stables is for keeping horse records and is about the same age. Will either of those work or will you need a better one?"

"I'll need a better one." He detailed the specs he needed. "And two software applications, *Web Builders Pro* and *Amazing Graphics Plus*."

"Okay. Go to *All Pro Computers* in town and use my account to buy what you need. If they have questions, have them call me. Bring everything back here, set it up in my study, and we'll discuss the specifics for the website."

He danced a jig. "Yip, yip, yippee."

Harold hurriedly drove out to the road, and Gene Wilcox drove in.

Why did he come to the ranch? He could have called.

He got out of his car and dipped his head toward my temporary arena. "I see you're working to hone your skills. I heard Beth and Kim and the Murray family are here, too."

The sun peeked through the clouds and lit up the corral.

"How's the planning for Mr. Hancock's rodeo coming along?" I asked.

"I've accounted for all the pieces and contacted several folks. Most are available to help. I asked Mr. Hancock to extend the date into March, but he's against it. The February date doesn't give much time."

It was Gene who suggested February. "What about the livestock? Are you able to round up enough animals?"

"Pretty much all of them. Everything is coming together. Are Beth and Kim ready?"

"Beth is withdrawing because she fractured her leg."

He winced. "I'm sorry to hear that. What about the Murray and Barton girls?"

"Everyone is working hard to be ready for the rodeo."

He shuffled his feet on the driveway's crushed rock. "I came to tell you there's been a change of plans."

Uh oh. "What's my bad luck?"

"Mr. Edwards can't haul your horses. You'll have to find your own transportation like everyone else."

"What's going on, Gene? JoAnn clearly said he could transport everything, including my horses, and you agreed it was okay."

He wobbled his head. "I know. This is outside of my control. I called Mr. Edwards, and he confirmed that with all my livestock and equipment going to the rodeo, he won't have enough trailers to haul yours. That's why I came in person to tell you that you'll need to find your own. I can't do anything about it."

I spread my hands. "What are we going to do? There are seven horses, plus all the tack and feed. Where will we find trailers?"

"It's a problem, I know. If you know someone, you better call and see if they'll loan theirs."

"Look, Gene. This is putting me in a tough spot. My ladies and the others were expecting Mr. Edwards to provide transportation."

"I'm truly sorry, Phil. I understand your situation, but I can't do anything about it."

Was he lying or not? If it weren't for my debt, I wouldn't go, but all the ladies were depending on me. I needed a lot of help and a ton of wisdom.

***

Monday, January 11th, evening

While Kim was putting the supper dishes back in the cupboard and Beth was reading a story to her boys, I retired to my study to work on finances. My cell chimed. "Hello."

"Hey, Phil, this is Marston. I just got back from Arizona and wanted to call."

"How was your trip? Did you have a great time with your grandparents?"

"Yeah, we did. Everyone was good, and we had a fabulous time together. Dad stuffed us in the car this morning amongst the luggage and drove straight through from Tempe. It was a long ride, but he needed to clear up a business issue at work tomorrow."

"Tell him I said hi. I'm glad you're back. Things have been happening fast around here, and I need you to start on several projects in the morning."

"Ah, not quite. That's why I'm calling. I know it'll put you in a bind, but I'm not coming back to work."

Oh boy. Another problem. "Why? Do you need more time off?"

"I'm going to college next week. Dad's been haranguing me to get a degree, but I didn't want to leave you in the lurch. While we were in Arizona, Dad coerced Grandpa McGwin to pay for my first year of college, provided I started right away. If I maintain a 3.5 GPA or better, he'll pay for the second year, and so on. This isn't fair to you, but I can't pass up a chance for a full-ride scholarship."

"I was really depending on you, Marston."

"I'm sorry, Phil, but if Grandpa pays for my college degree, I won't have a huge debt. What would you do in my situation?"

"I agree. You shouldn't let the chance slip away, and I don't blame you. But it'll be tough to find someone else to help around here. While you were gone, I got married."

"Wow, that was sudden. Who did you marry?"

"Kim Ryan. I believe you know her."

"Yeah, I know pretty Kim."

"She is lovely. I'm happy you got a college scholarship. What's your major?"

"The usual classes for the first year. But I'm aiming to get a mechanical engineering degree."

"You always kept my machinery in top shape. You'll be good at it."

"Thanks, Phil. I've got to cut this call short because Dad needs my help. Sorry to leave you hanging like this."

"I understand."

He clicked off.

Kim stuck her head into the den. "Who were you talking to?"

"Marston. He just got back from Arizona."

"That's great. What job do you want him to work on in the morning?"

"He quit and won't be back. His grandfather gave him a full-ride scholarship if he started college right away."

"Wow. That's great for him, but what are we going to do?"

"Limp along like the past few weeks. You're here, and Beth can help in the house, so it won't be a total loss."

At least, I hoped not.

Chapter 40

Wednesday, January 13th, noon

Beth, Kim, and I kept busy contacting rodeo associations, asking for a copy of their last year's contestants. We started at the top of our combined list and began calling.

Harold hammered out a great website, including a link to download entry forms. He searched for rodeo websites and asked them to put in a link for Mr. Hancock's rodeo and a blurb to advertise.

With everyone's hard work, the rodeo planning moved forward.

After calling around for horse trailers, I came up empty. The folks who had them couldn't loan them for a variety of reasons.

"What are we going to do?" asked Kim.

Beth stopped writing an email to listen.

"I don't know," I said. "Everyone locally can't or won't loan theirs. I located two trailers in Lubbock, Texas. But they won't be enough and would mean a long round trip, twice."

"We could take Challenger and Fargo in your trailer," said Kim. "I could ride in the barrel race, and you could enter the calf cutting event. Wouldn't that work?"

I shook my head. "What about Candy and her girls or the Barton girls? We shouldn't go if they can't."

"Honey, call Mr. Hancock and tell him about our trailer problem. Maybe he can help."

"It's senseless to call just for a trailer."

"Then share how much we've accomplished with the rodeo. We've got more than a dozen who have signed up, and many others are interested."

"Do we actually have that many? It's only been a few days."

"We do," said Beth. "Harold tracks the downloaded entry forms, and who has returned them with their entry fee?"

Kim picked up a sheet of paper. "We have over twelve hundred names and have contacted a tenth of them. If this keeps up, the rodeo will be a success."

Harold came from the den. "Look at this." He handed me a printout. "Since the URA has given provisional accreditation for the rodeo, Jeff Roth from Utah has sent in his entry form."

I browsed the printout. "I met him two years ago. He's a bull rider and has been the top winner for three straight years." I tapped the sheet. "Put his name on the website. His celebrity status will attract attention."

Harold returned to my study.

"See, Dad," said Beth, pointing toward Harold. "That's more good news to tell Mr. Hancock, and why you should ask for transportation for the horses."

"But Gene said—"

"We shouldn't trust Gene," said Kim. "He lied before and could be lying now."

"He wants me to compete to pay him what I owe. If he's lying, he'd be stacking the deck against me just to get Challenger, and it makes no sense."

"Calling Mr. Hancock shouldn't hurt, will it? He'll only confirm it."

"I suppose so, and I don't know what else to do." I fished out my phone and punched in Woody's number.

It rang once, and he answered. "Phil, I was about to call you. What's the progress in getting the word out?"

I gave him a brief rundown of the responses we'd received. "That's the status so far. I'm sure more people will sign up because the URA gave their approval for accreditation, and we've put their logo on the website."

"Fantastic. I talked to the URA the other day and mentioned your and Gene's names. They called Gene and said they'd talked to the Professional Rodeo Cowboys Association, the PRCA, about my rodeo. Could you call the PRCA and let them know that Jeff Roth is coming? If they endorse the rodeo, too, it might attract others."

"I'll do that. If the PRCA gives its approval, it'll let cowboys earn competition points for the year. It'll be a huge plus."

"Sounds good. How's your roping coming? I'm looking forward to seeing you compete."

"Ah, that's another problem. Gene said there aren't enough trailers to haul my horses, and I'm supposed to find my own transportation."

"Huh? That's not true. Edwards Trucking Company has plenty of trailers."

"Gene said they don't. They only have enough trailers to haul his stuff."

"That's not true. Spence has the equipment to transport whatever you need."

Then Gene is a bald-faced liar. "Can you help?"

"Not directly, because I don't have horse trailers. Ask JoAnn. She's working on the transportation side of things. Maybe she told Gene something, and he didn't understand correctly."

"It's possible." *But doubtful.* "I'll check with her."

What was wrong with Gene?

Chapter 41

I disconnected my call to Mr. Hancock and wanted to thump Gene. He'd demolished any trust I'd given him.

Kim asked, "What did Mr. Hancock say?"

"He's excited about our work."

"What about trailers and a truck?"

I shared what Mr. Hancock said. "Gene told an outright lie."

"Are you absolutely sure?" asked Beth.

"Gene said there weren't enough trailers, and Mr. Hancock said there are. Gene had to have lied."

"Then call JoAnn," said Kim, "and ask her."

"Okay." I searched through my contacts and punched in her number.

She answered, and I asked, "JoAnn, do you have the Edwards Trucking Company's phone number? You promised to give it to me."

"Oops, my bad. Do you have a pen?" She gave me two work numbers for Mr. Edwards, a private number, and a mailing address. "Call him. He's a great guy and will make sure you're taken care of." She disconnected.

I shared with the ladies what JoAnn had said before I called the number.

A woman answered. "Edwards Trucking Company, how may I help?"

"I'm Phil York. Could I talk to Spence Edwards?"

"What's it about, sir? Is he expecting your call?"

"It's about the charity rodeo in Atlantic. Mr. Edwards was supposed to come to my ranch and transport my horses."

"One moment, sir." She placed me on hold to a background song of *Six Days on the Road* by Dave Dudley.

Kim laughed at me. "Why are you bobbing your head?"

I grinned. "I'm on hold and listening to an old-time trucking song. It has a good beat and reminds me of my brother. Rest his soul."

"I always remember Uncle Charlie after he got back from a road trip," said Beth. "He gave us jelly beans and would mess around with us until he had to drive again."

The woman came back on line. "Mr. York, I'm transferring your call."

The line clicked two times, and a deep voice said, "This is Spence Edwards. Mr. York, how may I help you?"

"Gene Wilcox promised me transportation to Woody Hancock's rodeo, but he said you didn't have enough trailers for my horses."

"Hmmm," his voice rumbled. "I talked with Mr. Wilcox the other day. He said you had your own means of transportation and wouldn't need my services."

Would Gene's lies ever end? "Well, I need transportation for my horses. I've looked around and can't find any available trailers."

"How many horses do you have?"

"Three of my own and four other horses boarding at my ranch."

"I've got another trailer, so don't worry. I'll call Mr. Wilcox and let him know about the change."

"Mr. Edwards, if it's okay with you, don't go through him. Could we work this out between us?"

"Maybe we could. What's your location?"

I gave him my address and directions to the ranch. "I'll take care of things on this end. There's no reason to contact Gene."

Spence and I worked out the details, and he hung up.

"I heard you say to bypass Gene," said Kim.

"You know why, because he's been lying to us."

"Didn't Aunt JoAnn and Gene say there'd be transportation for our horses?" asked Beth.

"They did. I'm not working with Gene anymore. Mr. Edwards has agreed to haul everything. From now on, I'm dealing directly with him and Mr. Hancock."

"Are you letting Gene know?" asked Kim.

"No, I can't trust him."

My phone chimed, and I checked the caller ID—First National Bank. "Hello."

"Phil, this is Craig Jones. I'm getting back to you about your credit freeze."

"What did you find out? I hope it is good news."

"I've been calling around to find out what's causing your credit lock. It's like someone built a wall around your finances. Nobody knows anything."

Or no one is telling. "Did you contact the credit companies?"

"Yes. All three said the same thing. You owe $5000 to *Argus Security Solutions* and are nine months delinquent."

"I've never done business with them, nor have I heard of the company."

"Well, your credit will stay frozen until we clear this up. I tried to contact *Argus*. No one answered the phone or responded to emails. It's likely a shell company. I'm stymied."

"You know my credit is good. Couldn't you loan the money until we get this sorted out?"

"I'd like to, but I can't. The bank president could get into hot water with the Federal Reserve Board."

"I could pay it back before the end of the year. You know I'm good for it."

"I know you are. But I can't give you a loan. I'll keep checking, and if I learn anything, I'll let you know as soon as I hear something." He hung up.

Blast it. Would my problems never end? Something smelled rotten in Denmark.

Chapter 42

Monday, February 15th, night

The ladies and I kept busy for several weeks, collecting names of people to contact. Harold administered the website, processed application forms, and forwarded them to Mr. Hancock.

The four-inch snow in the first week of February was beautiful, but the muddy arena kept everyone from practicing for two days.

The snow melted, and Kim continued circling the cloverleaf. Candy's girls and the Barton girls came regularly.

One night, when Kim and I crawled into bed, she said, "The girls call themselves the Four Cowgirls of York Riding Ranch."

"Interesting. Are they giving Challenger a run for his money?"

"Uh-huh, they are. I shortened his stride, and he's quick around the barrels and better than Lindy. But the girls' horses are tough to beat. I watched you and Candy. You're a good team."

"Yeah. But she's not as good as Judith."

"I see the tension when you work with her. How bad are your memories?"

"Terrible. When bursting out of the box, I imagine Challenger is chasing the calf, and Judith reigning him to pull it around for me to loop its hind feet. I'm hesitant because Pigeon doesn't move the same way. It takes an instant to register the difference."

"Can't Candy adjust?"

"We've talked about it, but Pigeon won't change. I'm trying to compensate."

"Work with Candy. She's a good roper."

"I know she is. But in my head, I picture her as Judith on Challenger. She isn't, and I fear it'll mess me up in the competition."

If I didn't win by roping with Candy and Gene sued for Challenger, my memories of Judith on him would tear me up.

Winning was the only way to keep him.

***

The next day, while giving Fargo a good brush down, my cell phone rang. "Hello?"

"Phil, this is Gene. How's your search for horse trailers coming along?"

Keep your mouth shut, Phil. I leaned against the wall. "I've not found any and don't see how I can go."

"Woody wants you there."

Hmmm. Gene was on a first-name basis with Mr. Hancock and had been talking about me. "First, you said there'd be trucks, then you said there wouldn't. I located a couple in Lubbock, but they're not enough."

"You've got a trailer to take Fargo."

He knows that one horse won't win enough for what I owe. So what's he trying to pull? "Not hardly. I need someone for team roping, remember? And the Barton and the Murray horses need to go. I can't compete without transportation."

"Then I'm coming for Challenger. The rodeo is your only chance to pay off the debt."

I was waiting for him to mention this. "You want me to compete but won't provide transportation. It's like you don't want me to go. Then you bludgeon me with the trailer mishap."

Gene's voice rose. "I'm minus a trailer, and I'll take Challenger or whatever is necessary to get one."

"*Take*? There's a difference between right and wrong."

"Don't get uppity with me. If you don't go to the rodeo, then I'm suing. Or hand Challenger over and walk away from this mess."

"I'm not walking away, so don't count me out. We'll get to the rodeo."

"You can't. I mean, I hope you will. I'd love to see you in action again."

Was that a slip of the tongue? "Gene, I'll find transportation without your help. Goodbye." I hung up on him.

I stomped into the house, and Kim met me at the door. "You're angry about something. Are the horses okay?"

"The horses are fine. Gene called and said if I don't compete, he's starting legal action to take Challenger."

"Did you tell him you'd talked to Mr. Edwards?"

"I didn't. He wants me there but won't supply trailers. It makes no sense. Something has changed with him."

Kim took my hands. "Take a breath."

I did.

"Let it out slowly and relax."

"I'll try. I wouldn't be in this situation if that kid hadn't unhitched the trailer."

"What he did was stupid, but you're still responsible for it."

"I know. But Gene is using it as a club."

She looked toward our bedroom. "You should go pray about it."

"Do you mean right now?"

"That's what I was thinking."

"I will if you pray with me."

She glanced toward Beth. "Let me tell Beth what we're doing. You go into our room, and I'll be there in a minute."

I did and plopped down on the corner of the bed.

In a minute, Kim sat beside me. "I'm here. Tell the Lord what's on your heart."

I held her hand and closed my eyes. "Lord, you know what I'm thinking. I want to thump Gene. It isn't right, but it's what I want. Because of my debt and the situation with Challenger, I don't know what to do. Help me fix everything. Amen."

Kim squeezed my hand. "Dear God, you control everything. Give Phil peace to know that whatever happens is because you're in charge. Amen."

Kim was watching as I opened my eyes. She said, "Promise you'll pray."

"I'll keep praying about him."

"I didn't mean just about Challenger. The Bible says to pray wherever you are, no matter what's happening. Promise you'll pray."

"Judith sometimes asked me to do that."

Kim lowered her chin. "She's not here, and I'm your current wife. I'm asking you to talk to God. If you're happy, rejoice with the Lord. If you're angry, tell him what's going on and why you feel that way. Talk to him a lot. Will you promise?"

"I'll pray when I can."

"Don't back away from what God asks. I prayed for you and Judith for years and am continuing to pray as your wife. Always talk to God. I'm asking you to promise me."

"For you, I promise."

"Thank you. If God wants us to keep Challenger, he will. Until then, we wait."

Chapter 43

Wednesday, February 17th, morning

I'd just finished the morning chores when a car turned into the driveway, and Jerry Dunlap stopped next to the fence.

Oh great. I waited by the stables with my hands on my hips. "What evil deed dragged you out of bed before seven in the morning?"

"You really hate me."

"Your reputation speaks for itself. Liking you is a quality that's fallen off the table. What did you want?"

"Your horse, Challenger. My offer still stands."

"What would you do with a horse? It has nothing to do with your shady financial deals."

He raised his eyebrows. "My business doings are none of your concern. I hear through the grapevine that Gene Wilcox wants Challenger for your debt. If you take my offer, you could pay him and have money in your pocket."

"Then I'd be without Judith's horse. No thanks."

He snorted. "You should step back and take a better look at what I'm willing to pay. It's rumored that you can't get a loan from the bank because of a credit lock. Tsk tsk tsk."

How did this crook know that?

"Phil, it means that you can't get a loan to pay Gene and are hurting financially. He'll sue if you don't give him Challenger, and I'll get the horse from him."

"Was it you who monkeyed with my credit?"

He held up his hands. "Whoa. Don't accuse me of something you can't prove."

"Maybe I can't prove it, but I don't doubt that it's something you'd do."

"Your opinion of me is clouding your thinking. I'm not the evil person you make me out to be."

"I don't know a single person who trusts you. Get off my ranch."

He eyed me before opening the car door. "Phil, if you believe you'll win enough money in Hancock's rodeo, think hard. I've got my fingers in a lot of things and will guarantee you won't. Take my offer. It won't be on the table much longer."

How can he guarantee that? I squinted and took a step.

He hurriedly got in the car and wiggled his fingers at me through the windshield before driving away.

All my problems revolved around horses. *Help me, Lord. What do I do?*

***

Candy's car sped up my drive in the middle of the afternoon, sliding to a stop. She and her girls jumped out. "Phil," she said, "you have a bunch of steers out. When we crossed the bridge, they were cavorting in the creek and running through the underbrush."

"How many did you see?"

"At least a couple of dozen. There's probably more."

Lord, help me think clearly. "If you ladies will saddle your horses and bring mine into the stables, I'll get Kim and Harold to help."

I returned with Kim and Harold, and we finished saddling the horses. I fetched my lassos from the tack room. "Candy, here, use this. Kim and I'll use the other two."

We trotted the horses into the timber and down to the creek near the bridge. The widely scattered herd resembled puzzle pieces dumped on a table. I had eighty-four range-fed steers, and it would take the rest of the day to get them in.

"How did they get out?" asked Candy.

"Good question. The fence must be down somewhere." I said to Harold, "There's a gate just over this hill. Open it, and we'll herd the cattle toward it. Everyone, be on the lookout for a broken fence."

The rest of us bunched the steers and angled them toward the gate.

Harold returned. "The gate came unhooked and was swinging back and forth. It might be how they got out. I propped it open."

Did someone open the gate? I seldom used it. I said to everyone, "Don't worry about a stubborn cow. Let's herd the bulk of them through the gate and then come back for the stragglers."

Everyone worked to herd the cows through the gate, and Candy closed it behind them.

By my estimate, we'd rounded up seventy-three steers.

"I counted seventy-two cows," said Candy. "How many head do you have?"

"I should have eighty-four," I said. "Let's recount because my number doesn't match."

We recounted and compared the totals.

"Seventy-four," said Kim.

Sharon said, "I agree. That's my number, too."

"It means ten are in the underbrush. Harold, go with your mom. When you find a steer, herd it so she can rope it. Sharon, you work with my wife. Shelly, you're with me. Let's go in different directions."

Shelly and I angled toward the bridge and walked our horses through two feet of water to the other side.

"Mr. York," said Shelly, "there's a group of us girls, and we talk about different stuff. Lately, it's mostly about you and Kim. They want to know why you married her. She's way too young, isn't she?"

Oh, joy. The rumors are circulating. "Why do your friends say she's too young?"

"You're over fifty."

"Not hardly. I'm forty-two. Kim will have her twenty-fourth birthday in a few days. Our age differences may not be common, but there's nothing wrong with it."

"They asked why you didn't marry Mom. She needs someone."

I angled Fargo around a tree. "Is this a question from you or your friends?"

"Kinda both. They wanted me to ask if I got a chance."

"Why do they believe your mom and I should be a couple?"

"You know each other, and she likes you."

"Your mother and I like each other as friends. She's a great woman, but relationships aren't about marrying someone who's available. Values and morals must mesh. Personalities should balance."

"Are you saying Mom wouldn't be good for you?"

I raised an eyebrow. "These questions are kind of personal. Should you be asking them?"

She shrugged. "I don't know. Our friends talk about it and wanted me to ask."

"Why do you want your mom to get married?"

"Because of Dad. He yelled at her a lot, and at us kids, too." She hesitated before saying with a thin voice, "He hit her, too. One time I found her crying, and she said marrying him was a mistake. She was never happy when he was around."

"I've never seen her sad."

"She tucks it inside. When you got her the farm job, she was really excited and singing. If you could make her happy, I thought you and Mom should marry."

"Your mom is a great woman. But God directed me to marry Kim." I pointed through the trees. "Let's get that steer. You herd him into the clearing."

She worked it toward me, and I swung my loop and caught him. Together, we dragged the reluctant steer back inside the gate.

I said, "One down and nine to go."

"Here come Mom and Harold with one. I don't see Sharon and Kim."

"They're probably further down the creek. Let's go back to the bridge to find another one."

As we returned to the area near the bridge, I said, "Your horse is a natural when cutting a cow. He's got cow sense. Let him have his head when we rope the next one."

"He's fast in the barrel race," said Shelly. "Would he be a good cutting horse?"

"He might be if you give him the right training."

"Would you train him?"

"I'm pretty busy these days with the rodeo and all."

"Yeah, I'm excited about going. Anyway, you're a good roper. You caught the last steer really quick."

"Then let's find the others, so I can practice my roping."

We caught the last steer just as the sun set, and the western sky was a beautiful mosaic of pinks and purples. The temperature had dropped, and everyone pulled their coats tighter.

The six of us gathered by the gate as I secured it. "Thanks, everyone. Head back to the stables while I check the fence."

"I'm going with you," said Kim. "If you find the fence down, you'll need help."

"Alright. Candy, Harold, and girls, thanks for helping round up the steers."

"Glad we could help," said Candy. "I had fun rounding them up with the horses."

They walked their horses through the trees toward the stables.

Kim and I headed along the fence, checking it as we rode.

"Sharon wanted you to date her mom," said Kim. "According to her, Candy is looking for someone, and you'd be perfect for her."

"Yeah. Shelly said their girlfriends wondered if I should have married Candy, too."

"Are you sorry you married me?"

I grinned. "Terribly. I'm stuck with a young wife and I can't control her."

She playfully slapped my shoulder. "You're sure full of it. Sharon said that folks have questioned why we got married and wondered if I was pregnant."

"Did you correct the assumption?"

"I hope we have children, but I told her that wasn't the reason."

"Are you sure you love me, or am I just another notch in your corset?"

She grinned. "That's enough of your sarcasm."

I hopped off Fargo to check the fence, then I remounted. "Gene and Jerry seem intent on taking Challenger from us."

"If they do, what will it do to your memories of Judith?"

"Scramble them like a tangled ball of yarn, and that scares me."

"Don't forget to pray." She patted Challenger. "Have you considered giving him up?"

"I have, but have tossed it out the window. He was Judith's horse, and she raised him from a colt. They're stuck together in my head. I can't give him up."

"You're being overly sentimental about this horse."

"He and Judith are entrenched together. Being sentimental is part of the territory."

"At least Mr. Wilcox is giving you a chance to earn money at the rodeo," said Kim.

"It's one way of looking at it. But I feel like I'm being set up. Either he, Mr. Dunlap, or both have stacked the deck against me. If they have, I may not have a chance."

"I see the tension bothering you all the time. You're never relaxed."

"I know. Since Judith died, problems seem to follow me wherever I go."

"Keep talking to God. Always pray."

Chapter 44

Thursday, February 18th, night

Kim and I had just gotten into bed when my cell phone chimed. "Hello?"

"Phil, this is Spence Edwards. I'll be at your ranch in half an hour. Can you tell me where to park my trucks and trailer for the night?"

"I wasn't expecting you until tomorrow."

"I hope this won't inconvenience you. We got an early start and didn't have heavy traffic coming through Omaha. My horse trailer is fifty feet long, and the truck is forty. I trust you have space for both vehicles."

"There'll be room when you get here. I'll have to move the tractor and equipment."

"Thanks. I'll be there shortly." He hung up.

"Who was that?" asked Kim.

"Spence Edwards. He'll be here in thirty minutes." I started pulling on my clothes.

She quickly dressed, and we went outside and moved the farm equipment into the shed.

I turned on the yard light and was turning on every light around the stables when Mr. Edwards eased his trucks into the driveway. Kim directed them to park the horse trailer in front of the stables and the other truck by the shed.

He jumped down from the truck and was about six feet tall with gray hair. A woman about the same height as me was with him. He held her hand, and he limped slightly as they approached. "You must be Phil. I'm Spence Edwards, and this is my wife, Patti." He shook my hand.

"Welcome, Spence and Patti." I pointed to Kim. "This is my wife, Kim."

"Patti, your silver-gray hair is beautiful," said Kim.

Her smile reached her eyes, lighting her face. "Thank you. You're too kind. I wish I had your blonde hair." She said to me, "Mr. York, you have a beautiful ranch. I hadn't imagined it looked like this."

"Thanks. We worked hard to make it as you see it." I said to Spence, "I hope you didn't have trouble finding my place."

"Your directions were great. I pulled the route up on the internet and printed it out."

The driver of the other truck, a slender woman of about five feet eight with short reddish-brown hair, joined us.

"Christy is our daughter," said Spence, "the oldest of the family. She's never been to a rodeo and asked to use this trip as her vacation."

"We've been expecting you," said Kim, "and made up the beds this morning. Everyone must be tired after the long drive."

"There's no reason to put us up," said Patti. "The horse trailer has a small room with a double bed. The other truck has a sleeper. We'll be fine."

"No. We insist," said Kim. "You're our guests. Bring your bags to the house. Everything is ready."

"I noticed fast food wrappers on the seat when you hopped down from the cab," I said. "We'll fix a quick meal, and it'll give us time to chat before we turn in."

"You're sure?" said Patti. "We don't want to put you out."

"We're sure, and we won't have it any other way."

In the house, Patti and Christy followed Kim to the kitchen. I could hear them chatting as Spence and I sat at the dining room table.

I said, "My daughter, Beth, and her two boys are sleeping in the bedroom above us. You and your wife will sleep in the room across the hall. Christy will have the smaller room at the end of the hall."

"We were prepared to rough it with the beds in the trucks."

"While you're here, you're our guests."

"We hadn't expected such kindness." He removed a flyer from his pocket and spread it on the table. "This flyer paints an impressive picture of the rodeo. *Riding for the Lord* is a tremendous theme."

"We featured that phrase on the website. Do you know Mr. Hancock?"

"His name is Woodrow, but he prefers Woody. Mine is Spencer, but call me Spence."

"I'll do that. I've chatted with Woody a few times, and he sounds like a great guy."

"He's a super friendly man. I did business with him a few months back, and we've become friends. He walks with a straight leg because someone shot him in the knee."

"Ouch. That's not good. What happened?"

"A former worker didn't like him building the homes for pregnant girls. Ask him if you want the details. The doctors fused his knee, and he hobbles with a cane until they replace it."

"It must be hard for him." I pointed out the window at the trucks. "What's the plan of attack for tomorrow?"

Spence checked his watch. "It's later than I expected, and we're all tired. I'd like to sleep late if it's okay with you folks. We'll load the supplies into the truck in the afternoon. Then stay another night and load the horses early the next morning. That'll give us time to get to Atlantic and unload before dark."

"Okay. I'll make calls to let the Murray and Barton girls know what's happening."

Kim, Patti, and Christy brought in a large pan of macaroni and cheese and a plate of hotdogs.

Kim set out paper plates. "This was quick and easy. I'll cook something better tomorrow."

"This will do just fine," said Spence.

Christy said, "Dad, it's a lot better than the fast food you've been forcing on us."

He wrinkled his nose.

I said a brief prayer of thanks.

"How many horses do you have?" asked Christy. "Dad said seven, or is it eight?"

"Seven. Ed Barton's two daughters, Trish and Tracy, will be here to help load them. They're finicky about who handles them. Candy Murray has two horses. She and her girls will be here to help. Then my three."

"Why do you have three? There are only two of you."

"My daughter planned to go to the rodeo but broke her leg. After her mishap, she loaned her horse, Isabel, to one of Candy's girls. Kim will ride Challenger in the barrel race. I'll ride Fargo for team roping and the calf-cutting events."

Christy pointed to the hot dogs. "Could you pass them, please?"

I did.

Patti nudged Spence. "Tell Phil about the phone call."

I sat up straight.

"Honey," he said, "you shouldn't have said anything."

"It concerns him, and he should know." She glanced at me. "Spence, he's waiting."

He sighed. "I received a strange call from a man I don't know. His name was Jerry Dunlap, and from the way he talked, I assume you know him. He asked if I'd had contact with you about hauling your horses to the rodeo."

"I know him and can't say anything nice about him. Did you tell him I'd talked to you?"

Spence wobbled his head. "He said if you asked for a trailer, I was to say none were available. If you didn't show up at the rodeo, he'd pay me $500. I simply reiterated that Gene said you'd be finding your own transportation."

My fingers tightened around a fork. "He's a scoundrel and wants to buy my horse for half what he's worth. I don't trust him."

"He sounded off-kilter when he talked with me. I'd rather deal with reliable people. Woody said you're a Christian, and JoAnn Allen said you're a straight-up man."

"Thank you. I try to honor the Lord."

"Thanks for trusting Phil instead of Mr. Dunlap," said Kim. She squeezed my hand.

Would he cause trouble when I showed up at the rodeo? Would Gene Wilcox maintain his parade of lies?

Chapter 45

Friday, February 19th, afternoon

Spence and his family helped us load the feed and supplies, stacking them in the enclosed trailer. Ed Barton and his girls and Candy and her daughters arrived to organize their equipment. It was almost evening when we got everything loaded and secured.

Back in the house, Beth said, "Dad, if it's alright with you, the boys and I will stay at the ranch rather than go home until you return."

"That sounds fine, Princess. Someone should be at the ranch. The steers got out, and it seemed odd. So be on the lookout for mischief. Harold is doing the chores without Marston, and if he has problems, tell him where he can get help."

***

Saturday, February 20th, morning and afternoon

Very early the next morning, we loaded the horses in the trailer, and everyone hopped in their vehicles to follow Spence's trucks to Atlantic.

Seven hours later, our long line of vehicles finally exited the interstate near Atlantic and turned toward Hancock Village. I glanced at Kim in the passenger seat. "We're almost to Mr. Hancock's farm. Are you excited?"

"It's been five years since I competed in a rodeo. It feels different."

"Different? How?"

"You and I are married, and the girls may be competitors, but we've become good friends, too. They haven't said it, but I think they look up to me."

"Why do they?"

"Because I'm the wife of Phillip York, the owner of the best riding ranch in the state."

"I hadn't heard that. Why does it matter?"

"Because you're courteous and don't show favoritism. You've imprinted our ranch with an honest reputation."

"I try to be courteous but hadn't realized it amounted to much."

"It does. While I was growing up, when I came over to visit Beth, you always were like that."

Spence's trucks turned off the road into a long lane. I asked, "Will you beat the girls on Challenger?"

"Maybe. But if I don't win—wow." She pointed out the windshield. "Look at that house. It's a mansion. Is this where we're going?"

"It's Woody's colonial-style house. His uncle willed it to him."

"Oh, my gosh. It's gorgeous. I love the way it's lit up to display the four columns. Wow."

I pointed to our left. "Look at those buildings. They must be *The Meadows*. Further back, there's the rodeo arena. Whoa. It's bigger than I imagined."

A tall woman wearing a gray hooded sweatshirt, blue jeans, and buckle down overshoes directed Spence's trucks to park behind the arena. I followed the trucks and parked beside them.

A slender, blond man about six feet tall, wearing blue jeans, a western belt, and barnyard overshoes, hobbled up to my pickup.

He opened my door. "Welcome to Hancock Village." I stood, and we shook. "You must be Phil York. I'm Woody, the owner of this place. But really, it belongs to God."

"It's good to meet you, Woody."

Kim came around the pickup to join us.

"Who's this pretty lady?" asked Woody.

"This is my wife, Kim."

He dipped his head. "We're glad you're here, Kim. You'll be competing in the barrel race. Did I hear correctly?"

"Yes, Mr. Hancock."

"My name is Woody, not Mr. Hancock. First names are what I prefer."

Spence and Patti joined us. Spence said, "It's great to see you again, Woody."

Woody clasped arms with him. "Glad you made it safely."

"How's your wife?" asked Patti. "She's soon to deliver, isn't she?"

"Sally will give birth near the middle of March. She waddles around the house and is determined to be hospitable to everyone this week." He pointed to the far end of the arena. "Spence, your other trucks arrived yesterday. The men unloaded them and parked them over there. After you unload Phil's horses, park your rigs alongside them so that they'll be out of the way."

"Has Gene's crew set up everything inside?" asked Spence.

"His crew is working as we speak and should finish up tomorrow."

"Good. Things are moving right along. Your weather feels warmer compared to Sagely."

"We had two inches of snow last week, but it melted the next day. For most of this week, the forecaster said temperatures will be right at the freezing mark—chilly but not bad. Heavy cloud cover, though. It's a prelude to more snow for the weekend. We should have acceptable weather for the rodeo."

"Where is everyone staying?" asked Kim.

"Most of the cowboys will stay in town and travel out every day. They've packed the motels. A bunch of folks brought campers and tucked them behind the trees over there. You and Phil will stay with me and my wife in the house. The rest of your team," he pointed to Candy and the girls, "we've arranged for them to stay in the rooms on the lower level of a building you passed when driving in. It's a part of *The Meadows* that isn't fully occupied yet."

"We brought sleeping bags," I said, "and planned to bunk with the others."

"You and your are my guests and will stay at the house."

Gene Wilcox came out of the stables and spotted me. He joined our small group. "Phil, I didn't believe you'd make it."

"I wouldn't have if I hadn't called Spence. He had a trailer, and we worked it out."

"Gene," asked Woody, "what do you mean by not thinking Phil would make it? JoAnn Allen arranged for Spence to transport his horses."

Gene shrugged. "I heard somewhere that Phil had opted to find other transportation."

"Where did you hear it? You didn't hear it from me."

"I don't remember. It was a rumor floating around. It doesn't matter because he's arrived." He flipped his hand. "We're setting up positions for the TV crews to broadcast. I can't stay to discuss rumors." He walked away.

"He was evasive," said Woody.

"I thought the same thing," said Kim.

Jerry Dunlap exited a door to the arena. When he spotted us, he ducked his head and walked away.

What's he doing here?

"When I see that man," said Woody, "he goes in the other direction, almost like he's avoiding me. Do you know him?"

"Sadly, I do. He's Jerry Dunlap, a sports bookie and loan shark. I wouldn't trust him."

"That's what I thought, and it's not good. For now, get your horses unloaded and into the stables." He pointed to Candy and the four girls. "The ladies who arrived with you, I'll make sure they're settled in their rooms. Spence, I'm inviting you and your family to join us for supper."

Chapter 46

Saturday, February 20th, evening

At Woody Hancock's home, I scooted back from the table and patted my stomach. "Sally, your fried chicken was the best I've eaten."

"Thank you. It's a Southern recipe that Woody's mother gave me. She never told me where she got it."

"She never told me, either," said Woody. "Let's go to the main room and talk. We'll let the food settle before our apple pie dessert."

"More delicious food," said Spence as he stepped away from the table. "Are you trying to fatten us up for market?"

Woody smiled. "We're showing you good Iowa friendliness."

In the main room, Kim sat beside me on a couch. Spence, Patti, and Christy settled on the other one. Woody and Sally occupied the two recliners so he could stretch out his leg.

Patti asked, "Sally, do you need help in the kitchen? You look about ready to pop."

"Not really, but thanks for the offer. The ladies who work at the pregnancy center help me. I'll be glad when this baby comes."

"Do you know if it's a boy or girl?"

She winked at Woody. "He's a boy. Before Woody's uncle died, he wanted to wager that Woody would be married within a year and have a child on the way. If Woody had agreed to the wager, his uncle would have won."

"I didn't know you were newlyweds," said Kim. "I thought you'd been married longer."

"It'll be a year in May," said Woody. "Sally lost her first husband. We met through a long, crazy chain of events because of the COVID lockdown. I say she's my inherited wife. I'll share the story another time."

"Kim and I were married on January 2nd," I said. "I lost my first wife two years ago."

Spence lifted Patti's hand. "We married right out of high school. It's been close to forty-three years. Christy is our oldest, and we have four sturdy boys. They've all married and have families, and two are working for the trucking company."

"Just so everyone knows," said Christy, "Mom and Dad got married because of me."

"Christy," said Patti, "you didn't need to say anything."

"Why hide it? It's true." She looked at Woody. "I'm proud of my father, and he's the best father on earth. A boy date-raped Mom in high school, and Grandpa Adams demanded she get an abortion. Dad stepped into the batter's box and asked her to marry him. If he hadn't, I wouldn't be here."

"Wow," said Kim. "Spence, that was beautiful."

"It's the very reason we built *The Meadows*," said Sally. "We give unwed pregnant girls a place to stay. It gives them a chance to get their lives sorted out."

Woody leaned forward. "I'm sure we could all tell grand stories of how we met each other and how God has directed in our lives. But for now, let's talk about the rodeo. I plan to develop this into a yearly event to raise money for *The Meadows*. We want it to be a rodeo of God-honoring integrity. Though the rodeo won't begin until Monday, I already have reasons to believe it might not please the Lord."

"Reasons like what?" I asked.

"Gene Wilcox is doing a fantastic job of organizing. The pieces are coming together nicely, but …"

"What's the problem?" asked Patti.

"He lied to Sherry Sue about her father and lied to Phil about hauling his horses. He also told me that veterinarians wouldn't be necessary for the rodeo because his men could check on the animals. The URA requires licensed veterinarians, and I contacted three vets in Omaha. They'll be here Monday when we start."

"You said there's more than one reason. What else troubles you?" I asked.

"Jerry Dunlap. I didn't know who he was until you said he was a sports bookie. The last thing I want is a gambling ring."

"Then tell him to leave," said Spence. "Or call the police."

"The county sheriff permitted us to employ a security company to monitor the rodeo. We'll confront Jerry this evening and tell him to leave. I hope he hasn't set his gambling plans in motion. If he has, he could run it from somewhere else."

"You can't stop all gambling," I said. "A rodeo is a sporting event. People will make wagers."

"It's not the private ones that concern me. It's the full-blown professional enterprise I don't want."

"If you kick out the main conspirator, you'll be able to keep a handle on things."

"I hope so. I want this rodeo to be a family event that honors God."

"Woody," said Sally, "share why Gene's lie to Sherry Sue gives you concern."

"Phil, you know that Sherry Sue Settle works for my wife and gave birth to a boy. She asked Gene to make sure her father, Chris Settle, didn't come. She feared he'd make a scene because he despises the boy she slept with. Gene said that her father wouldn't be coming. Chris Settle is already here and told me that Gene invited him."

"Does Sherry Sue know he's here?"

"Yes," said Sally. "She and I have talked, and she's keeping out of the way, not sure what to do."

"Woody," I said, "if you fear a scene between her and Chris, you should also know that Brandon McCloud paid the entry fee to wrestle steers. If Chris detests Brandon, what'll happen if they meet?"

He snorted. "You know how to ruin my day." He looked at all of us. "I'm asking each of you to pray that Jerry Dunlap hasn't set up a gambling ring and won't cause trouble when I ask him to leave. Also, pray that Chris and Brandon don't meet up. If they do, it may not be pretty."

Chapter 47

Monday, February 22nd, morning

Dozens of family-filled cars arrived for the first day of the rodeo. Woody was smiling at the large turnout.

At the opening ceremony, someone sang the national anthem, and folks proudly covered their hearts. Cowboys and cowgirls, dressed in Western attire, paraded around the arena. A class of schoolchildren jumped to their feet and waved as they passed.

Candy and her girls led the procession. She carried the American flag on a pole, and Sharon and Shelly displayed the Iowa and Christian flags. The contestants of each event rode together and waved to the spectators as the announcer identified them and the upcoming events: bronc riding, bull riding, steer wrestling, calf roping, team roping, breakaway roping, and barrel racing.

Jerry Dunlap had departed, and Gene kept his distance.

For the first two days of the rodeo, Gene hadn't scheduled an event for Candy, the girls, Kim, or me.

Kim and I watched the bronc riding and steer wrestling. "How are your memories?" she asked. "Are they bothering you?"

"You know they are, but I'm okay for now. These events don't dredge up recollections of Judith."

"How bad did they bother you when you roped with Candy?"

"They clouded my mind, and I struggled to stuff them. I thought about giving up and walking away. That would have been easy, but I'm not a quitter. Overcoming my memories is a fight I need to win."

"I'm beside you and will keep praying."

"Thank you. I need it."

A man behind me asked, "What are the rules for bull riding, and how is the scoring done?"

"The cowboy starts the ride," I said, "with his feet out front while gripping the bull rope with one hand. He must keep his free hand from touching the bull. The rider receives points for the power and agility of the bull and his ability to stay seated for eight seconds."

As we watched, the bull tossed the cowboy. Chris and another clown amused the audience by teasing the bull while herding it through a gate.

The lady behind me asked, "Why do rodeos have clowns?"

"During the slower moments, they entertain the crowd. In bull and bronc riding, after the cowboy dismounts or the bull tosses him, they distract the animal, allowing the rider to exit the arena safely."

"Oh. That's good."

On the second day of the rodeo, after the calf roping event, the high schoolers waited in the arena for the calf scramble. "They're supposed to catch the calf, but how do they do it?" asked the lady beside Kim. "What are the rules?"

"Each contestant is a 4-H or FFA member," Kim said, "and they give each one a halter. When they release the calves, the contestants try to catch one. If someone grabs a calf or is hanging on, no other contestant may interfere. If the calf breaks loose, it's considered free, and anyone can catch it."

Kim pointed to the referees. "They monitor the action to ensure the contestants play by the rules. Each kid tries to halter and pull a calf across the finish line in the middle of the arena. The calf becomes a 4-H or FFA project, and they're supposed to show it at the next fair."

The gatekeeper turned the calves loose, and the starter tossed his hat, signaling for the scramble to begin.

A tall teen girl grabbed the neck of a black calf and held on.

The lady behind us shouted, "That's my daughter. Hang on to it, Kathy!"

Kim and I shouted encouragement to Kathy.

The girl haltered the calf, but when she tried to pull it over the finish line, the calf refused to budge. Another contestant helped push the calf to the middle, where a referee marked it with Kathy's number. The smile on

Kathy's face and her arms raised in victory brought a smile to her mother.

Later, Candy and I found time to practice our roping.

"I'm a little edgy," she said while coiling her rope. "It's the first time I've competed in team roping."

If she was just edgy, my memories kept me wound up tighter than an antique clock. *Lord, clear my mind.* "Candy, it's no different from when we practiced."

"But tomorrow there'll be hundreds of people watching, and I'll get nervous."

"They can't interfere with the rope or the calf."

She wrinkled her mouth. "I don't want to disappoint you."

And I didn't want to disappoint her, but I feared I would. *Lord, please prevent these memories from ruining tomorrow.* "Candy, as long as we do our best, whatever happens, happens. I've been praying for the Lord to help us."

"Thank you. I need it." She glanced at the nearby pasture. "Look over there. My girls are practicing with Kim and the Barton girls, and they're having fun."

I flipped my rope to straighten it. "They should do great when they compete. Let's get back to work. I want to do well."

***

Wednesday, February 24th, morning

I saddled Fargo right after breakfast and rode to the arena to be ready for the team roping event. I hopped off and tightened the cinch.

Kim rode up on Challenger. "Your turn to rope is soon. Is Candy ready?"

"She went to saddle Pigeon and should be here shortly."

"Are you ready?"

"As much as I can. My memories won't leave me alone, and my muscles are tight. I've prayed that I won't ruin it for Candy."

"So have I. The Lord will help you." Kim watched Chris Settle and the other clown tease a cow. "The crowd is enjoying their antics, and the rodeo is going well."

"The attendance has pleased Woody. He hadn't expected the seats to be this full. There are youngsters of all ages, including teenagers, parents, and grandparents."

I glanced at a team of ropers as they fiddled with their lassos and said to Kim, "Hold on a second, let me talk to those folks." I approached them and asked, "Are you having problems with your rope?"

The woman said, "Someone gave Sam a rope last week, and he's having trouble dallying it."

I held out my hand, and he gave it to me. I hefted it and swung it back and forth. "This rope is a stiff grade. If you're not used to one, it'll be hard to handle, and if a finger catches in the slack, you're apt to lose it. A rope with medium stiffness would be easier to swing and dally around the saddle horn."

The woman said to a boy, "Get your father's old rope."

He hurried off.

I said, "Wear tight-fitting, tough gloves. They'll save your hands from rope burns."

"Thanks for the suggestion," said Sam. "We're grateful."

Shelly Murray ran up, huffing to catch her breath as I prepared to mount. "Mr. York, ... Mom can't ... Mom can't make it. She won't be here to team rope."

I glanced at the stables, and she wasn't in sight. "Why not?"

"Because someone opened Pigeon's stall and turned him loose. Mom's gone after him, but she won't be back in time."

Blast it. My lips tightened as I kicked the dirt.

Kim asked Shelly, "Do you need my help?"

"There's no need. The other girls have gone with Mom. Phil, she's sorry and should have saddled him sooner. Now they'll disqualify you."

Lord, don't do this. "Tell your mom I understand. I'll let the judges know."

Shelly hurried back to the stables.

Lord, what happens now?

Chapter 48

Since Candy wasn't able to make it in time to rope with me, it meant a disqualification unless ... A lightbulb lit up in my head.

"Kim, I need you to take Candy's place and rope with me."

Her eyes opened wide. "No way. I'm not a roper."

"How many times did you rope calves from Lindy after they got loose?"

"But Lindy wasn't racing, and team roping is a different animal."

"It's not much different. You could do it."

Her voice rose. "No, Phil. I haven't trained."

"Challenger knows what to do. You swing the loop and catch the calf. He'll do the rest."

"Will you stop this nonsense? I can't rope."

"It means a disqualification, and Gene will come after Challenger. If you rope, we at least have a chance."

She planted her hands on her hips. "You're putting me on the spot."

"I'm in a tough spot, too. What would you have me do?"

A judge appeared beside me and put his hand on my shoulder. "George Everly's team is roping next. You'll follow him. You and your partner," he nodded at Kim, "come to the line and be ready."

"Give us a second." I turned to Kim. "You and Sharon roped the calves that got out. You rode Challenger and know what he'll do. You can do it."

She closed her eyes. "I'll make a fool of myself."

"You're better than you know."

"Ma'am, are you roping or not?" asked the judge.

Kim glared at me and said to the judge, "I guess. We'll be there."

"Thanks." He walked away.

Kim said, "I hate you."

"No, you don't. You've told me a thousand times you love me."

"You better be an excellent teacher because I'm a greenhorn."

"When the calf breaks from the chute, spur Challenger and toss the rope over its head. Back up and keep the rope tight while I loop its hind feet. That stops the clock."

"What if I miss?"

"Coil your rope and try a second time. If you miss again, we're done."

"I can't rope fast."

"Forget the clock. Speed causes mistakes. Challenger knows the routine, so think it through and catch the calf on the first toss."

"Can I practice on a post?"

I pointed to the one behind us. "A couple of tosses is all the time you have. Swing a few to get a feel for it. I'll whistle when the judges call us."

She hurried to the post and started tossing.

I prayed. *Lord, help her do her best.*

Her first toss encircled the post perfectly. Her second throw fell short. The third toss side-slipped and hung up on the post. She prepared for a fourth throw as the loudspeaker called out George Everly's time. 16.4 seconds.

The judge pointed at me, letting me know it was our turn.

I whistled at Kim.

She glared at me while mounting Challenger.

"Are you ready?" I asked.

"I haven't any idea what I'm doing."

"You watched Judith and me a thousand times. Wait in the right-hand box, and I'll be in the left box. Watch for my signal. When you're ready, give a nod to the man in the chute, and he'll prod the calf. Don't break early.

Give the calf a head start. Forget the clock and concentrate on your toss."

"I'm scared."

"That means you're ready. Let's go."

She backed Challenger into the box and loosened her rope so it hung from her hand.

Lord, I'm scared, too. I gave Kim a nod, and her lips tightened.

She wiggled the rope and nodded toward the chute. The man released the calf, and as it burst out, she spurred Challenger. His long strides brought her close.

She twirled the rope three times, tossed it, and looped it over one horn and around the head, a half-head catch. Not perfect, but legal.

Challenger kept the rope tight and backed up, pulling the calf.

The calf resisted and hopped. My rope hit the ground, encircling its hind feet.

Fargo backed up, and Challenger faced me, stretching out the calf.

The judge dropped his flag, and the clock stopped.

Kim's eyes grew round. "I roped it. I really did."

Thaaaank yooou, Lord. She did better than she knew.

Chris Settle and the other clown unhooked our ropes from the calf and, with lots of antics, herded it into the holding pen.

Kim walked Challenger up beside Fargo while coiling her rope. "I can't believe I caught it on the first toss. What was our time?"

I looked at the time clock. "It's up there."

"Wow, 15.8 seconds. How did we do so good?"

"You were concentrating."

"It doesn't match what you and Judith did, but we beat the other team. Will it put us in the running?"

"Currently, it will. The teams following us may beat our time."

"When will we know for certain?"

"Soon. Let's get back to the stables and give our horses a rubdown. I want to find out about Pigeon and see if he's alright."

Chapter 49

Wednesday, February 24th, late afternoon

Kim pulled up a folding chair beside me outside Fargo's stall.

"While you were gone to the ladies' room," I said, "Candy came by and congratulated our third-place roping score. She was glad you could fill in for her, so they wouldn't disqualify me. Pigeon is back in the stables. He has cuts from barbed wire, but they aren't serious."

"Good. Did anyone see who let him out?"

"The security people saw the man and can identify him, but they haven't seen him since."

"Does she believe Pigeon was let loose to keep her from roping?"

"We can't prove it, but it's what we think. Because I didn't win in team roping, I suspect Jerry Dunlap planned this incident to ensure I would loss Challenger to Gene. Speaking of Gene, here he comes."

Gene walked up and planted his two hundred fifty pounds before us in a wide stance with his hands on his hips. "They posted your team roping score."

"We saw it earlier. What did you want?"

"If you remember, back in the meeting at your place, I said if you got first place in team roping and calf cutting, I'd accept your winnings as payment. You didn't, so I won't. I'm coming after Challenger."

"The rodeo's not over," said Kim. "Phil still has his calf cutting, and I've got the barrel race. We'll be able to win the ten thousand you want."

"That's not correct anymore. A horse trailer is fourteen thousand dollars—actually, it's almost fifteen. Even if you win, it won't be enough to buy a trailer."

I jumped to my feet. "You told everyone ten. It's highway robbery to raise it afterward."

"Everything has changed. The only payment I'll accept is for you to give me Challenger, or I'll take you to court."

"If we got loans from friends to make up the difference," said Kim, "then we'd have enough."

He snorted. "That won't happen by the end of the rodeo, and you know it. My original deadline was the end of January. February is almost over, and I'm calling in the debt at the close of the rodeo. The only way to satisfy me is to give me Challenger."

"It's dishonest," I said. "You're stacking the deck."

He inched closer. "I *have* to have Challenger."

"*Have* to have? What will you do with him?"

"I've lined up a buyer. His offer was, shall we say, substantial."

"It can only be Jerry Dunlap, and he's a crook."

"I didn't say who it was. It's none of your business."

I pointed a finger at him. "You didn't deny it, meaning it is. The way I figure it, Jerry wants Challenger, and I refuse to sell. Because I didn't win in team roping, he's using you to get around my roadblock."

"Stop guessing. You know nothing."

A lightbulb lit up in my head. "I'm guessing you owe Jerry a small fortune because of a gambling habit and can't pay it off. Jerry will cancel your debt if you get Challenger for him. Eazy peazy, lemon squeezy, as he likes to say."

He snarled, "You know nothing."

"It's a known fact that you bet on horses."

Spence and Patti strolled down the aisle and joined us. He said, "I heard loud voices. What's going on?"

"Gene wants to steal Challenger and has reneged on our agreement. He's increased the debt I owe just to get him."

"That's rotten," said Spence.

"He owes me for a horse trailer," said Gene, "and I need a replacement."

"If you sue for Challenger," said Kim, "you still won't have a trailer."

It took a couple of seconds for me to catch on to Kim's meaning.

Gene's jaw tightened. "Yes, I will. I've got a buyer lined up and will sell your horse for more than I need."

"No, you won't," I said. "If you sell Challenger to Jerry Dunlap, he'll cancel your gambling debt. But that's as far as it goes. You still won't have enough to buy a horse trailer."

He yelled, "You know nothing at all!"

"Your anger tells a different story."

"Will you just shut up?" He spun and walked away.

Chapter 50

Wednesday, February 24th, evening

Darkness surrounded Hancock village like a cloak, and the stables were awash with light as everyone fed their horses and settled them for the night. The rodeo arena was empty except for a few folks who stayed to talk to the cowboys.

I secured a pail of water in the corner of Fargo's stall and began cleaning up his manure. I called to Kim on the other side of the adjoining stall. "Hey, pretty lady, how about you and me sneak out of here for a secret nighttime tryst?"

"No way, Jose. It's cold outside. I'm married, and my husband would beat you to a pulp."

I smiled at her teasing tone. "Aw, come on. We won't tell. He'll never find out."

"You don't know my husband. He's a hard man and keeps a close rein on me. He refuses to let me out of his sight."

I heard the laughter in her voice. "If he's such a mean ogre, why did you agree to marry the ornery cuss?"

"I keep asking myself the same question. When he asked, I didn't have any other stallions in the barn."

"Stallion? Is he pretty active in that area?"

"He's not bad. He doesn't know it yet, but he got me pregnant."

My jaw fell open, and I dropped the pitchfork, sprinting around the corner into the next stall. "Were you joking?"

A smile graced her cheeks. "I'm late for my period, and I'm pretty sure I am."

I pulled her into a hug. "You beautiful woman. I'm so glad for you."

"Don't you mean for us?"

"Yes, for us. But this is part of your grand dream. That's what I meant."

"I know you did." She kissed me.

Woody stuck his head around the corner. "I hope I'm not interrupting an intimate moment between you two."

We separated, and I said, "Kim's pregnant. We're going to have a baby."

"Congratulations. It's great news." He waited until Kim and I came out of the stall and said, "I came to tell you that Gene is moving the calf cutting to tomorrow morning instead of the afternoon."

"Why the change?"

"Calf cutting isn't a high-excitement event. Bigger crowds have been coming in the afternoon. He's switching the order because breakaway roping will bring more excitement."

"Have you told Candy and the girls?"

"They're at the end of the aisle, and I'm making the rounds to tell everyone."

"Uh oh." Kim placed her hand on my arm and pointed toward the stable doorway. "Sherry Sue is here with her baby."

Woody said, "Sally talked to Sherry Sue and suggested she introduce her baby to her father. Sherry Sue is afraid there could be fireworks."

"Should we stop her?" I asked.

"No, I agree with Sally. Their meeting has to take place, and it might as well be now."

As Sherry Sue walked slowly past us, she said to Woody, "Sally wants me to talk to Daddy, but I don't know how he'll react. Could you come just in case something happens?"

"Stay calm. We'll be right there with you."

She stepped inside Chris's horse stall and leaned against the wall.

Chris glanced at her but continued brushing his horse.

"Hello, Daddy."

Chris looked over the back of the horse at her and then at us. He tightened his lips before returning his attention to his brushing.

She adjusted the baby on her shoulder. "Daddy, isn't Lee beautiful?"

He grunted and disappeared behind the horse.

"Don't ignore me, Daddy."

From behind the horse, he said, "Don't expect me to accept what you did."

"What I did was wrong. I admit it."

He stood. "Your baby doesn't have a father. You don't have a husband, and I can't accept those things. You refused to get an abortion, as I asked."

"Getting pregnant was wrong. But killing a baby is a greater wrong."

He came around from behind the horse and pointed at the baby. "If you'd gotten an abortion as I asked, you wouldn't have the evidence of your wild ways."

"I'm not wild, and I keep saying I made a mistake. It was wrong, and I shouldn't have done it. I'm trying to make it right."

"I warned you, and you should have stayed away from the filthy bastard. But no, you had to sow your wild oats. What you brought into this world is evidence of your sin."

"Daddy, I keep saying it was wrong. I met Jesus while working here and am turning my life around."

"It doesn't wipe the slate clean."

"Jesus forgave me and made my life clean. I ask you to forgive me, too."

"Why should I? Who'd want a soiled dove?"

"Leslie would. He works here, and we've been dating. He knows what I did and still likes me. I think he's really nice, and he's a Christian, too. If he asks, I'll marry him."

"Do you believe marrying him will erase everything?"

"It won't erase my past, but it'll give me a new start."

Chris jammed a finger against his chest. "What about my reputation? People will say he's got a slutty daughter."

"She's trying to make it right," said Woody, "and she's asking for forgiveness so she can start over."

"It sounds great, but I doubt she can do it."

"She's putting forth the effort, and she wants you to put forth an effort, too."

"I want my daughter back like she was before."

"Nobody can change my past," said Sherry Sue. "Please forgive me. I said it was wrong."

"Consider what she's asking," said Woody. "Open your heart."

"How can I? What she did has me wound up tighter than a drum."

Woody stepped closer. "Calm down. She's your daughter, and I'm sure you love her."

"I don't like what she did."

"You shouldn't like what she did. But show her love like the father of the Prodigal Son. His wayward son squandered money with loose living, yet his father received him back with open arms. Sherry Sue is asking you to receive her back with open arms, just like that father."

Chris closed his eyes. "I hadn't thought of it like that. Let me think it over."

"The Lord will forgive us as we forgive others, so let him work in your heart."

"I'll try."

"Daddy," asked Sherry Sue, "can we please talk?"

He pursed his lips. "I guess, but let me sleep on it."

"May I bring Lee back tomorrow to meet his grandpa?"

He flexed his hand. "I don't know, probably. His daddy's a downright dirty scoundrel." His arm snapped out as he pointed. "There's the filthy bastard. McCloud, you're a low-down reprobate scumbag."

Brandon McCloud jerked around to face Chris. "Reprobate? I never know'd a third-rate rodeo clown even know'd such a god-awful word. You never know'd which end of a cow to grab hold of."

"You got my daughter pregnant!" Chris roared.

"I did nuthin' to your little bitch. Ain't true."

"Liar!" Chris yelled.

Throughout the stables, folks turned to watch. Others stuck their heads into the aisle to see what was going on.

"Calm down," I said to Chris. "He's not worth it,"

"McCloud's a no-good, low-down, sleazebag reprobate," said Chris. "All he wants is to get in girls' pants."

I put a hand on his chest. "Take it easy, Chris."

"You can't prove I got your ugly bitch pregnant," yelled Brandon. "I dare you to prove it."

Sherry Sue stepped out of the stall with Lee in her arms. "I'm not ugly, Brandon, because you said I was beautiful when we had sex. Our son is proof of what we did."

"You were supposed to get the little twit aborted, and I want nuthin' to do with it."

"I didn't go to the clinic, and *The Meadows* helped me."

"Your baby is a little twit, and I ain't got no obligation to it," he snarled. "I want nuthin' to do with the little bastard."

"Brandon, you've got your wish," said Woody. "Because you refuse to take responsibility for fathering a child, I'm ordering you to leave the rodeo tonight."

"I'm in calf cutting tomorrow."

"Not anymore. I'm removing your name from the roster."

"You can't do nuthin' with your bum leg. You, and who else?"

I stepped beside Woody. "Chris and I are here. Look around. Others heard your nasty remarks to Sherry Sue."

"Pack your suitcase and load up your horse," said Woody. "If you need a ride to town, I'll pull your horse trailer, but I want you out of here tonight."

"What about my winnings from steer rasslin'? You gonna steal those from me?"

"I've got the address that you put on your entry form. I'll mail you a check, and you'll have it in a few days." He pointed to the door. "Go collect your belongings and leave."

Brandon gave Woody the one-finger salute and displayed the gesture to everyone before stomping out the door.

"His reputation will precede him," I said. "It's doubtful any rodeo will let him enter."

Chris said to Sherry Sue, "Do you see what he's like? He just wanted in your pants."

"He wasn't like this before. Now I see what you meant."

Chapter 51

Wednesday, February 24th, night

I pushed back from the supper table. "Those meatballs were great, Sally. Could Kim and I get the recipe?"

"It's nothing fancy. I just threw it together. Swedish meatballs over fettuccini."

"I enjoyed the three-bean salad," said Spence. "It was delicious."

Woody said to Sally, "Honey, forget about cleaning up. Get off your feet. I'll pick up the table later and stick the dishes in the dishwasher." He turned to us. "Let's go to the other room and sit for a while."

In the living room, he said, "Phil, you're in the calf-cutting event in the morning. I don't understand how the judging works because it isn't to beat the clock. Could you fill me in?"

Everyone focused on me. "The judges allow a rider two and a half minutes to cut two calves out of a herd. The rider must cut one calf from deep within the herd and peel the other calf from the edges."

"You said two calves," said Spence. "I heard it was three."

"There's no hard-and-fast rule. It just depends on the rodeo. Gene is using the standard most common in our area. Once the rider has selected a calf and edged it out of the herd, he drops the reins and gives the horse its head. The horse works to keep it from returning to the herd."

"What are the judges looking for?" asked Woody. "What are the criteria for scoring?"

"The biggest factor is the horse: his attitude, attention, and quickness. He must be able to deal with a difficult calf. That's what the judges like to see. The horse must do it without visible control from the rider. The horse's ears must be alert, and his eyes must be on the calf. They watch how it spaces his legs in anticipation of the calf's direction. Mostly, the scoring focuses on the horse."

"How are points allocated?" asked Patti.

"The rider starts with a score of seventy, and the judges add or subtract points, but the score stays between sixty and eighty. I'm usually in the high seventies. I've never received a perfect score, but I know someone who has."

"Phil's horse, Fargo," said Kim, "has an instinctive knack for knowing what a calf will do. Some horses have it, others don't."

"If the horse is so smart," Christy asked, "and does all the work, why is the cowboy there?"

"The rider reins the horse," said Kim, "directing it to select a calf and edging it out of the herd. When that's accomplished, the horse goes to work, and the rider sits."

"Wow," said Christy. "Phil, do you believe you'll win?"

"I have a good chance. The best horses didn't sign up for this rodeo. If they had, their competition would be tough."

Chapter 52

As we chatted in Woody's living room after the evening meal, the doorbell chimed.

"I'll answer it," said Sally. At the door, she spoke with someone. She turned to Woody. "You better take care of this. The security detail detained the man who let Candy's horse out."

Woody reached for his cane and said, "Phil, please join me."

"May I come?" asked Kim.

"You might as well."

In the machine shed office, a blond young man in his late teens sat in a folding chair. He kept his hands in his lap while three security men guarded him.

Woody said to one of the security men, "Thanks, Peter. What did your men see?"

"They spotted him walking around and recognized him as the one who let Mrs. Murray's horse out. When they detained him, he kept saying, 'I've done nothing wrong.'"

"I didn't do nuthin' wrong," said the man. "Do you have a arrest warrant?"

"Who is he?" asked Woody.

Peter handed Woody a billfold. "I took this from him, and his ID is inside."

Woody flipped it open and removed a driver's license.

I looked past his shoulder. "Shane Wilcox is from Lincoln, Nebraska. Interesting. May I question him?"

"Be my guest."

I grabbed a folding chair and sat in front of Shane.

He spotted Kim by the wall and winked. "Hey, sexy lady. After I get out of here, how about you and me go off someplace kinda private like?"

Her lips thinned. "You're not going anywhere, and I've got this." She wiggled her ring.

"Back off, Shane," I said. "My wife is not an accomplishment for your reputation."

"Awe, man, that sucks. I'll bet your Mrs. Perky Tits is hot in the sack."

Kim's face hardened. "Wash your mouth out with soap. I'm a person, not a thing for you to play with."

I gripped his knee. "Take your infantile mind out of the gutter. Enough of your playboy act. Is Gene Wilcox related to you?"

He shrugged. "My uncle will have me outta here in no time."

"Thanks for clarifying Gene as your uncle. Why did you travel from Lincoln?"

"He told me to hop a train and git my butt out here. He had somethin' for me to do."

"When did you arrive?"

"A couple days."

"What did you do for him?"

He shrugged. "What's it to you?"

"You better talk," said Peter. "My men saw you turn a horse loose and chase it down the road. If Woody presses charges, they're willing to testify."

"You said 'if.' You mean maybe he won't?"

"Maybe, maybe not," I said. "Why did you let the horse loose?"

"I ain't talking. I ain't incriminatin' myself."

"Peter," said Woody, "he's not talking, so get the sheriff. I'm pressing charges. We have enough evidence."

Shane jerked erect. "Wait, wait. You can't do that."

"You bet I can."

"I didn't do nothin' wrong and was followin' orders."

Woody stood over him. "Harassing livestock on my farm by releasing a horse is count one. Illegally interfering with the rodeo's operation is count two. If Mrs. Murry presses charges, that's count three. We have enough to call the sheriff. Why was the horse let loose?"

Shane's shoulders sagged. "Uncle Gene paid me to do it."

"It doesn't tell us why," said Woody.

"He told me to let the horses in stalls seventeen and forty-nine out and chase them down the road. He said no one registered them to the rodeo, and they shouldn't be here. I just chased one horse cause the other weren't in the stall."

"Woody," I said, "number seventeen is Fargo's stall. I had him out early to be ready for the team roping."

"You were lucky, then."

"Shane, where's your uncle now?" I asked.

"Dunno. Prob'ly sleeping in his room."

Woody said to Peter, "Keep Shane here. I'll send word later about what to do with him."

"Are you callin' the sheriff?" asked Shane.

"He's a pervert," said Kim. "Lock him up."

"Phil, let's go talk to Gene," said Woody. "What we do depends on what he says. I can't have a black mark attached to my rodeo."

Chapter 53

Woody knocked on Gene's door at the rodeo while Kim and I stood behind him. He said, "I hope he answers. It's late."

"I see a light," said Kim.

Gene opened the door in his pajamas, rubbing the sleep out of his eyes, and noted Kim and me. "Is there trouble?"

"May we come in to discuss a problem?" asked Woody.

He looked at each of us. "Can't it wait until morning?"

"No, I brought Phil because it concerns him."

Gene's lips twitched. "Yeah, I guess we can talk." He glanced at Kim. "Let me change my clothes for the lady."

He seems nervous.

"You're presentable in your PJs," said Kim.

"Are you sure?"

"You're dressed appropriately. Don't change on my account, it's unnecessary."

"If you say so." He opened the door, and we entered.

Kim and I took the couch, Gene plopped in a folding chair, and Woody sat on a bar stool with his leg extended.

"What problem is so important," asked Gene, "that you came at this late hour?"

"We came to discuss Candy Murray's horse getting loose," said Woody.

"I'm aware of it. The security men asked where I was and what I was doing. I was in the announcer's booth checking the schedule." He played with his fingers.

Does he suspect why we came?

"They've kept me abreast of their investigation," said Woody. "What concerns us is that it canceled Phil's roping event."

Gene shook his head. "No, it didn't. He roped, and I thought he and Kim did pretty good coming in third."

"If she hadn't roped with me," I said, "they'd have disqualified me."

"She made it good, then. You make it sound like it's wrong."

"Let me ask something else," said Woody. "Did you visit Phil and Kim afterward to discuss a horse trailer?"

"Phil owes me for one, and I want him to pay up when the rodeo is over."

"Originally, if I got first place," I said, "you agreed to accept my winnings as payment instead of taking Challenger."

"True." He nodded. "That was our initial agreement."

"But you changed the agreement," said Kim, "and upped the price."

Gene's eyes flicked back and forth. "Things are different. I had to change it."

"Why?" asked Woody. "Was it so you could take his horse?"

"If he pays what he owes, I won't need Challenger." He frowned. "How does Phil's debt have anything to do with Mrs. Murray's horse? You make it sound as if it's my fault."

Woody raised his eyebrows. "Isn't it?"

Gene spread his hands. "How could it be my fault? I was somewhere else."

"We caught the person who let Candy's horse loose."

He jerked. "You ... you did? Who was it?"

"Your nephew, Shane."

He glanced at the door. "You're mistaken. Shane lives in Lincoln."

Woody removed Shane's ID from his pocket and held it out for Gene to see. "You're the mistaken one. He admitted to letting the horse loose."

Gene swallowed. "He's a teenager and sowing his wild oats. I never thought he'd do something like that."

I waited until he looked at me. "That's a lie, Gene. You paid him to do it, and six people heard him say it."

He mumbled, "Damn. I warned him to keep his mouth shut."

"Why?" asked Woody.

He fidgeted. "You'll find out anyway. I've got a gambling debt with Jerry Dunlap. He'll cancel it if I get Phil's horse for him, and he threatened me if I didn't."

"And you threatened me to take Challenger," I said.

"I didn't have a choice. What else could I do?"

"You hired Shane to do something illegal at my rodeo," said Woody. "That breaks the integrity clause in your contract that stipulated the rodeo would be fair and honest."

"Will you take me to court?"

"I'm considering whether to call the sheriff."

He put his hands together. "Don't put me in jail. Give me time, and I'll make it up."

"You can't make up Phil's lost opportunity to rope, and the Bible calls that sin."

"You sound like a hellfire preacher."

"How would you know what a preacher sounds like?" said Woody. "You don't go to church."

He shrugged. "I used to. Maybe I don't now."

Kim tapped my leg.

I understood and caught Woody's eye, pointing to myself and Gene.

Woody dipped his head. "Go ahead, Phil, explain."

I asked Gene, "If you've gone to church in the past, what did you learn?"

"I learned the Bible talks about God."

"Are you on good terms with God?"

"I think so. I'm a good person, and I don't steal stuff or kill people."

"Arranging for Candy's horse to get loose and by breaking Woody's contract, are those good things?"

He wrinkled his mouth. "I don't want to think about it."

"You better think about it." I leaned forward. "You also implied I was the father of Sherry Sue's baby."

He looked down. "I thought you could have been. When I talked to Woody later, I learned you weren't."

Kim stood, and her voice rose. "Why didn't you tell Phil and me when you found out? It would have erased the smear from his reputation."

"Sit down, Kim," I said.

"He should have corrected the lie."

"I agree, but let me handle this." I turned back to Gene. "You lied, saying that Spence didn't have enough trailers. Why?"

Gene mumbled, "It was to keep you from coming to the rodeo."

"So you could pressure me into giving you Challenger?"

He squirmed. "Yeah, that's why I lied about them."

"There's no law against lying, but you destroyed any trust we had in you, and you've also broken Woody's contract. What do you think we should do for all the damage you've caused?"

Gene hammered his leg. "You've proved I'm not perfect, but don't put me in jail."

"Tell us how you'll make up for what you've done?"

"I don't know." He was quiet for a moment. "Woody, if I apologize to Candy, will that be enough not to call the sheriff?"

"To say you're sorry would be a starting point," said Woody.

"What else should I do? I don't want to go to jail."

"An apology won't erase Candy's lost opportunity," I said.

"I'm willing to apologize, but I don't know what else to do."

"Would you say you are sorry in front of witnesses?"

Gene grimaced. "That stinks."

"Lots of people know what happened," said Woody. "We're asking for one publicly."

"I'll apologize in front of people if you won't call the sheriff."

"That is only a start. What about the mess of compromising the rodeo's integrity?"

He thought for a minute. "I could step aside as the rodeo organizer. Would you accept that?"

Woody nodded. "Excellent idea. Tomorrow, over the loudspeaker, say you made a mistake affecting the integrity of the rodeo and are handing it over to one of your workers. At the end of the rodeo, your crew will load your animals and equipment, and Spence will return them."

"Candy and I will be at the stables in the morning," I said, "waiting for you."

"I'll be there, but you owe me for the trailer."

"True. So how do we handle that?"

"Jerry threatened me if I didn't get Challenger, but because the debt is mine, I won't sue for him."

Kim smiled. "Thank you."

I relaxed. "Thank you. About the trailer, if you're agreeable, I'll send my winnings to pay what I can and make up the difference as I'm able."

"That's fair. I shouldn't have pressured you.

"Before we leave, there's something else," said Woody. "You did a fantastic job of putting together and organizing my first rodeo. If you clear up things with Candy and follow through with both public apologies, I'll consider using your services next year."

Gene straightened. "You're willing to trust me?"

"Because of your excellent work, I'll offer a second chance, provided you make an admission of guilt, you don't lie again, and you honor your word going forward."

"I don't deserve it, but thank you."

"I'll be checking. Don't disappoint. I'll release your nephew, but I don't want to see him again."

"You won't." He removed a packet of papers from a drawer. "Phil, here."

"What is it?"

"They said to give this to you after I got Challenger. Read it. You'll know what to do."

Outside, Kim asked, "What are the papers for?"

I stood under a window with the light shining down. "It's about my credit freeze. This states that someone paid off my fictitious account with *Argus Security Systems*. If this is valid, then the bank can unlock my credit."

"Was Gene the cause of it?"

"The cover letter states Gene was to deliver these papers. He's the messenger. The other signatures aren't familiar. Craig Jones should be able to decipher it."

"Hopefully it's legitimate, and we can get it cleared up." She said to Woody, "It's not fair that Candy missed roping with Phil. Can you do anything about it?"

"Hmmm, that's a good point. Let me sleep on it. I'll let you know in the morning."

Chapter 54

Thursday, February 25th, morning

At the stables, Kim and I told the girls and Chris about Gene coming to apologize. We asked them to be witnesses to his confession.

Gene slowly approached as Candy and I waited. He swallowed. "Mrs. Murray, I'm the person responsible for your horse getting loose. It was my fault that you couldn't rope with Phil. I did it for selfish reasons, and it took away your opportunity to compete."

He looked down and shuffled his feet. "It was wrong, and I can't correct what I did. An apology is all I can give. I ask for your forgiveness and am leaving the rodeo in the hands of someone better suited. I'm truly sorry for what I did."

He walked away, and she spoke to his back. "Thank you for admitting that it was your fault. I accept your apology."

He faced her again. "I hadn't expected you to accept it, and I don't deserve your kindness." He walked hesitantly to the stable's exit.

She said to me, "I didn't see that coming from a mile away. I never imagined he'd admit to doing something dishonest."

"Jerry Dunlap was applying pressure because of a gambling debt. Gene had to keep you and me from roping so he could take Challenger. My horse was the chit Jerry was requiring."

"Huh? Why would that crook want a Quarter Horse?"

"I don't know. It's a question that no one may have an answer."

"True. He's secretive about what he does."

Kim exited stall number seventeen, leading Fargo toward me.

"Candy, how's Pigeon?" I asked. "Is he ready for this afternoon?"

"Uh-huh. He's rested and raring to go."

Kim handed me Fargo's reins, and I kissed her. "Thanks, dear." To Candy, I said, "He better have enough energy. He's slated for two events."

"Huh? Two? What's the other event?"

"There's been a schedule change. After the breakaway event, Woody will let you prove your skill in team roping. If you do well, you could win a purse."

"How can you compete again? You and Kim came in third."

"I'm not. You are. I'll only assist by riding Challenger. The judges will watch your skill, not mine."

"Wow. Thank you, thank you, thank you. This is great news."

"Are you coming to watch me in the calf cutting?"

"You bet. I don't want to miss it when you win."

She walked beside Kim and me to the arena, and the four girls followed us, sitting in the half-full bleachers.

A chute handler said to me, "Wait with the others behind the gate for your turn."

"I'm cutting first because I drew position number one."

"Then go to the middle of the arena and wait for the judge's signal."

Kim and Candy stood behind the fence, watching the workers bunch thirty calves inside the arena.

I patted Fargo's neck. "Are you ready, boy?"

He tossed his head.

The judge signaled, and the clock began ticking off the seconds.

I eased Fargo up to the herd and spotted a large brindled calf. He'd be tough. I eased him out of the herd and dropped the reins, gripping the saddle horn.

Fargo lurched, spun, and twisted, always focusing on keeping the calf away from the herd.

I predicted his moves as he turned and rotated. When it was time to select a second calf, I took the reins and chose one that seemed feisty.

Again, Fargo worked to prevent the second calf from returning to the herd.

The clock spun down, and I drew in the reins, patting his neck. "Good boy." We waited by the fence where Kim and Candy stood.

The scoreboard flashed my score: 79.

"You did great," said Kim.

"Let's see if it stays on top," I said.

"It will," said Candy.

For the rest of the morning, we watched the other cowboys compete. No one topped my first-place score.

***

Thursday, February 25th, afternoon

The breakaway roping event began right after lunch.

Candy's turn was twelfth, and she backed Pigeon into the box, giving a nod to the judge. The calf burst out, with Pigeon right behind. She swung her loop once and roped the calf.

Overhead, the scoreboard blinked 2.4 seconds.

I whistled and said to Kim, "If she does this well with me, she'll not only earn a blue ribbon, but they'll give her a belt buckle."

Candy walked Pigeon up to Kim and me, grinning. "The calf ran right into my loop. I didn't have to do anything."

"You did something right," I said.

"My toss was sweet. I've never done that well."

Looking up, I checked the scoreboard. "There are eleven more contestants to finish the event. When you rope with me, if you do as well as you just did, you'll take first prize."

"Phil, if you don't do well with me, anything I do won't amount to a hill of beans."

"True." *Lord, help me help Candy get all the credit.* "Go outside to cool Pigeon off and get him rested. We'll rope in about ninety minutes."

From behind the fence, Kim and I watched the rest of the breakaway ropers. At the event's completion, Candy brought Pigeon back inside and waited beside us.

I pointed to the scoreboard. "You won."

She checked the times of the contestants. "Not by much. Pam Syverson caught hers in 2.6 seconds."

"She's in second place, and you're in first. That's all it takes."

I patted Pigeon and ran my hand down his leg. "He's relaxed and raring to go."

"His ears are forward, and his eyes are alert," said Kim. "He knows he'll be running again."

"He's smart like Challenger," said Candy.

The loudspeaker announced the winners of the breakaway roping event. "And folks, don't go away. We're not finished yet. We've got a special treat that's not on the schedule. Candy Murray just captured first prize in the breakaway roping and will pair up with Phil York in a special display of team roping. Sit back as the rodeo crew sets up everything. They're changing out the calves and bringing in a fresh one for this spectacular display of skill.

This ought to be one for the books, folks. We've paired the best female roper in this rodeo with a top-notch horseman. I believe we'll be in for a real treat."

"Oh, great," I said. "He piled it on thick."

Kim laughed. "There's nothing like a heaping helping of adulation, is there?"

"There are lots of things we must do right," I said. "Let's pray for the Lord to be honored."

We bowed our heads and asked God to help us do our best.

Candy and I rechecked our saddles, cinches, and ropes.

The announcer said, "Alright, folks. Here come Candy Murray and Phil York. Let's give them a big hand and watch the action."

The judge motioned for us to take our positions. Candy backed Pigeon into the box, and I got Challenger positioned on the other side.

I willed my arms to relax and patted Challenger. With my rope at the ready, I spread the loop and nodded to Candy.

She closed her eyes, and her lips moved. After glancing at me, she nodded to the judge, and the calf burst out.

Candy and I spurred our horses and were right behind it.

She swung once and tossed the loop over its horns.

Pigeon turned the calf, and it jumped.

My loop caught its hind feet, and Pigeon and Challenger backed up, facing each other.

The judge dropped his flag, and the clock stopped.

As we slackened our ropes, someone shouted from the doorway, "Calves are running wild in the playground, and the kids are screaming. Somebody, please help them."

Lord, protect the children. I dropped the rope attached to the calf, and in Challenger's race to the exit, I snatched another off someone's saddle.

Chapter 55

In Challenger's race to the arena door, Chris Settle, in his baggy clown outfit, flagged me down and shouted, "Let me help!" He latched on to my extended arm, swung up behind me, and yelled in my ear, "Get me inside the playground. You get the kids. I'll bunch the calves in a corner."

In the playground, the children were clinging to the equipment and trying to stay out of the way of the calves as they wildly raced about, bumping into everything.

I gave Challenger his head. He must have sensed the urgency, because he didn't slacken his pace while racing through the narrow gate.

Chris slid off Challenger's rump and began herding the calves to the far end.

The calves raced past the merry-go-round, spinning it like a whirlpool. A woman circled past and shouted, "Save my daughter, please." She handed her little girl up.

I seated the girl securely in front of me and said to the woman, "Don't get off. You're safe right there."

I angled Challenger toward the jungle gym as a calf raced beneath a boy hanging by one hand. I snatched the boy off the ladder just as he was about to let go.

A quick canter brought Challenger to the chain-link fence, and I deposited both children in Kim's arms.

Chris had moved most of the calves into the corner, but two of them continued their wild race around the playground.

A boy poked his head out of a tube. I hopped off and hefted him up on Challenger.

A girl, about ten years old, hunkered under a seesaw with her hands covering her face. I grabbed her and placed her behind the boy before angling Challenger toward Kim. "Take care of these kids. Give me your rope."

She did.

People shouted at me, but I ignored them and focused on protecting the children.

One calf circled the climbing equipment and slid to a halt in front of me. I swung the loop and snubbed him to a pole. He kicked and squirmed, entangling himself until he couldn't move.

With the calf secured, a boy jumped off the climbing equipment and ran to me. I directed him toward Candy, who was coming through the gate. "Run to the lady. Don't stop."

The boy raced to Candy, and she closed the gate behind him.

She joined me with her rope, and I said, "Use Challenger to catch the other calf while I get the children out."

Candy mounted and sped off.

The other clown, in baggy pants, joined Chris, and they kept the calves bunched in a corner.

A crying girl on the climbing equipment reached out. I lifted her off, and she clung to me.

Candy had worked the calf toward a corner at the far end. So I said to the girl, "There's the gate. Those people will get you. Run."

She ran as if a bear was chasing her.

The remaining calf sped away when Candy got close. He evaded her by running through the swing set, twirling a boy in a bucket swing.

I lifted the boy from the swing and handed him to a man on the other side of the fence.

Near Chris, a boy bounced on a spring rider, not crying but not knowing what to do. Chris helped him off and pointed at me. The boy ran, and I hefted him over the fence into someone's arms.

Woody joined me on the playground. "I was sitting in the stands and couldn't get through the crowd because of this bum leg. What can I do?"

Candy had roped the calf, and Challenger was pulling it to the far side.

I said, "Check for more children and get them out of here. Once they're safe, the rodeo crew can get the calves back to where they belong."

He and another man checked around and found a boy at the top of the slide and two girls high in one of the tubes. They were the last children.

Kim joined me. "Are you alright?"

"No. I'm a mental wreck. I feared the boy on the jungle gym would fall off as the calf raced under him. This should never have happened."

The crowd thinned as people drifted away.

With every child accounted for, the rodeo workers scurried about, assembling sections of the portable fence and forming a lane to return the calves to their pens.

Chris joined us and pointed to the other clown. "Abe said that the place where the calves got out, the fence was wide open."

"Did someone forget to secure it?"

"He doesn't believe so. The crew had put the calves from the breakaway event into a temporary holding pen and would take care of them later. When they returned, the fence was wide open, and the calves were gone. It shouldn't have been unchained."

Something didn't smell right.

Candy handed me Challenger's reins and asked, "Were any children injured?"

"Their parents took them to the medical station for the doctor to check," said Kim. "There don't appear to be any injuries, but the doctor will let us know after examining them."

Woody returned, and I asked, "What else do you need me to do?"

"Nothing. We'll put everything back in order, and I'll ask the security team what they saw." He glanced at Kim and said to me, "Today's rodeo is over. You and your wife take care of your horses and come to the house. I'll announce that the barrel race will be tomorrow."

Chapter 56

Kim, Candy, and I helped the rodeo crew move the calves out of the playground before walking our horses to the stables. Candy led Pigeon to the far end, and Kim put Fargo in his stall. I opened the gate to Challenger's stall and jerked to a halt.

Jerry Dunlap faced me from inside. "It's about time you got here. You were supposed to have ridden Fargo. If you had, I'd have been long gone."

"You were told to leave the rodeo and not return," I said.

With a thin smile, he said, "I came to collect what's mine."

He reached for Challenger's reins, and I backed up. "He doesn't belong to you."

His eyes turned cold. "This horse is most definitely mine."

A thick, heavy-set man stepped out of the shadows.

Jerry pointed at the man. "Duane came as insurance to prevent you from causing trouble. The sheriff has deputized him, and he has full authority."

Duane glanced at Jerry with a frown before folding his arms.

Kim, in Fargo's stall, asked, "Phil, is something wrong with Challenger?"

I shouted, "Call the security team and get Woody. We've got big trouble." I'd never used this tone, and I prayed she realized something wasn't right.

She hesitated before running outside.

Jerry's eyes narrowed. "You're stupid. Calling for help won't do any good."

"We'll see. I haven't sold Challenger, least of all to you."

"What you say doesn't mean squat." He patted his pocket. "These papers say otherwise. I want my horse." He said to Duane, "Get Challenger and take him to the trailer."

In a single motion, I mounted and backed him up.

Duane came to the middle of the aisle. Jerry exited the stall and said, "You're not very smart. You're avoiding the inevitable. You could end up behind bars. Five years is about right for grand larceny."

Woody's security chief, Peter, entered the stables. "Your wife asked me to get here fast. What's going on?"

I pointed at Jerry and said, "He's trying to steal my horse."

"This horse belongs to me," said Jerry. "I came to claim my rightful property."

I squinted down at Jerry. "I never sold him."

"A judge has signed and notarized these documents, saying the horse is definitely mine."

"May I see the papers?" asked Peter.

Jerry handed them to him.

Three members of the security team entered, and Peter said, "Stick around, guys. I'm not sure what's going on yet." He stepped under an overhead light and opened the papers. "Hmm. These look valid, but I'm not a legal eagle. A lawyer should examine these."

Jerry snatched the papers from him. "These say the horse belongs to me, and I've got a trailer to load him up."

Peter held up his hand. "Sit tight. Let's not be in a hurry. We'll let Mr. Hancock decide how to handle this."

Kim ran into the stables, panting. "I got Woody, and he's right behind me."

Woody hurriedly hobbled through the doorway. "I'm here, Kim. Mr. Dunlap, you and I had an agreement that you weren't to return."

"I came to get a horse. Then I'll be gone. You have my word."

When did his word mean anything?

"I see," said Woody. "Who's the man with you?"

"Duane Strickland. He's here to load Challenger into his trailer, and we should have been gone by now. The sheriff deputized him in case of trouble."

"Were you expecting trouble?"

"Mr. York is causing trouble by resisting my claim to this horse. I planned to slip in and out during the rodeo activities before anyone noticed. These documents prove the horse is mine."

I reined Challenger in a circle to be further from Jerry. "I didn't sell Challenger to you or anyone else."

"This horse belongs to me," said Kim.

Jerry grinned wickedly. "Not hardly, lady. You've got no ownership papers, as I have."

Several people walked up to our group.

Peter said to his men, "Keep the bystanders back until we settle this issue."

They shifted to route the people behind me.

"Mr. Dunlap," asked Woody, "if you have ownership documents, may I see them?"

He handed them to Woody.

"It can't be real," I said. "I never sold Challenger."

"Calm down, Phil. Let me look at this." He carefully read the documents, taking his time to examine them. "Uh-huh." He flipped to the next page. "Interesting. I know Judge William Deardorff, and it's his signature. He married Sally and me."

Woody shifted his stance, turned to the third page, and carefully read it. "Fascinating. These documents are valid." He handed them back to Mr. Dunlap. "But you can't enforce them."

"Yes, I can, and I brought Duane."

"Your papers say you got this horse from Gene Wilcox, not Phillip York."

Jerry tapped the papers. "You saw page three. Gene Wilcox signed the horse over to me after he took ownership. Go ask him if you don't believe me."

"We can't. I fired him. Before he left, he relinquished his claim to Challenger, so the horse was never in his possession."

"What? It ain't possible. These papers say he got ownership."

"He didn't because several people heard him give up his claim. Your documents aren't worth the paper they're written on."

"See, Jerry," said Duane. "Your plan is full of holes. We came for nothing. Where's the money you promised?"

Jerry shoved him. "Shut your mouth."

"Make me, Jerry." Duane turned to Woody. "Those calves got loose because Jerry opened the fence. He wanted people away from the stables while we got the horse. I was only supposed to load the horse, nothing else. I ain't breaking the law for this son of a bitch."

Jerry took a step toward him. "I told you to shut up."

"I'm speaking the truth, and you know it."

Jerry cocked his fist, and Peter jumped between them. "Alright, let's stay civil."

Woody said to me, "Put the horse in the stall. No one is taking him tonight. Peter, station someone to watch."

Peter pointed to one of his men. "Guard the horse. Make sure no one takes him out of the stall." To the other security officers, he said, "Take Mr. Dunlap and Mr. Strickland to different locations for questioning."

Chapter 57

Kim and I got Challenger and Fargo settled at the stables.

"I'll stay close," said the security man, "and make sure nobody takes this horse."

"Thank you," said Kim.

We left the stables and climbed the steps to the house.

Sally opened the door. "You had quite an afternoon."

"Yeah," I said, "and I'm wound up like a twisted ball of yarn."

"Sally, are you alright?" asked Kim. "You look kind of pale. Are you sick, or is your baby coming?"

"I've got acid reflux. A lady from our staff is taking courses to become a maternity nurse. She checked on me a while ago and gave me antacids to settle my stomach. I'm not supposed to eat anything spicy or rich."

"I'm glad you've got a nurse close by," I said.

"So am I. Cherri is a blessing." Sally ushered us into the main room. "You can relax. Woody is questioning the men. I'll put the food on the table shortly, and I asked Candy and her girls to join us for supper."

"Do you need any help in the kitchen?" asked Kim.

"Let's take it easy. I've already cooked the food and only need to set it on the table."

We settled on the couch.

"Sally, have you heard anything about the kids in the playground?" asked Kim

"From what Woody told me, none of the children had physical injuries. Our pastor, Robin Shenefelt, is a trained counselor and met with them and their parents. One boy was terrified, and Robin was calming the child down. The other children were afraid but excited to see the calves up close. Robin is mostly talking to the parents."

"I've been praying for them," I said. "It's good you have someone to help them work through their ordeal."

"Robin is excellent. He's a regular around here and counsels the pregnant girls to help with their situations."

The doorbell chimed, and Sally said, "Let me answer it. It's probably Candy and her girls. Then I'll set supper on the table."

Shelly and Sharon pranced across the room toward Kim and me. They giggled and high-fived each other.

Shelly said, "Mr. York, you did great."

"If you're talking about the playground," I said, "lots of people helped the kids."

"Calm down, girls," said Candy. "He hasn't heard the news."

"What news?" asked Kim.

Candy shooed her girls away. "Go sit, or find something to do." She sat on the arm of the other couch. "What do you think our team roping score was?"

"Oh, I forgot about it. I don't know. About what Kim and I did, eleven or twelve seconds."

She laughed. "You're not even close. We roped the calf in 5.1 seconds."

"No way," said Kim. "Top professional ropers might do it in as little as four."

"The official timers clocked us, and all three recorded 5.1. It's certified."

"We can't be that good," I said. "It's not possible because the world record is 3.3."

"Yes, it is possible. Sharon recorded our run on her phone, and I watched it over and over. We roped the calf so fast that it was over before it started."

"Wow. You got the credit, not me."

"Don't be so humble. I couldn't have done it without you."

Lord, I give her all the credit.

"Food is on the table," said Sally. "Let's sit and eat."

Woody came in just as we sat at the table. "Go ahead and pray. I'll wash up and be right there."

He returned and dished up a mound of mashed potatoes.

"What did you learn from questioning those men?" asked Candy.

"What I've already suspected—Jerry Dunlap is a snake in the grass."

I put my fork down. "Did he say anything?"

"No, except to reiterate that Challenger was his, and the documents proved his ownership. He refused to believe that Gene hadn't taken possession of him. Other than that, he was silent as Clarabelle the Clown. Duane Strickland did all the talking."

"What did Duane say?" asked Sally.

"Jerry hired him to load a horse and haul it. Nothing more. When Jerry said someone had deputized Duane, Duane realized something was fishy, but he stayed quiet because the pay was extra good."

"What about the documents?" I asked.

"Duane thought they were legit. It surprised him that no one could enforce them. He hadn't hired on to do something illegal, and that's when he said that Jerry had let the calves out. Folks would be away from the stables, rounding up the calves. No one would be around to prevent him from loading the horse."

"What about the playground?" asked Candy. "Was it part of his plan, too?"

"Duane wasn't sure. Jerry saw the playground gate was open, but he made no move to shut it."

"That's evil. I'm glad the calves didn't hurt anyone."

Praise the Lord. "So am I," I said. "So am I."

"What about Challenger?" asked Kim. "If Jerry can't take possession of him, what's going to happen? Are we free to take him home?"

Woody nodded. "Gene gave up his claim, making Jerry's documents worthless. He's your horse."

"Why did Jerry want Challenger?" I asked. "He doesn't use horses in his business."

"Peter asked Duane that very question. Duane said it was about a wager Jerry had with someone in Denver. The other guy saw Challenger compete two years ago, and if Jerry could get Challenger for him, the other guy would pay him a small fortune."

"What are you doing with the men?" asked Sally.

"The sheriff took Jerry away. I'm pressing charges because the calves could have hurt someone. There was no evidence that Duane had done anything except be with Jerry. He took off down the road with his horse trailer."

He pointed his fork at me. "I must thank you for saving those kids this afternoon. You reached the playground in record time."

"Chris and Abe helped. Candy was there. Kim and a few others helped calm the kids."

"You took charge. That's what I needed because I couldn't have gotten there in time."

Chapter 58

Thursday, February 25th, late at night

Kim and I crawled into bed, and I scooted close, wrapping my arms around her.

"What did you learn when you called Craig Jones today?" she asked.

"I faxed him the papers, and he said the signatures were from a questionable shell company. He did a quick search on the internet, and the men could have a link to Jerry Dunlap."

"Was Jerry behind your credit lock?"

"It's possible, but Craig said it's not provable. He'll contact the credit companies and send them the letter. He'll also request that they remove *Argus Security Solutions* from my credit report and prevent the company from taking any future action. It may take a week or two, but it should clear up everything."

"That's good." She was quiet for a bit. "Phil, you've changed while we've been here at Woody's farm."

"No, I haven't."

"Yes, you have. You're calmer, you don't get upset as easily, and you help others. They appreciate you going out of your way and have told me so. What changed?"

"I don't know. My crazy wife suggested something I'm working on. Where is she?"

She lightly slapped my arm. "Your wife isn't crazy."

"Uh-huh, she is. She slaps me for no good reason."

Kim elbowed me. "She doesn't either. What's your wife's suggestion?"

"I don't know if I should say anything because she might get a swelled head."

Kim pivoted to face me. "Tell me, husband of mine. If I'm crazy and helped you change—for the better, I might add—I want to know what secret switch I flipped."

I looked into her eyes. "You're beautiful."

"You didn't answer my question. Tell me, or I'll tickle you."

"Do you remember what happened that time you tickled me?"

She tapped my nose. "There isn't a pile of manure nearby, so just tell me."

"I don't know. You suggested I pray, and I have been."

"Really? Am I so influential as to have caused such a change?"

"Indubitably."

"Wow. That's a big word to say, absolutely. Why did you say it?"

"I'm feeling good, and it just came out."

"What have you been praying about?"

"Oh, mostly about the mess with Jerry and Gene. It calmed me and kept me from being upset. I left my problems in God's hands and didn't worry about them."

"Have you prayed about anything else?"

"Yeah. The playground and the kids. There wasn't much time to react, and I said a quick prayer for everyone's safety. I've also been praying for the girls, Candy, and my crazy wife to do their best in competitions tomorrow."

"If my suggestion of prayer makes you calmer, I love being crazy."

"You helped heal my life."

"Judith's death wounded it, didn't it?"

"Uh-huh. When she died, I was like a baby bird that had fallen out of the nest. I floundered around and didn't know what to do. You gave my heart a home."

"What about your memories of her on Challenger?"

"I wondered when you'd ask. You took Candy's place in team roping, remember? It changed everything."

"How do you mean?"

"When you rode Challenger, I didn't see Judith. I saw Kimberly Ann. You broke Judith's connection with him, and it was wonderful seeing you instead of her."

"Why didn't you say this before?"

"I wanted to make sure it was real, and it is."

"I love you, Phil. There were times I felt like the second woman in your life."

"Marrying Kimberly Ann Ryan was the best prescription for healing my life. I love you for sewing me together. I married a woman who is beautiful inside."

Chapter 59

Friday, February 26th, morning

On the last day of the rodeo, I helped Kim get Challenger ready for the barrel race.

Patti Edwards came to the stall as Kim cinched the saddle. "Kim, I've been chatting with the girls at the far end of the stables and wishing them luck. They think you'll beat them. Do you think you will?"

"All four girls are great competitors, and any of us could win. It's the other women in the rodeo that I know nothing about. They could beat us."

"Aren't there men in barrel racing? I've only seen women."

"Not on the rodeo circuit. I don't know why exactly. It just is. Boys will compete in the younger leagues."

"You're using a different saddle, aren't you?"

Kim pointed to the saddles sitting astride the wall. "It makes a difference when you use a lighter barrel racing saddle. It doesn't have all the frills of a roping saddle."

"What's the most important thing when you're racing?" asked Patti.

Kim thought for a moment. "For me, it's my relationship with Challenger and knowing what he's capable of. We have to trust each other."

"I've heard the term 'changing the lead' and don't understand it. What does it mean?"

"When a horse is about to enter a turn, the rider reins him to plant his hooves differently."

I said, "Honey, they just announced the start of barrel racing. We better get to the arena."

"I didn't mean to keep you," Patti said. "I'll be watching. It should be exciting, and I wish you the best."

"Thank you," said Kim. She grabbed Challenger's reins and led him out of the stables.

She took her position in the line, sixteenth in a field of thirty-one contestants.

"Are you ready?" I asked.

"I think so." She patted Challenger's neck. "He's easier to work with than Lindy. He knows what to do before I ask, and I want to try something."

"What do you want to try?"

"When practicing through the turns, it's like he wants me to give him his head."

"He's a smart horse. You could consider it." I pointed with my chin. "Trish is first in line. I hope she does well."

"Oh, she will. She's never tipped a barrel. Tracy has done that sometimes."

The loudspeaker announced Patricia Barton as the first contestant.

Kim mounted Challenger to get a better view over the heads of everyone.

I prayed silently. *Lord, help Trish do her best.*

"There she goes," said Kim. "She's started her run,"

The crowd shouted encouragement as she sped through the cloverleaf course.

Trish completed her run, and the electronic timer flashed 16.78 seconds.

"Wow, wee," said Kim. "What a great run. I'm not sure anyone will beat her."

I prayed for the other girls as they raced around the barrels. Sharon circled them in 17.43 seconds. Tracy completed her run in 17.55 seconds, and Shelly on Isabel, 16.99.

"Trish is in first place," said Kim. "They're all doing great. None of us raced faster than seventeen when we practiced."

"You can. I know you can."

The next three riders tipped over barrels, adding five seconds to their score. Currently, Trish and Shelly were in first and second place. A girl further back in the line said she wouldn't have a chance against those times.

When Kim's turn arrived, she took her place and waited for the official.

Lord, Kim is in your hands. Keep her mind clear and help her strive for her best.

The official directed Kim to start whenever she was ready.

She backed Challenger against the fence so he'd be moving when he triggered the electronic timer. Kim clicked to Challenger and kicked her heels. He exploded forward.

At the first barrel, Kim's leg brushed against it. It wobbled but didn't tip. At the second barrel, Challenger turned so abruptly that Kim's hat flew off.

Lord, she's doing great. Don't let her tip the third barrel.

At the third barrel, his turn was smooth and swift. She put her heels to his flanks, and he shot like a bullet the last hundred feet to cross the finish line.

I retrieved her hat.

Kim hammered her thigh. "Let's get out of here. There's no reason to stick around."

"Why? Wait for them to post your time."

"I didn't do great, that's why. His run was awkward. I gave him his head and figured he'd do better, but it was a mistake."

"He didn't make any mistakes."

"I almost tipped the first barrel because he cut it too short. His turn around the second barrel was wide, and he pivoted too quickly. On the third, he slowed down. Beth was right. Isabel is faster than Challenger."

I glanced at the scoreboard over our heads. It blinked several times to adjust the contestants' rankings. Kimberly York flashed to the top of the scoreboard with 16.78 seconds. "Kim, you're—"

Trish, Tracy, Sharon, and Shelly exploded out of nowhere to surround Kim.

"The Cowgirls of York Riding Ranch really rock," said Sharon.

Tracy pumped her fist. "Kim, you had a great run."

"You're tied with me," said Trish. "Your run was perfect."

Kim blinked. "It was not. You guys are teasing."

Trish pointed up. "Look at the time clock. We're in first place."

She looked at the scoreboard. "They made a mistake."

"Kim, it's your score for real," I said. "Challenger made the difference."

"How could it? His turns around the barrels were wrong."

"His turns weren't wrong. You and Challenger connected."

Her eyebrows rose. "Did we really?"

"Uh-huh. You did great."

"Wow." She hugged Challenger's neck. "We did it, big boy. I didn't believe it."

"Believe it," I said. "Look at the stands. Woody and Sally are applauding. Spence and Patti are cheering."

Shelly tugged at Kim's sleeve. "Let's go celebrate."

"Let's party," said Tracy.

I glanced at the other contestants waiting for their runs. I flipped my hand. "The other riders won't beat you. Go have fun with the Four Cowgirls of York Riding Ranch. Maybe we should say the five girls."

Kim grinned, and I kissed her.

Trish made a face. "Ewwww, smooching."

Tracy laughed. "Wait till you have a boyfriend."

Chapter 60

Friday, February 26th, afternoon

Outside the arena, as we prepared to go in for the awards ceremony, Kim adjusted my shirt and straightened my hat. "I want you to be presentable on the last day. Everyone will be watching." She pointed at my boots. "You should have shined them."

"For goodness' sake, we're in a rodeo. Everything gets dirty and messed up."

"Not my husband. He's a gentleman."

"I am not."

"You most certainly are and have to look like one."

From behind us, Candy said, "Quit arguing, Phil. She's right. Don't slouch in the saddle, either. Everyone wants to see tall cowboys."

"Will you ladies quit ganging up?"

"No," said Kim. "Come. There's the signal for everyone to enter the arena."

We mounted and paraded past the crowded bleachers.

A little girl shouted, "There's the cowboy, Daddy. That's him."

I couldn't identify the girl's location. With all the riders, there was no telling who she'd spotted.

The loudspeakers crackled. "Folks, I'm Woody Hancock. Welcome this afternoon to the last day of a thrilling rodeo week. It's been exciting, hasn't it?"

The crowd applauded.

"This is the time we recognize the achievements of the folks who competed. In today's show, we'll recognize the top winners of each event."

The loudspeakers crackled as Woody whispered to someone in the announcer's booth.

"Alright folks, they've handed me the list, and here are the winners. In bull riding, Jeff Roth. As I call your name, come to the front and remain there until I call everyone's name. In steer wrestling, Samuel Jenkins won first place."

Samuel rode up beside Jeff as the audience applauded.

"In bronc riding," said Woody. "Paul Slatten came out on top."

Paul angled his horse up beside Samuel to receive more applause.

"Danny Roberts won the calf roping event."

"With breakaway roping, Candy Murray amazed everyone with a fantastic run."

She rode Pigeon up next to Danny.

I said to Kim, "Get ready, your name will be next."

She smiled. "And yours will be called, too."

"And in barrel racing," announced Woody, "we had a tie for first place: Patricia Barton and Kim York. Come to the front, ladies."

Kim and Trish rode forward, holding each other's hands high.

The loudspeaker crackled as Woody said, "In team roping, Mark Conway and Stacey Andrews were the best team. But here's the kicker: we had a special roping event because of a foul-up, and a contestant couldn't compete. To make it fair, Candy Murray tried her hand, and she didn't disappoint. She teamed up with Phil York, and together they had the top score. According to our rodeo rules, we can't give Candy the first-place award, but the judges say she earned a purse as if she had."

Mark and Stacey moved their horses forward to stand beside the others.

A burst of applause and whistles erupted from the audience.

Woody said over the loudspeaker, "Phil York was the winner of the calf cutting competition. Ride up and join the others. We saved his name for last."

"Huh?" I rode Fargo up between Kim and Candy. "What did he mean by that?"

"Shhh," said Candy.

"Just listen," said Kim.

The loudspeaker crackled again. "Folks, I received a letter this morning and want to read it. You'll see why in a moment. The writer wishes to remain anonymous."

Dear Mr. Hancock,

Before this week, I'd never seen a rodeo and never wanted to. I grew up believing cowboys were cruel to animals and punished them for their own aggrandizement.

My daughter came home from her Christian school with tickets to your rodeo and wanted me to take her for her birthday. I'd promised her whatever she wanted, and I was determined to keep my promise despite my unsettled feelings.

In this rodeo, I expected to see the animals treated harshly and the riders being big showoffs. I was mistaken. A rodeo veterinarian and I chatted, and he assuaged my fears. I saw no one mistreating any animals. Instead, they treated them with respect. The workers and cowboys took care to ensure none were injured. They pulled animals from the lineup if they weren't healthy.

The riders weren't braggadocious, nor did they strut around pounding their chests. They were courteous and helpful, and they encouraged each other.

I was wrong about rodeos and was pleasantly surprised. My daughter had a wonderful time watching the action, being around the animals, and talking to the cowboys and cowgirls. Only one bad thing happened, which brings me to the last part of this letter.

My daughter was on the playground when two dozen calves invaded it. She crawled under the seesaw and prayed for an angel to protect her. Phil York was her angel, plucking her from her hiding place and sweeping her to safety on his horse. I'd seen him before, and I began asking others about him.

Everyone said Phil is a gentleman and always treats the women in his orbit with the utmost courtesy. He was helpful to the other contestants, offering suggestions to assist in their events. I asked around and learned that when he roped the first time, his partner was a rank amateur, and yet they placed third. Genius. The second time he roped, he showed excellent skill. I can't say enough about Phil York.

If this rodeo has an award for the most outstanding cowboy, I unabashedly nominate him for the honor. The man is a remarkable Christian, and his love of God and people shows through in everything he does.

Mr. Hancock, I'm donating $25,000 to The Meadows in Phil York's name. Please thank him for me. His walk with the Lord made your rodeo a God-honoring event.

Thank you for putting on this rodeo as a Christian ministry. I look forward to attending next year.

Yours in Christ and Christian service,

Anonymous.

The TV crew shone a spotlight on me.

Oh, great. I had no rock to crawl under. Another person should get the praise, like Jeff, Samuel, Candy, or Trish.

Lord, let any honor be yours.

The other competitors had crowded around, giving me no chance to escape. The applause from the audience drowned out whatever Woody said over the loudspeaker.

Kim must have sensed my embarrassment and edged Challenger up against Fargo to put her arm through mine. "I love you, Phillip York. What the letter said is what I've always known about you: a man who walks step by step with God."

"... and gentlemen! Ladies and gentlemen!" shouted Woody over the PA system.

The noise subsided.

"Ladies and gentlemen, we're not done yet. There's another award."

The applause died away.

I knew what was coming and was sure Kim knew because she wouldn't let go of my arm.

Lord, keep me humble. I surrender to you.

Woody came out of the announcer's booth and mounted a raised platform holding a portable microphone. "Phil, please come forward."

Kim and I walked our horses up to the fence in front of Woody.

I whispered to Kim, "I'm not perfect."

She whispered back, "You are to me."

"Phillip York," said Woody, "as the sponsor of the Hancock Rodeo of 2021, it gives me great pleasure to present the Christian Cowboy Award to an outstanding man. You're an excellent competitor, and your Christian attitude was a shining example of how this world should live."

Let me live as your example, Lord.

He handed me a large wooden plaque with a polished brass plate engraved with my name.

"Thank you, Woody," I said.

"No, I thank you." He faced the crowd. "Phil's presence created the spirit of Christian competition I hoped would permeate this rodeo, and it has." He spun and saluted me.

Epilogue

Friday, February 26th, night

While we held each other in bed, Kim whispered, "Phil, are you awake?"

"No, I'm talking in my sleep," I said.

"You're full of sarcasm and must be feeling good. I can't sleep either."

"Tomorrow we'll be busy loading the horses and going home. We should get some sleep."

"I'm having trouble getting my mind around what happened today."

"This week has been full. What will you do with your gold cup? Beth will be jealous that Challenger beat Isabel."

She sighed. "I've been thinking. To put it in the den beside her silver cup wouldn't be fair. She couldn't compete against me, and I don't want to gloat over her misfortune."

"Where will you put it?"

"In our closet. You better hang your plaque in the den."

"I don't want to gloat, either."

"You're not. You're praising the Lord and putting him on display."

"I'll think about it."

She scooted closer. "No, you won't think about it. I'll hang it on the wall if you don't."

"Alright. I know when I'm overruled. You can hang it."

"Thank you." Kim was quiet for a moment. "With Marston gone, we need help at the ranch."

"I know and have been thinking about who might be available, but I don't know of anyone."

"I know of two, and they'd be good."

"Two? Who?"

"Trish and Tracy. They know about Marston quitting and have been begging their father to let them work for us."

"Do I sense you've already agreed?"

"They pleaded with their father to call me. He did, and we talked. He's okay with them working, but they're still in school. As long as they get their schoolwork done and they always work together, they can work part time, provided I supervise them and you give your approval."

"But we need someone full-time," I said.

"Part-time for only three months. After graduating in May, they'd work full time."

"I'm guessing they want to work with the horses. Would they be able to handle the heavier tasks, like haying, lugging feed sacks, and working with the machinery?"

"I know they can," said Kim. "If you agree, could I tell them in the morning?"

"I feel like I'm being ganged up on."

"You are, because I know they're good workers."

"I'm okay with it if they prove they can do the heavy work. Let's give them a trial period and see how it goes."

"Thank you. They'll prove themselves," said Kim. "Honey, I was thinking about Gene. Are you angry with him?"

"I'm not angry, but hurt by his lies and attempt to take Challenger. Let's invite him to church."

"Good idea, because he could use the Lord's help. Don't invite Shane."

"I won't. You know, honey, I've been thinking."

"About what?"

"How God used you to yank me back to the land of the living. Living on memories soured me like a rebel horse. I wasn't aware how depressed I'd become until you kissed me on New Year's Eve."

"Have I healed your heart? Or is Judith tucked away to come between us in the future?" When I didn't answer, she said, "And don't answer with sarcasm. Give me an honest answer."

I kissed her. "I wasn't going to, and I was examining myself. Judith will always be in my heart, but God is back on the throne, and you and I stand before him hand in hand.

Judith is watching from heaven as we place Christ at the head of our home."

"I like your answer. If Christ is the head of our home, how many children could we have? I'm hoping for at least four."

"While you and I stay healthy, I'm agreeable to as many children as God gives us."

She wrapped her arms around my neck. "I love you for saying that."

I grinned. "When I retire, I'll turn the job of raising our kids over to you and just put my feet up."

She slid her fist up under my jaw. "I hope you're teasing."

"You know I'm joking. Besides, a rancher never retires, and I expect our kids will help on the ranch."

"Phil, how much do you love me?"

"Oh, I don't know. Maybe, as the song says, *I love you a bushel and a peck and a hug around the neck*. I love you enough to wish we'd married sooner. If we had, you'd have kept me from wallowing in the mire."

She kissed me. "Let's get some sleep. We have a long day tomorrow."

"Goodnight, pretty wife," I said as I lay on my back with my arm under her head.

"Goodnight, perfect husband." Her breathing evened.

Lord, thank you for giving me an ocean of love for Kim. Thank you so much for using her to heal my wounded heart. Thank you for everything, and may you receive all the glory for everything I do. Goodnight, Lord.

Acknowledgments

Foremost, praises and thanks to God the Almighty, for his showers of blessings through the months, and for keeping me focused on bringing this story to completion.

To my caring, loving, and supportive wife, Lottie. My deepest gratitude goes to her for allowing me the time to hibernate in my man cave, pounding the computer keys to my heart's content. It was a great comfort and relief to know she gave me a quiet place while I completed my work. My heartfelt thanks.

I wish to offer a huge thanks to the many people who helped me improve this manuscript and cover design. If I failed to mention someone, I offer my humblest apologies.

Amanda Paez

Baylee Frisinger

Brittany Eldridge

Grace Nims

Harshita Sharma

Jamie Factor

Lisbeth Sando Pedersen

Mel Hughes

Sarah Karwisch

Shelby Ward

Thanks to the community of helpers who helped hone this manuscript. Their eagle-eyed insights and kind suggestions have strengthened this story and my writing.

About the Author

Michael R Emmert, after graduating from McPherson College, spent fifteen years as a missionary and writing newsletters from far-off places like Tanzania, Swaziland, Zululand, and Navajo land.

During this time, he shifted his writing talents to make up fictional Christian love stories for readers' entertainment. He's been a member of American Christian Fiction Writers (ACFW), East of the Web's (EOTW) Uncut writing group, and now The Writer's View (TWV) as a panelist.

When not writing, Michael lives in the greater Atlanta area with his wife, daughter, and seven grandkids. His better half strives to keep him on the straight-and-narrow (without success).

Fueled by popcorn, he writes well-loved relationship stories. His current novels include "Shunning Ida Mae," "Deception and Depravity," "Three Strikes," "Wounded Heart," and now "One thing remains the same: Love always wins out. Just ask his family and sleepy desk cat.

Books by The Author

Shunning Ida Mae

In 1886, Ida Lapp, a plucky Pennsylvania woman, secretly loves an Englisher, something strictly forbidden by the Amish Ordnung. When discovered by her parents, her penalty forever changes her life and sends her on a journey to face persecution. At the same time, she desires the impossible—to return home to a family who despises her.

On an Iowa farm, Anna dies and leaves Joseph Melroy with the daunting task of raising two small children. Faced with the heartache of losing his wife, looming financial troubles, and a promise he is loath to keep, he must do something he'd not thought possible to survive the attempts of the area's only unmarried woman to corral him before a preacher and to do it before she ruins everything.

Ida seeks the job of caring for Joseph's youngsters and discovers that only marriage to the English outsider can extract her from a homeless situation. She agrees to a loveless union on the condition she can walk away.

Immersed in a local setting where few people comprehend her Amish background, she endures whispers, side-glances, and outright hatred from the town's gossip who claims matrimonial rights to Joseph. The woman learns of the late-night wedding and spews her venom against Ida.

Shunned by her family, and circumventing barbs by those who don't approve of her, Ida must navigate the corridors of a vastly different culture. Will she stick with Joseph? Will Joseph save the farm? Will Ida return home to her parents who want nothing to do with her?

Three Strikes

In 1978, Spencer (Spence) Edwards hasn't been on a date in over a year and is ultra-picky about who he'll ask out because he promised his mother to honor God. In their annual wager, his best friend bets that if Spence asked Patti, the most beautiful girl in the senior class, on a date, she would refuse him three times. When a teacher partners Patti with Spence on a class project and he ventures to ask her, she says 'no' (Strike One).

But after forbidden circumstances place them together, his stellar reputation takes a nosedive. Angry parents, horse rides, friends chanting rumors, semi-trucks, and snow storms generate friction that inserts a wedge between him and Patti. Romance must take a back seat while he sorts through a myriad of roadblocks to win the wager. God seems to have withdrawn, and after he's falsely accused of the unthinkable, he considers giving up … almost.

Gifted Heart

In 1947, Ray Petriani flees Texas in the middle of the night with a wife and young family. Desperate for work, he takes a job in California and his boss sends him to inland China on a business venture. A gift exchange with the local potentate provides him with two things he doesn't want, things he cannot reject, and things he agreed to protect. Those gifts transform his life.

His research of the first item, a gilded antique music box said to have belonged to a Chinese Emperor, only uncovers additional shrouded historical doubts that raise further problems as to its actual intent. Ray refuses to give up his investigation and believes the meaning of its significance lies hidden in the way they presented to him.

But it's the possession of the second gift, a pretty female slave, which rocks his world and generates friction with his wife that reaches atomic proportions and plants a minefield of impossible complications. Town people, officials, family, and associates, all full of righteous hatred toward Orientals because of the war, seek to purge the area of this Asian beauty who doesn't belong, but who is forbidden from returning to her homeland.

Can Ray, his family, and this newly freed slave navigate the corridors of bitter animosity from the people of their two countries, attempts on their lives from both sides of the Pacific, and bungling government bureaucracy, to uncover the deep Chinese secrets that entwine their lives?

Inherited Wife

Woodrow (Woody) Hancock's uncle offers him two wagers. First, he could make Woody find a wife sooner than he wants, and second, Woody would build the home for unwed pregnant girls they've both dreamed about, and both would happen by the end of next year. But Woody declines the outrageous wagers because he's not ready to get married, nor does he have the funds to build the home.

When his uncle dies just after the new year, Woody inherits his uncle's beautiful farm. In addition, $186 million could become his, plus $23 million for a home for unwed pregnant girls, but if he's married by July, or forfeit all the money to an abortion clinic, a place he abhors. Fortune seekers hound Woody, forcing him into hiding. He takes a job at a pregnancy center. The COVID-19 pandemic sweeps the country, and the center moves to Woody's farm, where he's secluded with four lovely women. But despite the women's deceptions and secrets, he hurries to woo one of them as his lucky bride.

When he selects a woman, and they marry, his problems multiply. As Woody and his inherited wife attempt to fulfill his uncle's second wager of building the home for pregnant girls, they must endure threats, fire, lawyers, inspections, and a gun. They struggle to maintain their sanity against someone who vows their downfall. Can they survive the ever-increasing turmoil before they lose it all, or worse?

Deception and Depravity

Mr. Johansen, a successful businessman, connives a circus-style job fair to replace his executive assistant. Charlotte applies to his online advertisement, and things don't proceed well when his partner viciously opposes her Christian beliefs.

During the application process, Matthew escorts Charlotte through a myriad of difficulties, but when Mr. Johansen selects Charlotte as one of the top three candidates, his partner unleashes a whirlwind of chaos which sends her to the hospital. After a judge issues a subpoena, her life takes off in a direction she never imagined, and is forced into seclusion. While she's hiding with Matthew, his youthful past resurfaces to entangle her in sordid events he believed were long forgotten.

Can Charlotte extricate herself from the enmeshing web of Matthew's childhood? Can she land the top job she's only dreamed about? Can Matthew forgive himself for the sins of his past? Can Charlotte forgive him for his deception?

Rabbit Tails

I grew up on a family farm near central Iowa, where Corn, Beans, Dairy, Beef, Chickens, Pigs, and a Horse were part of my upbringing. The rural area and the Christian community stamped me as an outdoor person. Hunting rabbits was as much a part of me as was plowing, making hay, and caring for livestock. Part of my life involved raising the lovable animals as pets and for the dinner table.

As a boy, I picked up the "handle" of Rabbit after catching seven of the furry animals without a gun.

Made in the USA
Columbia, SC
29 July 2024